PRAISE FOR BILL YENNE

Bill Yenne writes "with cinematic vividness."

ROGER MCGRATH, *THE WALL STREET JOURNAL*

I can guarantee that you will be engaged by [Bill Yenne's] master storytelling from his opening words to the very last page.

COLONEL WALTER BOYNE, SMITHSONIAN NATIONAL AIR & SPACE MUSEUM

Bill Yenne is a perfect example what happens when a child reads too many books and doesn't watch enough television. He ended up with an imagination.

JOHN SMITHERS OF MONTANA'S *MISSOULIAN*

HUNTING SEASON IN LOGAN COUNTY

HUNTING SEASON IN LOGAN COUNTY

COUNTY

JIM HAMMER
BOOK 1

BILL YENNE

ROUGH
EDGES
PRESS

Hunting Season in Logan County
Paperback Edition
Copyright © 2025 Bill Yenne

Rough Edges Press
An Imprint of Wolfpack Publishing
1707 E. Diana Street
Tampa, FL 33610

roughedgespress.com

This book is a work of fiction. References to historical events, real
people, or real places are used fictitiously. Any similarity to real
persons, living or dead, is purely coincidental and not intended by the
author.

All brand names and product names used in this book are trademarks,
registered trademarks, or trade names of their respective holders.
Wolfpack Publishing is not associated with any product or vendor in
this book.

Paperback ISBN 978-1-68549-375-2
Ebook ISBN 978-1-68549-374-5

HUNTING SEASON IN LOGAN COUNTY

PROLOGUE

"C'MON, BABY," Mark Edredin whispered as the sun rose into the sky over his left shoulder. "I know you're out there...let's see you."

"Shuddup," Steve Coe replied in a barely audible hiss. "You'll scare 'em all away."

The two men were not out here in the vast and remote plains of Logan County, Montana, to admire the sunrise, nor the sudden splash of vivid orange light on the distant Buffalo Jaw Mountains. No, they were out here because it was the first day of antelope season.

The two longtime friends had been hunting together since high school and had not missed an opening day of antelope season—or deer season either, for that matter—in at least a quarter century. This patch of land on the old Tredquist place had been one of their favorites throughout all those years. One time, when they were barely out of their teens, they had even hunted with Old Man Tredquist himself, but this was a long time ago.

Edredin peeled his eyes for the nearest ridgeline and snuggled the stock of his bolt-action Remington 780 into his shoulder. There was a gully running parallel to the ridge but it was barely discernible in the tall grass rolling across the plains between here and there. Pronghorns like to hide in gullies like those, so he put his eye to the glass of his Burris HD 2 scope and took a closer look.

Coe watched carefully but did not raise his own binoculars. Edredin was right. You don't want to spook an antelope, and Coe did not want to be the one to jinx his own luck. He had already lost the coin toss to be the first of the two to take the season's first shot, so all he could do was breathe—as softly as possible.

Gradually, the light from the rising sun crept down the slope toward the shadows of the gully.

Suddenly, as if conjured out of Edredin's imagination, a large pronghorn buck emerged into the sunlight from the gully and looked around.

Trophy quality, Edredin said to himself as he admired the buck's nicely curving twelve-inch horns and lined up his shot.

At this moment, both men heard the crunch of something moving behind them, and just as suddenly as the buck had appeared, he was gone.

"*What the…*" Edredin cursed angrily as both men rolled over from their prone position and started to get up.

They saw two men about forty feet away who were moving toward them with long strides.

"What do you think you're doin' out here?" Coe demanded with the same level of rage Edredin was displaying in his own angry face.

The approaching men were clean shaven and well-dressed, as though they had just opened the Amazon box containing their North Face outerwear this morning. They each wore a blue ball cap bearing a patch emblazoned with a teal-blue stylized image of a sun. It was the kind of logo you'd take to be just a generic picture, the kind of thing you see on the bargain table at Walmart, except these two had matching caps.

Edredin was about to make a crack about their mamma dressing them alike when the man with close-cropped red hair spoke first.

"You're trespassing," he said with a sternness bordering on aggressive. "We're here to ask you nicely, and to ask you nicely *only once*, to get back into your old pickup and get the hell off this land."

"We've been hunting out here on the Tredquist place our whole lives," Cole said indignantly, match the man's aggressive tone. "It's you clowns who better be getting to back under whatever rock you woke up under this morning."

"You cost me a trophy buck," Edredin said, getting into the conversation. "My patience is not worn thin, it damn well expired when you come trompin' up. Now beat it before I tell the Tredquists you're out here interfering with opening day."

"This is not Tredquist property," the other man asserted. "It stopped being Tredquist property seven weeks ago when the family sold the entire parcel and transferred the title."

"Sold it to you assholes?" Coe said skeptically. "I never heard anything about this."

"What you heard and didn't hear is none of our concern," the man said, edging closer and practically shouting into Coe's. "We are here to see you get off this land and do it now...without any further argument."

Impulsively, Coe reached out and shoved the man as hard as he could.

With a startled expression, the man stepped back, caught his foot on something and toppled to the ground.

The redheaded man quickly pulled the Glock G19

pistol from his nylon tactical holster and squeezed the trigger.

The 9mm high-velocity round sliced into Coe's left shoulder, and his hunting rifle tumbled from his arms. A blank, frozen expression clouded his face, and he fell backward into the sagebrush.

After a split second of stunned astonishment gripped Edredin, he reacted on impulse and started to raise his Remington to defend his friend.

"I don't recommend it," the red-haired man said, aiming his pistol directly at Edredin from a distance of about ten feet.

"Drop your rifle," the other man demanded.

Edredin hated himself for having no other choice.

"Now, gather up this bloody mess and get the hell out of here before we stop playing nice!"

CHAPTER
ONE

SHERIFF KYLE FAHR squinted through the glare of the sunrise on the windshield of his Dodge Durango and wished he'd taken the time to hose it down yesterday. He'd gotten back late from a wellness check in a remote part of the county and had pulled the early shift today when his deputy called in sick. Fahr figured it might have something to do with the first day of antelope season.

Fahr had been the sheriff of Logan County for a dozen years, but he had grown up in the county. After a couple of decades as a detective on the mean streets of Denver and an acrimonious failed marriage, he had been ready to go back to a place where nothing ever happened—at least almost.

His was not a complicated job, there were several office buildings in Denver with a population greater than Logan County, but it was a *big* job. Montana has more than a dozen counties bigger than Rhode Island and Delaware combined, and Logan is one of them. He had rolled over the odometer in his Crown Vic, and he was now pushing six figures in the Durango. A lot of this was on dirt and gravel, but this morning, he was just cruising the two-lane blacktop in the south of the county.

As he was about to click off his window washers, he saw a car approaching in the distance. Out here, you could see cars coming a few miles off, but this one was closing the distance in a hurry. A dark-gray Chevy Colorado practically leaped out of the swale in the road ahead and raced past the Durango in a split-second *mmmmzzzzing.*

Fahr jerked his SUV into a tight turn, lit up his lights and siren, and floored the accelerator. In a state where even the smallest of county roads are posted at seventy, speeding was never high on Fahr's list of misdeeds to be dealt with, but someone doing north of ninety was someone who could not be ignored.

The pursuit was over faster than Fahr had imagined, and he was glad for this. The twin-cab pickup had pulled off the road and was parked with its flashers going—not what you'd expect for a drunk or somebody running from the law.

As the sheriff cautiously approached on foot, the driver rolled down his window.

"Mark Edredin!" Fahr exclaimed. "What the hell are you doing..."

"Steve's been shot! Steve Coe. He's bleedin' bad."

"Hunting accident?"

"*No. They shot him!* I'll tell you all about later. Gotta get him to the hospital in Obsidian!"

"Okay," Fahr said, turning to dash back to the Durango. "Follow me!"

With his siren yelping and blue lights flashing, Fahr didn't let the red needle get below the century mark until he reached the flashing amber at the edge of town. He had radioed his station and told Holly to phone the Logan County Hospital to say he was coming in hot.

They were ready. They slid Steve Coe out of the back cab of the pickup, put him on a gurney and had him through the swinging doors in a heartbeat. They knew what to do.

Fahr followed Edredin through the ER entrance and was with him when the medics told him he could go no farther.

Edredin was a wreck.

The sheriff gently maneuvered the distraught man to one of the worn green vinyl sofas in the waiting room and sat him down.

"Can I get you some coffee?"

"Whiskey," was Edredin's one-word reply.

"We'll work on it for later," Fahr said as he poured him a cup from the half-empty water cooler. Handing it over, he poured one for himself and sat down. He took a deep breath and waited for Edredin's gasping breath to level out before he said anything.

"You feel up to talking about the shooting?"

"Yeah. I guess so."

After a long pause, he started forming the words.

"Okay. So we were hunting. First day of antelope season. We were out at the Tredquist place, you know?"

"Yeah, I do."

"I had a buck in my sights. Ready to shoot when this fella came along and spooked him."

"What fella?"

"There were two of 'em. Well-dressed. Real expensive lookin' jackets. They came on like they owned the place, and well, y'know, they said they *do* own the place."

"They own the place?" Fahr asked quizzically. "How can they say they own the Tredquist place when the Tredquists own the Tredquist place?"

"Everybody knows this. But I'm telling you what they told us."

Edredin took a sip of water and continued.

"They demanded we had to leave right now. They got really mean about it too. One of 'em walked right up to Steve. The redheaded one. He got so close you could see his spit hittin' Steve as he yelled at him. He tripped over his own feet and fell backward. The other guy pulled a gun and shot Steve in the arm."

"Just like that?"

"Just *exactly* like that. Then he pointed the gun at me and told me to drop my rifle and get Steve outta there. What could I do?"

Fahr just nodded.

"Steve could walk, but just barely. It took us a long time to get to my truck. I put on a tourniquet. I hope it helped."

"I'm sure it did. You did the right thing."

"Then I just drove like a bat outta hell and you know the rest."

"I better get out there and talk to those two," Fahr said. "You have any idea where I might find them out there? The Tredquist place in a really big place."

"There's those summer tourist cabins next to the ranch house on the gravel road leading up from the county road. I saw several vehicles parked around there when we passed by."

"I better get going, then," Fahr said as he stood. "I'd hate to get out there and find they'd done a runner."

———

Out of force of habit, Kyle Fahr ejected and reinserted the mag in his SIG P320 before he fastened his seat belt. The details of all those troubled nights in Denver were buried in his brain. He had done this before. He'd do it again. Bringing in perps was one thing, but bringing in perps who had just put a man in the hospital was a whole other level of precarious.

As he approached the cluster of buildings which comprised what remained of the old Tredquist compound, he saw the vehicles Edredin mentioned. He noticed a pair of big white Toyota Tundras with logos on their doors. He saw no people around but figured they had seen him. By the star on his door, he knew they knew what happened next.

As he climbed out of the Durango, the door to the main building swung open and two men stepped out. They were both wearing expensive-looking jackets and he saw one had short red hair. The man who shot Steve Coe.

"Hello, Sheriff," he said, betraying no emotion.

"Hello gentlemen," Fahr replied. "I believe you know why I'm here, so I'll dispense with the bullshit. I understand you shot a man this morning, and I'm going to have to take you into custody."

"For shooting an armed trespasser who threatened me? I don't think so."

"As I'm sure you understand, you're not the one wearing the badge here," Fahr explained. "I'm placing both of you under arrest. Now, if you'd please unfasten those nice gun belts and carefully place them on the ground, I'll need to cuff you and take you into town."

Both men were in the process of complying when they all heard the roar of an oncoming vehicle. There was a screeching spray of gravel as the gloss-black Cadillac Escalade came to an abrupt stop near Fahr's Durango. It was tricked out with tinted windows and a menacing-looking push guard, and it bristled with antennae.

Two men in suits were out of the vehicle practically before it came to a stop.

"Federal agents," one of the men announced as both

of them produced badges and federal ID. "Sheriff, I'm Special Agent Vincent Milino, and this is agent Aron Kruegher. We're taking charge of the situation."

"What interest does the ATF have in *this*?" Fahr asked.

"I'm not at liberty to say. But as I *did* say, we're taking charge of this situation, and pursuant to that, I'm asking you to stand down immediately."

"I'm sorry," he said. "These men were involved in a shooting that put a man into the hospital. I'm placing them under arrest and will be transporting them to the county jail in Obsidian."

"Apparently you did not understand what I said," the man said. "*We* are taking charge of this and I have asked you politely to stand down. As I'm sure you understand, federal jurisdiction trumps local jurisdiction. I am therefore *telling* you, *one last time*, stand down and leave this property...*now*."

CHAPTER
TWO

JIM HAMMER NOTICED the forlorn little green sign reading "Obsidian 12," as he drove north in his old blue Chevy pickup with the camper shell and the hitch carrier on the back for his 1965 Norton N15CS.

It had been a dozen years since he'd been only twelve miles from this place this had been his only reality for the first eighteen years of his life—and longer than eighteen since he had been here for more than just a day. He might have stayed here longer last time if not for an emergency deployment, but there would be no more of those. Jim Hammer, formerly Captain Jim Hammer, had mustered out of the US Army after two decades, most of them spent in special operations from South America to Southeast Asia.

He had been one of the last out of Afghanistan. After the calamitous American withdrawal, Hammer and his team had stayed back—for a long time. Officially, they weren't even there. Unofficially, a lot of what they did was unknown, even to those in the deep world of the covert unknown who had left them there.

They were well aware of the dark world of malevolent

Taliban warlords and opium brokers who for reasons unknown had been declared off-limits by those calling the shots from Washington. Gradually, they had penetrated the web of wrongdoing in which the Taliban gangsters were entwined with, and under the protection of rogue factions deep the Pentagon bureaucracy. Gradually, the malefactors in Afghanistan began turning up as fatalities in inexplicable accidents—or suffering from untraceable, but fatal, head wounds.

When they had done all they could, Hammer and his team—who were by now not officially there—had walked out of Afghanistan, crossing the Hindu Kush on the cusp of winter.

When he left the service, Hammer had entertained a number of job offers from private security firms, but he had decided to go on the road for a while instead, and this road was now leading him toward Obsidian.

After his parents passed several years back, he had stayed in touch with his aunt, Charlotte Hendricksen, who still lived in Obsidian. She had repeatedly told him of her spare room, mentioning it in the same sentence as phrases like "if you ever want to take a break from your roller coaster." His reply had always contained a phrase such as "one of these days."

Today, if his plans held, would finally be "one of these days."

"This will be a welcome change of pace," Hammer said to himself. Nothing ever happens in Logan County. It's the most boring place in the world. That's why he had left twenty years ago, and why he's glad to be going back. And it *was* antelope season, and this was appealing. It had been a long time for this kind of hunting.

Hammer saw the grain elevators long before he saw the flashing amber light hanging over the intersection at the edge of town. The woeful wail of a freight train passing through town reminded him of when he was a kid. He and his friends used to hop the freights and ride them down to Miles City for fun. They talked about going all the way to Chicago, but they never did. At least not on a freight.

Hammer made a right at the light and headed a couple of tree-lined blocks to downtown Obsidian. Main Street consisted of a couple of blocks of once-important brick storefronts still proudly turning their century-old faces to a once-busy, now quiet, thoroughfare. The fancy haberdashery was now a craft shop. It had been something else the last time he was here. The high-end shoe store was now a used bookshop, a purveyor of recycled ideas, for which there was apparently still a market. At the end of the street stood the way-too-ornate county courthouse. Some things will be around forever.

The Shiny Rock Café had not changed since he was a kid. It had always been the heart and soul of Obsidian. Even its name meant "Obsidian." It was the crossroads of all information which was deemed important. Every town has such a place. If something is worth knowing, you'll know it here, and you'll know it before anyone else, anywhere else for a radius of hundreds of miles.

He climbed out of his pickup, moved his sunglasses to his ball cap, the gray one with the logo of a Louisiana bait shop, and slammed the door. No need to lock it, especially here. He wore a gray wool shirt and a heavy gray canvas jacket, with plenty of pockets—especially inside pockets. Sometimes you needed to carry stuff and keep your hands free.

Everything he wore, except his jeans, and he always wore jeans, was gray. After all those years in the Army, Hammer had defaulted to a new uniform color. Not planned, but it had just worked out this way. His shoes, XCS hiking shoes, had started out black, but time had made them gray too. They were low-topped, and looked like regular shoes, until you saw the soles. You could climb Granite Peak up in the Beartooth country with those soles.

"Hammer! It can't be you."

He had barely made it inside, the jingling of the little bell on the front door alerting patrons and staff to his arrival, when he was recognized. It was not that he was hard to spot. A lot of other guys stood six-two, but his shoulders often got a second glance, either from women or from guys deciding not to pick a fight. The flecks of gray made his dark beard, which he trimmed occasionally, look scruffy to some, fearsome to others, and sexy—in an untouchable sort of way—to a lot of women.

Time stopped. The woman in the red plaid shirt and the big glass coffee carafe remained motionless, frozen in her tracks. Only her eyes moved, as she looked him over.

Everyone else in place also stopped what they were doing. They stared at him and at her, deeply engaged in the theater of what would come next.

"It *is* you. Isn't it?"

"Yeah Kristin, it's me."

"When was this?" Kristin asked. "Last time you came in here? It seems like last week and it seems like a hundred years ago."

"Just a dozen years," he said.

"Can I getcha some coffee?"

"Sure, thanks," he said, taking a seat at the counter.

"We stopped serving breakfast a half hour ago, but I know he's got eggs back there so I can getcha anything you want."

"I'll just have a burger and fries, and a bottle of pop."

"It comes in cans nowadays, old timer."

As Kristen turned away to put in the order and go pour coffee at the booths near the windows of the diner, the man two stools from Hammer turned to introduce himself.

"Good morning, sir," he said, extending his hand in that quasi-formal way locals in small towns often greet strangers. "My name's Mike Fellowes. If you don't mind me eavesdropping, it sounds like you're a former regular at this counter."

"I'm Jim Hammer," he said, taking his hand. "I grew up here in Obsidian. Left about twenty years ago."

"I've been here almost fifteen myself," he said. "I'm a city boy from over in Great Falls."

"I played basketball in the Great Falls High gym once," Hammer said.

"The Bison had a great team back in the day," the man said with a smile.

"We didn't play you guys," Hammer said with a chuckle. "The state championships were there that year. You guys were class double-A. We were triple-C.

"I didn't know there *was* a triple-C," Fellowes said quizzically.

"There isn't. It was just a joke we used to tell. All the small schools are C. We just used to say triple-C because we were *so* small. You guys had algebra classes bigger than our whole enrollment. Well, not really. Probably. It's another exaggeration for effect."

The ice thus broken with a joke and a chuckle, Hammer made conversation by asking why Fellowes had come to this remote corner of nowhere.

"Love," was the one-word answer. "I met a gal from here at Montana State. Maybe you know her?"

"Maybe…"

"Jenna Tolliver?"

Names from deep in your past, when suddenly articulated after time, always spark a synapse. Hammer hadn't thought about her in years. She had been in his class.

Jenna was the queen bee who ran everything. Student body president. Yearbook editor. On every committee. Never the prom queen—but chair of the prom committee for two or three years in a row.

"Yeah, I knew Jenna," Hammer said with a smile. "She was a character. Always organizing things. I'm surprised she isn't the mayor of Obsidian by now."

"She's the Chair of the County Commissioners."

"Well, I'm sure not surprised," Hammer said. This sounded like exactly where Jenna Tolliver was headed all those years ago.

"You'll get a chance to see her," Fellowes said. "She's meeting me here in about five minutes...well, wait a minute, I just saw her car pull up."

Jenna Tolliver Fellowes was every bit the ball of fire she always had been, one of those who filled a room by her presence. She came through the door in her Indian-print fleece jacket and an expensive-looking tote bag brimming with paperwork, and glasses perched on her head. She had put on a few pounds, but not many, and her eyes were filled with the familiar Jenna fire.

"Jenna, I'd like to have you meet a new friend of mine," Mike said. "You might know him...Jim Hammer."

"Hammer?" Jenna said, looking him over before extending her hand. "Jim Hammer. I thought you were dead."

"Hmm," Hammer said as Mike cringed at the directness of his wife's assertion. "Sorry to disappoint."

"Not a disappointment, just a surprise," she said without taking her eyes off his face. "We heard you were killed over in Afghanistan...years ago."

"I took a lot of incoming over there," he assured her indifferently. "But I guess they missed me same as I missed hearing this particular rumor."

She continued to stare at him as though unconvinced, so he changed the subject.

"So what about you, Jenna? Mike was telling me you got a county job."

"Well, I try to keep things together here, while Mike runs his five-hundred-or-so head of Angus."

Kristen arrived with the burgers, and Mike invited Hammer to join him and his wife at one of the booths.

"How *are* things here in the county these days?" Hammer asked.

"Same old, same old, for the most part," Jenna replied, taking a sip of coffee. "I guess the big news is they sold the Tredquist place."

"I used to hunt out there," Hammer recalled.

"So did I," Jenna replied. "In fact, Mike and I were out there for whitetail last year."

"It came as a big surprise," Mike interjected. "Not much notice. It happened over the summer. The last of the Tredquists moved away some years ago, so I guess the family...wherever they are...decided to get rid of it."

"Who bought it?" Hammer asked. "Somebody local?"

"It was a land company down in Billings," Jenna said. "That's all I know. The rumor going around is it was the Chinese."

"The *Chinese*?" Hammer asked.

"Yeah, it's something that has got a lot of folks out here in the middle of this country worried these days," Mike interjected. "Chinese companies are buying thousands of acres of farmland. There was a big fuss a couple of years ago when a Chinese company bought land near Grand Forks AFB over in North Dakota."

"Yeah, I guess I did hear about it on the radio or some podcast," Hammer said. "The Air Force has Global Hawks based over there...their super long-range recon drones...but the Tredquist place?"

"You might not remember the Air Force built a 10,000-foot runway out there back in the fifties," Jenna said. "Back then, they had B-52 bases all across the northern tier of the country...Spokane, Glasgow, Minot..."

"And the one over at Grand Forks was built for B-52s," Hammer reminded her. "But I sure don't remember a bomber base on the Tredquist place!"

"It wasn't a base," Jenna clarified. "It was an auxiliary landing field. Just a runway. By the time we came along, it had been abandoned for years. The Tredquist place is so big you can walk all over it and never see the runway. Probably overgrown with sagebrush after all these decades."

"Are you sure it's the Chinese and not just some out-of-state zillionaire parking his money?" Hammer asked, unconvinced.

"A lot of people were skeptical like you," Fellowes said. "Until the Chinese girl walked into town."

"Chinese girl?"

"It was a couple three weeks ago," Jenna said, picking up the thread of the narrative. "She was a young Asian woman who walked into Obsidian one day looking frightened and lost. Some people took her here to the Shiny Rock and bought her lunch. They were trying to figure out what to do to help her when two men drove up in a big white Toyota Tundra. They apologized for any trouble she might have caused, left a couple of Benjamins on the counter and whisked her away."

"That's strange," Hammer said. "Did anybody recognize those guys?"

"Nope," Mike said. "But they do get a fair number of out-of-towners in here. There aren't many other places to stop for lunch for people driving on the state highway, and the café *does* have a billboard out there."

Hammer was taking a bite of his hamburger when

suddenly there was a flurry of activity. A small group of excited people had just burst into the diner. And an animated conversation ensued between them and the people at the counter.

"There's been a shooting!"

"Where?

"Out at the Tredquist place. A couple of hunters."

"Hunting accident?" Fellowes asked. "It *is* the first day of antelope season, you know."

"They said it was deliberate! Attempted murder."

"Who's 'they?' Who said that?"

"Folks at the hospital. They brought him in."

"Who got brought in?"

"Steve Coe. They said it was Steve Coe who got shot. Mark Edredin brought him in. He was bleedin' something fierce. They don't think he'll make it."

"Who said?"

"I don't know. That's what I heard."

Jim Hammer had heard enough. It was his turn to lay down some banknotes and leave the place in a hurry.

"I'm afraid I've gotta run," he said as he pulled on his coat. "We'll catch up again later. I've gotta get over to the hospital. Steve and Mark were friends of mine."

CHAPTER
THREE

ALL EYES in the ER waiting room turned as the stranger burst through the automatic doors in a blast of October cold.

By now, the scene at the hospital had calmed—from frantic to merely anxious. Mark Edredin's wife Jessica had gone to the local bank managed by Erin O'Malley, Steve Coe's girlfriend, to break the news. The two women were with Mark in the waiting room when Jim Hammer arrived.

"Hammer," Edredin said, looking up and recognizing a face from past memory, someone he had not seen in twenty years. "I didn't know you were in town."

"Just got here an hour ago. I was at the Shiny Rock when they said you had just brought Steve in here."

Edredin just nodded. His face was strained and worried.

The three men had once been more than friends. Long ago, this trio, and their cohesiveness as basketball players had been the mainstays of the Logan County High School varsity when they were sophomores, and they only got better and better in the two final years leading up to the state championship. Edredin and Coe had settled down here, while Hammer left the county and never came back —until now.

"How is…" Hammer started to ask.

"He's in surgery," Jessica replied. "They haven't told us much. My name's Jess. This is Erin."

"I'm Jim Hammer. I knew Mark and Steve…a long time ago."

"Pleased to meet you," Jessica said.

"Wish circumstances were different," Erin added, looking up with red, tear-filled eyes.

Hammer nodded agreement and took a seat.

"He took a bullet in the arm," Edredin said at last. "I got a tourniquet on, but he lost a lot of blood."

Hammer nodded. He had seen a lot of these—way too many—in Afghanistan and all over the world. Arms, legs, torsos, and heads. He never expected there would be one of these on his first day back in his hometown.

"How'd it happen?" Hammer asked at last.

"We were hunting out on the Tredquist place when these two guys came up and said they owned the place and wanted to kick us off. One of 'em was getting abusive with Steve and tripped himself onto the ground, and then the other guy pulled a gun and shot Steve."

"The guy who shot Steve, what did he look like?" Hammer asked.

"Tall. New jacket. Red hair. Nothing out of the ordinary."

"He wasn't Chinese?"

"*Chinese*?" Edredin replied. "Hell no."

"The sheriff went out to arrest the guy," Jessica said. "He escorted Mark in here and then went back out to the Tredquist place. That was a couple of hours ago. He ought to be coming back pretty soon."

It was about fifteen minutes later when Sheriff Kyle

Fahr arrived. He walked into the ER waiting room with a dejected look on his face.

"How did it go?" Jessica asked assertively. "Did you arrest them?"

"No, I did not," Fahr replied with a sense of embarrassment.

"Don't tell me they ran off!" Jessica roared. "Did you call the highway patrol to put out an APB?"

"No, they didn't run off. I found 'em and was in the middle of making an arrest when the feds showed up. They said they were taking charge of the scene."

"The feds?" Hammer asked incredulously. "What agency?"

"It was ATF."

"What reason did they give?"

"Because they can."

Everyone looked at everyone else in disbelief.

"I've already talked to Ryan Scott about getting a warrant which cuts the feds out of the picture," Fahr said, proud of himself for ratcheting up the heat and involving the county attorney. "Scott said he'd call the state attorney general in Helena and get him to go over their heads. I'll go back out there in a day or two. Don't worry."

"It's all bullshit!" Edredin said in a loud voice. "It's Tredquist land. It's *always* been Tredquist land, even if those jokers said it wasn't."

"What interest do the feds have in a shooting on private land?" Hammer asked rhetorically. "No matter who owns it?"

"And who are you?" Fahr said, squinting at Hammer.

"My name's Hammer, Jim Hammer," he said, extending his hand. "I was a friend of Mark and Steve back in high school."

"Hammer. Yeah, I remember your name. Captain of

the championship basketball team. I remember that year. The trophy's still in the glass case by the front door."

"I'm afraid I don't remember you, Sheriff Fahr," Hammer said, reading the sheriff's name tag.

"I was a few years ahead of you. We had a lousy team."

Just then, the swinging door opened and a man in scrubs came out.

"He's in recovery," the surgeon announced with an audible sense of relief. "It was touch and go for a while. We were sure concerned. But we got the bullet out. He came through. My compliments to whoever tied the tourniquet. That saved his life for sure."

Erin was leaning on Jessica now, tears pouring down her cheeks. Hammer even noticed a little dampness at the corner of Mark Edredin's eye.

"Family can go in now and see him," the doctor said as he turned on his heel to return through the swinging doors.

They all stood, expecting Erin to go through alone, but she held fast to Jessica's hand. Turning to her, Erin said:

"*You're* family...and you too, Mark."

As the three of them disappeared, Hammer found himself alone with the sheriff.

"What about the feds, then?" Hammer asked, going back to the matter at hand. "What were *they* doing out there?"

"They weren't there when I got there," Fahr replied. "I was making the arrest when they came screaming in with a big fed Escalade with aerials all over it. They just took over and gave me the boot."

"And you just left?"

"What could I do? Just so you know, federal agents

have jurisdiction over county sheriffs anywhere anytime. They have charge of the case now."

Hammer's bitter expression unnerved the sheriff.

"I see you don't like it, but this *is what it is.*"

"One more thing," Hammer said as he put on his coat. "These guys who were out there...were any of 'em Chinese?"

"No," Fahr said emphatically. "Why?"

"Nothing. I was just thinking out loud."

"Listen, Hammer," the sheriff said. "I can see the wheels turning in your head, and I need to tell you that you had better...if you know what's good for you, you best stay well clear of getting involved in this. I won't stand for civilians starting to take the law into their own hands."

"Of course," was the only thing Hammer could think to say—out loud. He wanted to say something about the phrase "won't stand for civilians," but decided this would serve no purpose—for the time being.

Excusing himself by telling Fahr that he needed to make contact with a relative who lived in town, Hammer wished the sheriff a "better rest of the day," and left the hospital flicking through his phone for Aunt Charlotte's number.

CHAPTER
FOUR

CHARLOTTE HENDRICKSEN WAS out the front door before her nephew had even set the parking brake on the pickup. She had anticipated his arrival by making a lasagna, knowing if he *didn't* show up—and her imagination gave her a lot of reasons why he might *not*—a lasagna would keep. Despite his phone call, it was not until she saw his truck a block away that she set the dial on the oven to 350 and pushed "start."

No reason to jinx it.

She showed him to his room. It was just a bed and a bathroom, but she had furnished it with a microwave and a minifridge, and it had its own separate outside entrance near the garage. There wasn't room for his pickup in the garage, but plenty of space in there to park the Norton. *Perfect*, he thought.

There was a lot of catching up, although the demise of the Taliban warlords was omitted, as were a lot of other events from the last many years. Charlotte brought out a photo album, but only one. She was sure he would rather not want to dip too deeply into the past.

No reason to jinx it.

They spoke about the future, and she told him he could stay as long as he wanted. He said he didn't have any firm plans and he might stay around for a while. She said it was fine. She did not want to say it was lonely being alone, because she did not want to have him feel pressured. She did use the phrase "I *will* let you know if you're getting underfoot"—albeit with a smile and a chuckle.

No reason to jinx it.

He mentioned it was the first day of antelope season, adding he was looking forward to going out "one of these days."

This naturally led to talk of what had happened at the Tredquist place earlier in the day.

"Oh my gosh, the Coe boy!" Charlotte exclaimed when her nephew had related a sanitized version of the story. "Will he be all right?"

"The doctor seemed to think so," Hammer said. "It was a close call. Mark Edredin's tourniquet tipped the odds in Steve's favor. I'm planning to swing by tomorrow and see if he's up to visitors."

"Please wish him well for me."

"I sure will."

"You say this happened out at the Tredquist place?" Charlotte asked. "I thought they allowed hunting out there."

"They did. For years. For as long as I can remember, but it seems the Tredquists sold the place last summer without telling anyone. Most people don't know. Mark and Steve sure did not."

"Who owns it now?"

"Nobody seems to know. Some people down at the Shiny Rock were talking about the Chinese."

"I've heard some people talk about the Chinese buying land," Charlotte said. "But this is the first I've heard about them buying the Tredquist place. I guess I'm like most people I didn't know it had been sold. What do they want with a patch of Montana range land? Have they run out of range land in their own?"

"It still isn't clear who bought it," Hammer clarified. "That angle just seems to be idle speculation."

"I know who you could ask," Charlotte said, he eyes brightening. "My friend Linda Stahling has a daughter who works down at the assessor's office. Maybe you knew her in school? Her name was Lauren."

Lauren Stahling? Suddenly, Hammer's past was not just trickling back into the present. It was a deluge.

Lauren Stahling!

———

If Jim Hammer was looking for an excuse *not* to drive down to the assessor's office on Tuesday morning, this was not to be found in a lack of parking places at the courthouse. He pulled into the fourth empty spot from the one directly in front of the main entrance. His twenty years in special operations had made not being conspicuous second nature.

Lauren Stahling.

Everyone has a name like this in their high school past, a name that links up with some variation on the well-worn tale of an innocent kiss between friends in the front seat one night behind the gym, a kiss that led to more, and then to a lot more in the back seat. And, of course, to the words that were said, to words burned into memories like words carved into picnic table benches.

As he stared up at the office directory inside the courthouse, he quickly realized Linda Stahling's daughter did not merely *work* in the assessor's office.

He made his way to the second floor and the big

carved wooden door with the gold lettering which read: "Lauren A. Stahling: Logan County Assessor."

"I'm here to see...um...the assessor," Hammer told the young man at the counter as he walked in.

"Do you have an appointment?"

"Nope."

"I'll see if she's available," he asked efficiently. "Could I have a name?"

"*Hammer*," came the voice from across the room.

There she stood.

Her face was that of a woman pushing forty but whose eyes had lost none of their piercing brilliance. Her perfectly proportioned body, unchanged in all those years, looked as good in her cinnamon-colored sweater dress as it did in Hammer's fondest memories. Very good. Not just good —*very* good. Her long brown hair tumbled across her shoulders the way her remembered. Her expression was one of poised confidence. In every way, she was one of those women who had improved with age.

"I heard you might be stopping in to see the assessor this morning," she said wryly as she gestured for him to come into her inner sanctum. "Please do come in."

"Looks like you're doing well," Hammer said, looking around her office. The huge carved desk flanked by the state and national flags made the place seem almost like the throne room of a castle—or a superior court bench.

"I've read through the years you've done well for yourself too," she replied as she closed the door. "Captain's bars in your twenties; the rumor that you would have made colonel if you would've taken a Pentagon desk job instead repeatedly volunteering to go back overseas. I liked that story. I sounded like you. Then there were all those medals and commendations. As I recall, there were three DSCs and how many Silver Stars?"

"Five."

"Congratulations. From what I read, you more than earned them."

"Thanks. I might have made major if I hadn't volunteered to spend all my time in the field."

"We read about you in the paper," she said. "*The Logan Tribune* was a big fan of yours. They really liked the 'hometown hero angle.' A lot of people were proud of you. A lot of people miss the *Tribune*. They folded a year ago. What brings you back to Obsidian?"

"Antelope season."

"Good answer. I heard the season didn't go well for Steve Coe yesterday."

"That's going to be my next stop this morning."

"I can imagine you're at least as pissed off as the rest of us by how the sheriff was shut down out there," Lauren said as she sat down and gestured for Hammer to do the same.

"News travels fast."

"It didn't have to travel far," she said. "The sheriff's office is in this building, as well as two jail cells that were empty last night."

"I can imagine you're as baffled as I am by what happened to Kyle Fahr out there."

"*You* work for the feds," she said. "What's your take?"

"Between you and me, I'm not a fan. I saw more than I'd like to remember of shady mischief done by federal bureaucrats, from Afghanistan to Cartagena to Washington...and as a point of clarification...I no longer work for the feds."

"On the retired list, then? What's next?"

"Like I said, it's antelope season."

"So it is," she said with a smile that seemed to look right into him. "But what brings you in *here* instead of Bob's Sporting Goods to get your hunting license?"

"I'd be a liar if I didn't say stopping in to see you was something I was hoping to do on this visit," Hammer said with a grin. "But I actually do have something I'd like to look up here in your office."

"I'd be a liar if I didn't say I'm happy you did," she said with a laugh. "But I also have to recall a lot of years since you 'stopped in.' I missed seeing you last time you were in town, which was also a long time ago, now."

"Unexpected deployment," he said with a shrug. "There's a lot of things I didn't get a chance to do on that trip."

"Uh-huh," she said, continuing to smile. "As for the thing you wanted to look up, your aunt told my mom, and I've already looked it up. The Tredquist place was sold to a company called Sunrise Land Holdings for just north of ten million dollars."

"That name's about as generic as skim milk," Hammer said.

"And not a lot of money for around two hundred thousand empty acres of the Big Sky Country out here a long way from anywhere touristy," Lauren added. "Unless they're planning to run cattle, I don't know why anyone would want it."

"Where is this Sunrise outfit from?" he asked. "Out of state?"

"Billings," Lauren said, handing him a document from her desk.

"Billings?" Hammer said with a laugh. "Big city folks, but at least they're from a local big city…kind of."

"They may have a front," she said. "With a name like theirs, you have to wonder."

"I'm sure you've heard this conspiracy theory going around about the Chinese buying up American range-land," he said. "I got an earful from Jenna Tolliver at the

Shiny Rock yesterday...about the time she said she thought I was dead."

"I've heard that conspiracy theory." Lauren laughed. "Actually both of them. The Chinese one comes and goes. Chinese companies with government connections really *are* doing this across more than two dozen states, but I think the talk has gotten a little out of hand. The USDA reports the total acreage is not as much as a lot of people say, but I know what you think of feds."

"Who knows?"

"I've looked. There does not seem to be anything as big as the Tredquist place...that is, that *I've* seen. I haven't seen any come across my desk in Logan County...yet. Did either Mark or the sheriff say anything about those people out there being Chinese?"

"No," Hammer replied. "But what about the Chinese girl who walked into Obsidian a few weeks ago?" Hammer asked.

"I heard about her. You think she's connected to all this...apart from her being Asian?"

"Well, apparently she was picked up pretty quickly by some guys in big double-cab that sounds a lot like the vehicles the sheriff saw out there yesterday."

"*Hmmmm*," Lauren said thoughtfully. "The mystery deepens. Questions unanswered..."

"And then there's the need to do right by Steve Coe," he said. "That's why I'm starting to think I'll postpone my hunting trip and do some digging. Maybe I'll take a little day trip down to Billings tomorrow and see what's behind this business."

"I thought you were going to say you were ready to go out there with your Winchester to spend your hunting season cleaning house," she said with a wink. "I could see the thoughts in your eyes, which are just as readable now as they were twenty years ago."

"You read right, but one of the several things I've learned in those twenty years is taking out foot soldiers never leads to the root of any problem. You've got to work your way to the top. There's a corporate ladder to climb and it seems to start in Billings. Do you have an address for the Sunrise outfit down there?"

For a moment, Lauren just stared thoughtfully into space as though she was about to say something. After a long, audible silence, she finally did say something.

"Hammer, would you like some company on this little trip down to Billings?" she said at last, tapping a folder on her desk. "I have some routine paperwork here which I need to get them to sign. I do have their address. They're in the First Interstate Bank building, in a suite on the eighteenth floor of Montana's tallest building. I just could mail it, but you've piqued *my* curiosity. Besides, I can't let you have *all* the fun."

She saw Hammer start to chuckle.

"I'll phone Tom R. Brach, the managing director, and say I'm already in Billings on other business and this will only take a minute. No offense, but I think someone who Brach knows in a business context will get farther with casual conversation and leading questions than a six-ten stranger with an aversion to shaving every day."

"Retired people aren't obligated to shave every day," he said with a smile. "I'm only six-two...*and* you have a very good idea."

"Thank you." She smiled. "I'll take this as a compliment. Wednesdays are slow days, and I have a bevy of assistants to cover for me here. Pick me up at my house in the morning...early. It's a few hours' drive, but with you at the wheel, I'm sure we can be there before the lunch hour...and by the way, I didn't mean what I said about shaving as *negative* criticism."

CHAPTER
FIVE

"NICE RIDE," Lauren Stahling said, nodding to Hammer's pickup as she emerged from her house carrying a large, official-looking, black leather bag. "Kentucky plates?"

"Bought it there on my way west."

He looked her over as she paused to inhale a breath of cool October air. She was certainly dressed for the part of a bureaucrat doing the county's business. Her hair was tied up stylishly and she wore a long black wool overcoat over a crisply pressed, high-collared shirt and a black pencil skirt.

"You look nice, Stahling," he said.

"Thank you."

"You wouldn't be out of place on a high-priced legal team going into a Manhattan skyscraper to skewer opposing counsel over a trillion-dollar contract."

"I can't let them think us girls from Logan County are hapless bumpkins."

"No chance of that happening."

They were southbound on the state highway as the sun clawed its way into the sky.

"I have an appointment with Sunrise Holdings for eleven a.m.," she said.

"Great. Did you have any trouble?"

"I didn't *ask* Brach whether it was convenient." Lauren laughed. "I just *told* him. If Sunrise is legit, or even if they're just trying to *appear* legit, they're not going to say no to a quick visit from the county assessor in the place where they own a couple hundred thousand acres."

Hammer laughed. He was really starting to like the way the grown-up Lauren Stahling did business.

Lauren asked Hammer about his hospital visit the previous day, and he explained that the prognosis for Steve Coe was a long, but probably full recovery. He and Erin were talking about starting to plan a wedding.

When Hammer told of meeting Mark Edredin at the Shiny Rock for a cup of coffee, Lauren saw his knuckles go white on the steering wheel as he recounted the narrative of the shooting.

"I had to talk him down from going out there guns blazing," Hammer explained.

"Which is exactly what I saw in *your* eyes yesterday," she said.

"To which I added that popping a couple of foot soldiers doesn't get you to the core of the problem. As we say in my business, it's a tactical solution to a strategic problem."

"Did you mention our field trip today?" Lauren asked.

"Nope. I don't want to say anything until we know more than we do now."

———

On the drive, talk inevitably wound its way around to what had happened to each of them since she was off to the University of Washington and he was off to Uncle Sam. Through all the years, they hadn't stayed in touch. It was just two friends talking a little about old times, but mainly about the arc of their respective lives over the past twenty years. Hers in Seattle. His all over the world doing things he mostly couldn't—or just *didn't*—talk about.

She'd graduated from U-Dub with an accounting degree and had a pretty good job. She'd been married for a dozen years and had come back to reclaim her roots in Obsidian after her husband was t-boned by a semi-truck. For his part, Hammer admitted he'd never been anywhere long enough to even let the thought of putting down roots pass through his mind.

After a couple of hours on the two-lane blacktop and one brief stop for coffee, Hammer merged onto Interstate 94. Ten minutes later they were on city streets with the First Interstate Bank building looming ahead.

"Wish me luck," she said as she exchanged her flat-soled shoes for a pair of three-inch heels and climbed out of the truck. Walking purposefully through the lobby, she really did look like she was on her way to skewer opposing counsel over a trillion-dollar contract.

Hammer took a quick drive-by of a non-descript, six-story modernish bank building a few blocks away, and came back to the First Interstate and parked half a block away. He was less interested in the modernish bank building than in its parking lot. Both the FBI and ATF had their Billings field offices in the building, and Hammer wanted to count the black Escalades outside. There were just two. Even assuming half of the fleet was out some-where—which was a stretch—this was a modest presence.

He got bored waiting in the truck and was just

starting to stroll down the sidewalk when Lauren emerged from the First Interstate.

"How did it go?" Hammer asked as they climbed back into the pickup and he turned the key in the ignition.

"Better than I expected," Lauren replied. "I got the papers signed, and Brach was willing to talk small talk. Honestly, it didn't look like much was going on. There were only two other people. A very friendly young woman at the reception desk and a man in a bright orange tie who looked bored."

"What did Brach have to say?"

"I started by asking him about him," she said. "People like to talk about themselves. I asked where in Montana he was from, and he said he wasn't. I had figured as much, but I learned he's from back east, the DC area. Has an ex-wife back there. I did get his card. You said you wanted something with a logo to compare to what Mark and Steve saw on the ball caps."

"Excellent."

"The company, Sunrise Land Holdings, which pays its property taxes out of this office here in Billings was formed two years ago, and it's owned by a holding company called the Hambledon Global Advocacy Group. It's an international charity group based in the UK, with their US office in McLean, Virginia."

"That's inside the DC Beltway on the way to Dulles Airport," Hammer observed. "Lots of lobbying outfits and companies doing business with the government are out there, especially ones where the people like to come and go to other parts of the world and have easy access to Dulles. Did he say what their people wanted with the Tredquist place?"

"He tried to bury me with a lot of flowery chatter about children and beautiful pristine open spaces. He even gave me a Hambledon Global brochure with lots of pictures of smiling children."

"Did he say anything about the old Air Force runway?"

"He was startled for a minute when I mentioned it, but then he said it was bringing in people to experience the pristine open spaces. I don't understand it unless they're planning to build some kind of resort, and when I asked him about it, he said those plans hadn't been finalized yet. He said it in a way that sounded like he was making it up on the spot."

"What's your call?" Hammer asked. "Is Sunrise a front for something?"

"Oh, let me see," Lauren said with a laugh. "It's a company so keen to appear legitimate that they take offices at the highest profile address in town, but when you get into those offices, nothing seems to actually be happening. There are no pictures on the walls and there's a paper shredder in the corner. Yes, I'd put my money on it being a front for something."

"What's your guess?" Hammer said. "A front for who or what?"

"It could still be a front for some kind of sinister Chinese takeover, but the only indication of an Asian connection was the girl who was picked up in a Sunrise pickup. Whoever they are, they're into something which needs a 10,000-mile runway in the middle of nowhere."

"A runway an hour south of a part of Canada that's even *more* in the middle of nowhere," Hammer added. "I don't think it's about smiling children."

"Drug smugglers?" Lauren replied, as much a statement as a question. "How can federal agents be so blatantly mixed up in supporting a drug operation on this scale?"

"I got a close-up look at this in Afghanistan. Opium

has been their number one industry forever, and their version of the opiate trade makes the Colombian and Mexican cartels look like street corner pushers. The Taliban are the biggest drug cartel in the world, but that's only part of it. Their operation is very much facilitated by people from crooked Pentagon hacks to NGOs that are fronts for just the sort of thing we suspect with Sunrise and its parent company. Each are doing their part and taking a cut. You can say 'conspiracy theory' if you want, but I saw it up close."

"How is this even possible?"

"Follow the money," Hammer said with an ironic grin.

"What can you do?" Lauren asked cynically.

"What can *I* do? Literally?"

"Sure."

"Like I did in Afghanistan. I decided it was hunting season. It was a war where the powers that be had lost track of an overall strategy or had been co-opted by corruption. We—me and my team—decided what needed to happen. Straightforward objectives clearly articulated. You can guess what happened next."

"And you're thinking *now* might be the time for hunting season here in Logan County?"

"First, I've got to get a better handle on what they're doing out there," Hammer said. "Can you get me a full-size assessor's map of the Tredquist property?"

"Of course," Lauren said, smiling. *Hunting season in Logan County.* She was really starting to like the way he did business. It was daunting—and more than a little bit scary—but why was she feeling more *excitement* than trepidation?

CHAPTER
SIX

JESSICA EDREDIN and Erin O'Malley sat down in one of the booths lining the front windows of the Shiny Rock Café.

"How's Steve?" Kristen asked as she brought them breakfast menus and glasses of water.

"We just came from the hospital," Jessica answered. "He's doing a lot better. Looks like he'll be discharged on Saturday morning."

"Kicking him out before the weekend," Erin said with a smile.

"How's Mark doing?" Kristen asked, looking at Jessica.

"He's mad as hell," Jessica admitted. "Blames himself for not shooting the guy when he shot Steve. Of course this would have made things so much worse, but still. Basically, he is depressed because he feels so helpless. Hasn't been back to work at the feed company since it happened."

"If there's anything I can do," Kristin said earnestly.

"Thank you...for now, coffee and a Denver omelet."

The little bell on the front door tinkled and Mark came into the café.

"There he is," Erin said cheerfully. She had more to be cheerful about than did her friend. Day by day, her man was on the mend, while Jessica's man was getting worse.

"How are you doing?" Erin asked as he sat down.

"Okay, I guess," he said, his tone of voice flat and lifeless.

They made small talk as they ate, with Mark saying very little. Mainly he just stared out the window as he nibbled around the edges of a plate of eggs. The threesome was nearly finished eating when the sheriff's car pulled up.

"There's Fahr," Mark said. "Hope he's got better news."

"What's the good word, Kyle?" Kristen asked, getting right to the point when the sheriff came in.

"The word's *not* good, Kristen," he said in a bitter tone. "There is no good word. The attorney general won't authorize a warrant."

"*Why?*" Kristen gasped.

"It's over their heads, damn it! The attorney general says it's over *his* head. The feds are in charge."

Everyone at the counter and those in the other booth heard what the sheriff had said and stared in disbelief.

"Don't look at me," Fahr said angrily. "There's *nothing* I can do."

"You want some coffee?" Kristen asked meekly.

"I think I need a shot of tequila," the sheriff said angrily.

"That's not a bad idea!" Mark Edredin said emphatically as he stood.

"*Mark!*" Jessica said. "Don't even talk like this! It's eight o'clock in the morning!"

The people in the café, their eyes shifting back and

forth between Edredin and Fahr, barely noticed as Jim
Hammer came through the front door.

"Am I interrupting something?" he asked, observing
all the staring that was in progress.

"Hi Hammer, good to see you," Kristen said calmly.
"Mark and Kyle are talking about shots of tequila and
Jessica was saying it's a little too early in the day."

"Well, it *is* early," Hammer said. "What's going on?"

Everyone spoke at once, but Jessica's voice came out
on top.

"Basically, the attorney general washed his hands of
issuing an arrest warrant to go over the feds' heads," she
said, nodding toward the sheriff. "Does this about sum
it up?"

"Don't look at me," Fahr repeated bitterly.

Hammer could see Mark Edredin was fuming but
impressed by how well he was controlling a boiling
temper, even as the sheriff was losing his.

"Let's talk about this," he said, putting his arm on
Edredin's shoulder and guiding him toward some empty
stools at the end of the counter.

"I know, I gotta get a grip," Edredin said. "But I feel
so out of control…so helpless."

"Remember the state championship game our senior
year?"

"They were undefeated, too."

"Remember how freaked we were? Remember how
we pulled together, even though we were just a bunch of
country kids?"

"We led by five at halftime and beat 'em by twelve,"
Edredin recalled.

"Yes, we did," Hammer confirmed. "We pulled
together and we did it. This time, we're up against an
undefeated team who doesn't even know there's a game

on. Like back then, they don't know who the hell they're dealing with."

"Let's do it, then," Edredin said firmly. "*Game on.*"

"Okay," Hammer said, taking the Sunrise Land Holdings business card out of his shirt pocket. "Is this the logo that was on those guys' ball caps?"

"Yeah, it was. Same teal-blue color. What does it say? Are they out of Billings?"

"Yup."

"It's like they're running roughshod over Logan County and we just can't fight back," Edredin said. "It's like rules of engagement in Afghanistan...you know I put in a tour over there too."

"Yeah, I heard that," Hammer said sympathetically. "Who were you with?"

"Infantry...the 503rd. It was nothing as heroic as you Special Forces guys, but I took some incoming and dished it back at 'em. More than a few times. Couple of Purple Hearts."

"Anybody who actually served in combat and brought back a Purple Heart from over there is heroic in my book."

"Yeah, but after all the combat, it's damned hard to come back and have to take this kind of abuse at home and not be able to fight back. Seeing Steve get shot brought back a lot of memories. Not all of them good. It just feels hopeless. I just wish I could do something."

"I know what you mean, *exactly*," Hammer said. "But I think we *can* do something. It's a long story."

"Okay, I'm all ears."

"Let's go for a little drive. I'll tell you in the car. Let's go get you some hope...c'mon. I have a map."

Edredin felt himself relax. There was something in Hammer's optimism which had already started to dilute his helplessness.

As the two men stood to leave the café, Jessica Edredin thought she detected the slightest spring in her husband's step.

"Where are you two going?" she asked.

"Going for a little drive," Hammer said. "Clear our heads."

———

They were about five miles out of town when Hammer pulled over and rolled the big assessor's map out on the hood of his pickup.

They studied how the property they knew as the Tredquist place lay in relation to the state highway and the paved, but less-traveled county road. They saw the graded gravel road long used by hunters, like themselves, to access the vast rolling hills on the south side of the property. They looked at the cluster of old ranch house buildings where the sheriff had his run-in with the feds. Edredin pointed to the spot where Steve Coe had been shot, and Hammer nodded as he compared the map with a satellite view he pulled up on his phone.

The two also scanned the less-familiar northern part of the land. They saw the old runway and the nearby barracks and commented on how remote these places were from any prying eyes of anyone who might be traveling paved roads. The Air Force had wanted it this way.

Noting the networks of dirt roads running across parts of the land with which they were unfamiliar, Hammer said, "Let's go exploring."

With Edredin using the map to navigate, they finally got close enough to put Hammer's high-power Oberwerk 10x42 HD II binoculars on the runway and the adjacent one-story buildings.

"There's people moving around out there," Edredin said, looking through the glass.

"So there are," Hammer said. "What do they look like?"

"There's a few in jackets and caps like the ones we saw when Steve was attacked, and a couple in suits, one guy there in a bright orange tie."

"See any Escalades?"

"Nope, but there's a couple of sedans."

The two friends went back to Hammer's pickup and continued to drive the dirt roads marked on the map. They were about an hour or so into their "exploration" when they saw a vehicle emerge from out of a side road partially obscured in a gully. There had been frost overnight and the ground was still damp, so there had been no dust to give them any warning.

"That's it!" Edredin said with alarm. "That's the Toyota Tundra those two guys were driving! It's coming right at us!"

"I guess we better stop so they can say hello," Hammer said as he pulled over.

When Hammer unfastened his seat belt, Edredin noticed he had a Colt M1911 .45 automatic in a holster under his coat. Edredin was a bit anxious about the prospects of what might happen next.

Hammer and Edredin stepped out and moved away from the pickup. Hammer's idea was this would lure the guys in the Tundra to do the same. It did.

"It's them," Edredin whispered. "That same two from three days ago. The redhead is the one who shot Steve."

The teal-blue logos on their caps were hard to miss. As Edredin had described them from before, each man had a tactical holster on his hip. The red-haired man, who was driving today, had a Glock G19. The other guy looked to be carrying the same or similar.

"Look who we have here, Brad," the red-haired man said in a mocking tone. "Our trespasser from the other day is back, and he brought a friend."

It did not surprise Hammer when the first man to shoot his weapon on Monday was the first to shoot off his mouth on Thursday.

Hammer said nothing. Nor did Brad, who looked a trifle ill at ease. Hammer did not glance over, but he suspected that Mark Edredin also looked a bit ill at ease.

"I told you this is private property and you are not wanted here, so I'm telling you assholes to get the hell out of here before we have more trouble!"

As he had in the previous encounter, "Red" couldn't help but take a couple of strides forward. His mistake was taking those steps toward Jim Hammer.

Hammer countered by taking two steps toward Red.

"You're out on bail pretty fast," Hammer said. "I heard the feds took charge of you after you shot a man on Monday. I figured you'd still be in federal lockup."

Hammer knew full well the feds had been called only to *prevent* Red from landing in jail.

"I guess you have friends in high places," Hammer continued.

"We got a wise guy here this morning, Brad," he said, laughing as he took several more steps toward Hammer. "Apparently, he forgot I was dealing with *armed trespassers* then. My life was in danger. Your buddy here is the one who ought to be in jail."

Hammer remained still as the red-haired man continued toward him. He wanted Red to have a sense of being in control.

This worked. He did have that *sense*, or in this case, the *misapprehension*, so he failed to notice when Hammer set his feet in a shooting stance.

Looking at Edredin, Red smiled and said, "I hope you

know where he put the keys, because you're gonna be driving out of here *again* with a limp friend in your trunk."

Turning back to Hammer, Red reached for his Glock.

He had only just closed his fingers on the grip and started to raise the weapon when he found himself staring into the muzzle of Hammer's Colt M1911. Red had not imagined Hammer would be armed.

It was a big mistake.

For someone used to the world of black polymer 9mm automatics, the Colt M1911 is an anachronism. Little in it had changed since the world wars. The weathered natural metal made it look like a relic out of Anzio or Iwo Jima. The Colt weighs more than a Glock G19 and has a recoil which is harder to master. They market those modern 9mm weapons as "light and easy to use." For someone like Hammer, who could bench press around 300 pounds, lightness and recoil are clearly irrelevant.

Red had not fully raised his Glock when Hammer pulled the trigger.

The bullet impacted Red just below his left eye socket, but this is neither here nor there because his entire skull exploded in a damp cloud, showering Brad with bits and pieces of skin and bone.

No need for a second round.

By this time, Brad had his own Glock raised, but he was so startled by the gunshot that opened the show that he hesitated.

Another big mistake.

Hammer's big lead lozenge caught him just behind his left temple, but this was irrelevant. Most of his head just wasn't there any longer.

Hammer holstered his weapon, picked up his two spent cartridges, and pocketed the cell phones and wallets carried by the two men.

"What can I do?" Edredin asked.

As he pulled a long-handled shovel and a Pulaski out of his camper shell, Hammer was pleased to see that Mark had regained his composure and was ready to go to work.

Hammer had plenty of experience cleaning up messes like this, and in less than half an hour, both bodies were in a six-foot trench under a bunch of rocks in a gully more than a hundred feet off the narrow dirt road. The patches of blood at the scene of the shooting had been carefully tilled in such a way that they would not be noticed by a casual passerby until the next rainstorm. After this, they'd be gone.

When the tools were stowed back in Hammer's truck, the two of them went over to take a look at the Toyota Tundra. It was fairly new, but otherwise not out of the ordinary. The two Montana boys who grew up thinking of pickups being defined by manual transmissions shook their heads at the automatic, and Edredin was the first to comment on the vehicle having a two-way radio.

"Probably because cell service is nonexistent out here," he quipped.

"Okay, we need to move the truck a long way from here, and as long as we're doing this, let's put it to work for us," Hammer said thoughtfully. "Here's what I'm think should happen next. You can take the Toyota, keep your gloves on, and drive back out to the county road. Turn north, away from Obsidian. You know the picnic area off the road up about eight or ten miles? Pull in there and park somewhere that can't be seen from the highway. Lock it up like you would if it was yours. Take the keys and walk back to the road. I'll pick you up."

"Just leave it?"

"Leave it where you would if you didn't want it found. When it *is* found there eventually, it will be like

Red and Brad parked it and took off out of the county. Rats abandoning their ship. If the feds happen to dust the cab for prints, they'll find only Red and Brad."

"Jim, stop me if I'm out of line here," Edredin said. "But if you're planning to go to war with this outfit, I want to be part of it. I do have an AR-15 and a SIG P226, and I know how to use them. Count me in. Just give the word."

"Thanks," Hammer said with a grin. "It's great to have a vet from the 503rd on the team."

CHAPTER
SEVEN

FRIDAY MORNING DAWNED drizzly in Logan County.

Tom R. Brach cursed the graded gravel road leading into the old Tredquist ranch house compound, where Sunrise Land Holdings had set up their field headquarters. The dampness had turned the road into a sloppy mess, which in turn was turning his gun-metal gray Mercedes E-Class into a sloppy mess.

He did not like this, nor did he like having to drive all the way up here from Billings to sort things out. For the past year, his Montana project, the scheme he designed and implemented, had been going smoothly. His bosses in McLean were delighted. Now everything was going sideways, like a skid in a turn on a patch of black ice. McLean was anxious.

All the way up to Logan County, he had gone through it in his mind. He had set up shop at a good address, arguably *the best* business address in Billings. He had set out to establish the legitimacy of Sunrise. He had brought Tony Stayton with him from the McLean office as an executive assistant to run day-to-day affairs in the office.

Stayton was diligent and loyal, but he had his quirks, such as always wearing a bright orange necktie. He was a proud alumnus of Oregon State.

Brach had been a realtor in Maryland and northern Virginia for years, and he knew the drill. He joined a local realtors' networking group when he got to Billings. He had joined the Rotary and got himself a seat on the board of the new performing arts center going in across the street.

He met a woman who liked him and liked his flash. She also liked his flesh, and he considered this a perk. He asked her to be his PA, gave her the title of "VP of Networking," and flashed a pretty good—for Montana—salary. Kally Stefano was a realtor of moderate success, but mainly she looked good and her smile certainly added to the Sunrise curb appeal. Brach never revealed the deep secrets of what Sunrise was really all about.

When it came time to make a move on the Tredquist property, she and Brach had flown down to Denver to wine, dine, and win over the cash-hungry heirs. Even Margaret Tredquist, the matriarch, who had a sentimental attachment to memories of the place, had succumbed to Kally's charm offensive.

Everything had been going so well that Brach should have known it couldn't last.

He couldn't believe it when Jason Nuemeyer, the Sunrise on-site manager at the former Tredquist property had phoned Monday morning in a panic.

"*Kenny Lathrope just shot a trespasser!*" Nuemeyer gasped.

In retrospect, maybe one of Brach's biggest mistakes was his wanting to keep the Tredquist deal under the radar. It hadn't been widely publicized, even in Logan County, so those local idiots still thought they could go hunting out there.

Then one of those locals got shot, of course they called the local sheriff.

Brach also phoned friends, and luckily, his friends had bigger badges.

But this came at a cost. By showing their badges, Vince Milino and his ATF crew had to show their hand. Brach's bosses at Hambledon Global in McLean were furious with Brach for getting the feds involved at such a critical early stage in the Montana project.

———

Brach parked next to the Toyota Tundra with the Sunrise logo and rapped on the door.

"Morning," Jason Nuemeyer said sheepishly as he answered. He was wearing one of the nearly new North Face jackets that were the uniform of the Sunrise workforce. "Wish it was under better circumstances."

"I wish I did not have to be here *at all*," Brach said. "Let's talk."

The three other men sitting around in the living room looked up as Brach came in but went back to what they were doing when Nuemeyer ushered Brach into his side office.

"I wish I did not have to be here," Brach repeated as the door was closed. "I hate this boring drive up from the city and I hate getting my car splattered with mud. Makes me look like a damned hillbilly. Mostly, I hate having to come up here to personally try to sort out this mess you've got us in up here."

"We knew Kenny Lathrope was high strung," Nuemeyer said. "Sometimes that red hair of his looked almost like flames, but I figured he had the kind of feisty personality that would convey the right message to any would-be intruder."

"Well he sure as hell conveyed a message with this one!" Brach growled. "Getting the feds mixed up in this to keep him out of jail cost me plenty of points. They're pissed off big time that the sheriff already knows they're part of this."

"But he's only the sheriff of Logan County," Nuemeyer insisted. "This is *nowhere*. This is a nothing place. Nobody in the real world cares about this place."

"Well, Logan County phoned the state attorney general in Helena asking for a warrant to countermand federal authority in this."

"Oh," Nuemeyer said hesitantly. "What happened with that?"

"The feds got him to stand down, but this is no longer a nowhere thing in a nowhere county. We better hope this blows over and blows over damned quick."

Brach took a long drink from the water bottle Nuemeyer had handed him and walked to the front window.

"Where's Lathrope now?" Brach demanded. "I need to fire his ass."

"He's out with Brad Shannin patrolling the back roads in the other Tundra. Especially out around the airfield."

"When will they be back?"

"Pretty soon," Nuemeyer said nervously. "Probably."

"*Probably...probably...probably!*" Brach seethed. "Get him on the phone!"

"There's no cell service out here, so we use two-way radios."

"Like old-school CB radios?"

"Yeah. Truckers still use 'em. They're more reliable than cell phones out here in the wide open spaces."

"Well get him on the CB and tell him to get back here *now!*"

Brach paced as Nuemeyer tried in vain to contact

Lathrope. Just as Nuemeyer was giving up, Brach saw a vehicle approaching.

"Is that them?" Brach asked.

"No," Nuemeyer said, staring at a mud-spattered blue pickup with a camper shell. "I never saw this truck before. No front license plate. Probably some local buffoon who couldn't be bothered. Nobody ever comes in here on this road."

"Except the hunters on Monday, and *these* trespassers today," Brach said pointedly. "Why are those guys in the other room not out there patrolling the place in the other Tundra. Some changes gotta be made."

"Maybe these people came here looking for jobs," one of the men suggested.

The two men in the ranch house had never seen Mark Edredin nor Jim Hammer before, and of course they couldn't have known Hammer had registered his truck in Kentucky because it was one of the few states which do not require a front license plate. Twenty years in special operations had made being inconspicuous second nature.

Brach and Nuemeyer stepped outside to size up the two scruffy-looking men walking toward the front door. They were each tall and fit. Even in their heavy coats, neither looked to be carrying any extra weight. Brach thought that if they *were* looking for work, they might be worth considering. They did not look like men who's spend the day slouching around a ranch house.

The three Sunrise employees who had been slouching inside, came out and stood facing the two strangers.

"Pat them down," Nuemeyer ordered before anyone had begun to exchange niceties. He was genuinely suspicious, but on another level, he was trying to show off a level of vigilance in order to ingratiate himself with Brach.

Hammer was glad he'd left the Colt under his seat.

"They're clean," the man doing the patting reported.

"I'm sorry, gentlemen," the amiable realtor from Billings said, putting on his salesman's charm and greeting the visitors with a smile and an extended hand. "It's just we weren't expecting you. I'm Tom R. Brach of Sunrise Holdings in Billings. This is Jason Nuemeyer, our on-site manager of this location. What can we do for you?"

Hammer and Edredin introduced themselves as they shook Brach's hand. Nuemeyer extended his own but did not smile. The other three stood apart from the cordialities. Hammer immediately recognized Brach's name as having been the man whom Lauren Stahling had met in Billings two days earlier.

"You may not recognize Mr. Edredin," Hammer began, "but he had a very unpleasant introduction to your organization on Monday, when a friend of ours was shot in the arm by a friend of *yours* while Mr. Edredin watched."

"Oh, that," Brach said. He was startled they had the audacity to just walk in here like this. He had to get rid of them. "You need to know Sunrise greatly regrets the incident…and the inconvenience…"

"What?" Edredin said angrily. *"Inconvenience?"*

"If there is anything we can do…" Brach started saying.

"To start with, Mr. Edredin and Mr. Coe had some property taken from them on Monday," Hammer said. "There were two hunting rifles…"

"And two scopes," Edredin interjected. "One of them is a Burris HD worth more than five hundred dollars… and a couple pairs of binoculars."

"Do we have these?" Brach asked Nuemeyer.

Nuemeyer just nodded, first to Brach, then to one of the other men, who went back into the house. Finally, he returned, carrying the binoculars and two bolt-action hunting rifles with scopes mounted, which he laid on a picnic table on the front lawn. He then proceeded to remove the bolts from each rifle, so they could not readily be fired.

"You may hand these over to Mr. Hammer," Brach said with a disingenuous smile. Hammer pocketed the bolts and took the binoculars and rifles in hand.

"Well, unless there's anything else..." Brach started to say.

"Actually, there is," Hammer said. "On Monday, the man who shot Mr. Edredin's hunting partner was about to be taken into custody when federal agents arrived on the scene. We assume he was placed into federal custody. That was four days ago and nobody has contacted Mr. Edredin about a witness statement."

Brach and Nuemeyer exchanged glances, perplexed expressions on their faces.

"We'd like to know where he's being held, and who Mr. Edredin should contact about volunteering *his* account of what happened."

"I don't have this information," Brach replied after a long pause. "I can certainly try to find out and let you know."

"Maybe we should make some calls? Billings office? Denver?" Hammer insisted.

"No, let me try to find out, and I'll give *you* a call," Brach replied. "If you could please give me your number?"

"Oh, I wish I could," Hammer said apologetically. "My cell phone got broken. These things just aren't made to last anymore. I'm still waiting for the replacement. Maybe you could give me *your* card? I'll phone you as soon as I get my new phone."

Eager to be rid of this disconcerting nuisance, Brach

handed over a business card with a promise to "look into it."

As they watched the two men back away from the ranch house in the old pickup, the charming Brach reverted to the irascible Brach.

"Instead of just sitting around the ranch house," he said irritably. "I want you out finding Lathrope and Shannin!"

"What if they don't want to be found?"

Both Brach and Nuemeyer turned their heads toward the man who spoke.

"*What?*"

"Maybe they did a runner," the man suggested. "Lathrope knows he screwed up big time. He shot a guy. The feds maybe kept him outta the county jail for now, but if somebody turns on the heat, he gets burned. Him and Shannin could be all the way to Denver by now...or Seattle...and still running."

As Brach and Nuemeyer looked at one another in consternation, they could hear the sound of a large turbo-prop airplane rumbling in the distance.

CHAPTER
EIGHT

"I GOT a hole in my shoulder, so they don't think I can walk," Steve Coe said, cracking a joke as an attendant pushed him toward the doors of the hospital in a wheelchair. Erin was with him, a smile on her face, carrying a "Get Well" balloon and a vase of two-day-old flowers. It was Saturday morning, and the hospital was turning its rooms.

"Sure glad to see you on the other side of this thing, man," Mark Edredin said.

"Not as glad as I am to be seen," Steve said, smiling.

Jessica gave him a hug, and Erin gripped the hand of his good arm with both hers and told him how good he looked.

He quipped something about being able to get used to all this friendliness and invited them all to come over to his house to have a beer.

Erin's first reaction was an expression which said, "I want you all to myself," but this quickly turned to a grin and a seconding of the cordial invitation.

Steve walked into the house on his own, although he

was a bit shaky after five hours of surgery and five days on his back connected to tubes and wires.

Lauren Stahling arrived a few minutes later, and the five of them sat around in the living room while Jessica served a store-bought coffee cake she had brought to share, and Erin made coffee. The conversation was friendly, even gregarious, with a strong undertone of sighs of relief.

After a while, as the women remained in the living room, Steve and Mark ended up in the kitchen. Steve took a couple of cans of Buffalo Jaw IPA out of the fridge and they sat down at the table.

Steve made jokes about how they wouldn't let him have beer in the hospital, but how Erin had sneaked one in the night before.

"So, how you doing?" Mark asked in a relaxed way after he'd taken a long, satisfying sip.

"Seriously?"

"Yeah," Mark answered, realizing Steve had turned more somber.

"How am I doing? Man, I'm lucky to be alive. I feel pretty good, all things considered, but knowing how I dodged a bullet...or how the bullet dodged parts of me that would've killed me...it makes me think. And I think about it all the time. You know, all the bullshit about borrowed time and making your life count. Realizing I'm in love with Erin, and we gotta get serious and settle down."

"Congratulations," Mark said, touching his friend's beer can with his own.

"You know I was lucky. A quarter of an inch either way...and all this. And man, you know, if you hadn't tied the tourniquet like you did, I'd have never made it to town."

"Glad I was there," Mark said, touching Steve's can again.

"I wish I could have returned fire," he said. "I can't really remember much about getting hit. I can't remember their faces. I guess it's a good thing. I'd sure hate to have this in my dreams. Even if the sheriff couldn't arrest the shooter, I hope he gets what he deserves."

"Yup."

That was all Mark could say. He wished he could tell Steve that the red-haired guy's skull had been shattered like cheap crockery and the rest of him was feeding coyotes from under a pile of rocks in a ditch, but he and Hammer had agreed nobody would ever know...

"I have a surprise for you," Mark said. "C'mon."

The two men walked out to Mark's car, where he popped the trunk and took out Steve's Remington.

"*Geez, Louise,*" I never thought I'd see this again! How..."

"Me and Jim Hammer took a little drive out there yesterday."

"Did you see those guys who attacked us?"

"No," Mark said succinctly.

"Is Hammer back for a while, or is he gonna disappear for twenty years again?"

"He's out of the Army and taking time off. He said he came for antelope season. I don't know what his plans are. I don't really know *he* knows."

"I'd like to see him again," Steve said with a grin. "Maybe we ought to think about getting the championship team back together again?"

CHAPTER
NINE

IT WAS a quiet Sunday morning in Obsidian. Aunt Charlotte had gone to church, and Jim Hammer was just parking the Norton in her garage, where it had lived since he'd been back in town. Suddenly, his phone rang. It was Lauren Stahling.

"You're up early," he answered in a sociable tone.

"I bet you'll tell me you were up earlier," she replied affably.

"I was just parking the Norton. I took a little ride this morning."

"Have you had coffee?"

"Due for more. I can meet you at the Shiny Rock."

"I just made some," she said. "Why don't you come here?"

He exchanged his leather jacket for the gray canvas one he usually wore, brushed off his jeans, washed his hands and face in the utility sink in the garage, and wheeled his motorcycle back out.

"Black with a touch of whitener?" Lauren said, recalling how he took his coffee as she opened her front door with a cup in hand. She was wearing jeans, not tight jeans exactly, but tight enough to accent the perfect curves of her body. She wore a flimsy top under a lavender, long-sleeved, button-up sweater.

"Just enough to make it behave," he said, repeating his usual recipe, which she'd heard before.

"I was over at Steve and Erin's house yesterday after he came home from the hospital," she said, gesturing for him to take a seat at the kitchen table.

"How is Steve doing?" Hammer asked. "If they cut him loose, I guess he's on the mend."

"Yeah, he seemed to be doing okay. When did you last see him?"

"Thursday morning. I was thinking of stopping by later this afternoon."

"That would be a good idea," Lauren said. "I know he'd like this. You were good friends with him and Mark."

"The dream team of Logan County High." Hammer laughed. "The heart of the State Championship team... long, long ago."

"Speaking of Mark, I heard you guys met my 'friend' Tom R. Brach out at the Tredquist place on Friday."

"He was like you described him. Slick salesman type. Suit, but no tie. Cordial enough, but real anxious to get rid of us. So much so that he handed over the hunting rifles without a fuss. This guy Nuemeyer who is their supervisor up there sure didn't want to do it. You could see it in his eyes. But Tom R. is the boss."

"Did you see the men who attacked Mark and Steve... the red-haired guy?"

"They weren't there, but I really touched a nerve by asking whether the redhead was in federal custody. I pressed him on wanting to know where the feds had the guy who shot Steve locked up. Told him Mark was ready to make a witness statement. Really caught old Tom R. off guard."

"I'll bet he was not expecting *this*," Lauren said with a laugh.

"Of course not, but that is what you'd 'normally' expect if the feds took over from county jurisdiction."

"What did he say?"

"He hemmed less than you might expect, but he came up with 'not having that information,' and saying he'd get back to us. Asked for my number. I said I'd call *him* and got another one of his cards."

"Will you call him?"

"Maybe. I'll probably get a burner phone at the drugstore tomorrow. I'm not in a hurry for fake information, and if I wait to call him, or even if I don't, that's another loose end for him to have in the back of his mind."

"Did you learn anything else?"

"I learned more from the expressions of Nuemeyer and the other three up there. I could see in their eyes that they've lost track of the redhead. I sensed by the way they were glancing at each other, a couple of them thought 'Red' and his buddy have taken off for parts unknown. Which I suppose is realistic under the circumstances."

"The shooting was certainly a topic of conversation yesterday when I was talking with Jess and Erin," Lauren said. "Where do *you* think he is."

"I don't think we'll be hearing from them," Hammer replied in a vaguely mysterious tone.

"Hmmm…is this like those nasty Taliban warlords you were telling me about?" Lauren asked after a long and thoughtful pause.

He just smiled and took another sip of coffee.

She nodded. She understood completely. He'd always known her to be a quick study.

"Is that where you were riding this morning?" Lauren asked.

"I took the bike because I wanted to keep a low profile and go off-road."

"What did you see?"

"The airport is in business. When Mark and I were out there on Thursday, there were no airplanes, a couple of vehicles and maybe a dozen people. There were no Escalades. Today, there were more vehicles, including an Escalade, more people and an airplane."

"What kind?"

"It was an ATR72 twin turboprop, a regional airliner made in France. About a dozen small airlines around the world have used them for years, and they're still making them. They also sell 'em to charter airlines and private users. It's big enough for around seventy-two passengers, which is how it gets its name. It's not so big, and it's not a jet. If you see it flying over, it looks just like another plane from one of those small feeder airlines around the state."

"What airline was this one from?"

"This one's painted solid white, like it just came from the factory. You see all kinds of all-white airplanes all over the world where they're being used by people who don't want to advertise who they are."

"Do you have any idea where it came from?"

"When we were talking about the runway on our car trip, I guessed picking a runway an hour south of Canada was part of the plan. This one had a tail number starting with 'C,' so it's registered up there. Fully loaded, an ATR72 had a range of up to a thousand miles, maybe less, maybe more, depending on load. Theoretically, they could fly contraband nonstop from an airstrip along the

British Columbia coast. Lot of deserted country up that way."

"And not get caught?" Lauren asked.

"The drug runners fly their stuff in from Mexico all the time, and the southern border is watched a lot better than this border up here."

"Could you tell what they were carrying?"

"They taxied in next to the buildings to unload, so I couldn't see, but an ATR72 has a payload of around seven tons. The street value of a load like this would be in the hundreds of millions of dollars. A few flights and it's into the billions."

"What are you going to do about it?" Lauren asked as though she expected him to resolve this situation.

"As we've learned the hard way, we can't just 'call the cops.' The black Escalades are already there," he said. "I'm going to go out again tomorrow and try to get a closer look."

"Are you going to involve Mark again? You should know he and Steve were talking yesterday about getting your old dream team back together again, but I don't think this was what Steve had in mind when he said it. They had put away a couple of beers by that time."

"I don't know what I'm going to do just yet," Hammer said. "But I just cannot let this go on here in Logan County. Maybe if they hadn't shot Steve, I might not feel so...I have to do *something*. If nobody else can do anything, maybe it *is* time for the championship team."

"All talk yesterday brought back a lot of memories," Lauren said. "All those lives...all *these* lives. All of us in the same room. Everybody except you...and everybody saying how much they had missed you."

"Being back here...I guess I realize now ...I *should have* stayed in touch," Hammer said. "But the longer it went, the farther away everybody seemed."

"We *did* miss you," she said in a way that had her immediately cursing herself for inadvertently opening a Pandora's box she had kept closed and had planned to *keep* closed.

Now, there came the moment that often comes up in a conversation, the moment when the inertia of the dialogue comes to a natural pause. And so it had.

With both of them seated at the corner of the kitchen table, they had not consciously noticed their faces had drifted so very close to one another.

It was Lauren who broke the tension.

"I'm ready for Sunday brunch," she said, standing up abruptly. "Let me buy you a stack of hotcakes down at the Rock."

———

Deputy Jamie Manderson headed north on the state highway in her Logan County Sheriff's Department Dodge Durango cruiser. Sheriff Kyle Fahr liked his weekends off, and this gave Jamie a chance to get out from behind the counter at the office.

On Saturday nights, when the few bars along the highway or in town let out, thinks could get lively, but Sunday mornings were the slowest time of the week.

There were no other cars on the highway when she'd turned onto it, and she had passed only two when she saw the school bus coming her way. Her first thought was it was funny to see a school bus on the road on a Sunday. Maybe it was some kind of field trip, like maybe they were taking kids down to Billings or over the Helena for some school event that started first thing Monday morning.

Mmmmzzzzzzing

"Okay, buddy," she said as the bus whizzed past. "You're goin' a little bit fast out here."

She glanced in her mirror. No hit of brake lights.

Time for a routine traffic stop to liven up her morning.

She cranked the Durango into a hard U-turn and set out to catch up with the bus. She clocked it at nearly seventy, which is legal for most vehicles on a two-lane Montana blacktop, but the school bus limit was lower.

Jamie snuggled the cruiser in behind the bus, and when the driver made no effort to slow down, she lit up the light bar.

This got the guy's attention and soon he was over on the shoulder with his flashers lit.

She should have called in the plate number, but she knew there was nobody back at the office. Sunday mornings *were* the slowest time of the week.

Grabbing her ticket book, she stepped out and looked the bus over. School buses belonging to districts or counties usually carried these markings on the side. This one was unmarked, meaning it was not a regular school district bus, but one belonging to one of those contract bus companies hired for field trips. That made sense with it being on the road on a Sunday.

As Jamie walked slowly toward the front of the bus, she glanced in and saw that they seemed to be mostly girls. Late teens. They all had dark hair, so she guessed they were probably native kids from one of the reservations up toward US Route 2.

The ones in the back of the bus were jumping around and trying to wave to her, but the ones toward the front were more well-behaved. Jamie chuckled. She had been a teenage girl once herself. It was hella boring on long bus trips.

She walked around to the door and signaled for the driver to open it.

"Sorry, Officer," the driver said apologetically, obviously trying to be nice. He was a skinny little guy about thirty, who was not in the mood to pick a fight. "I was trying to stay under the limit."

"Do you know how fast you were going?" Jamie asked, following procedure. She had all the time in the world.

"Under seventy," he replied, citing the posted limit.

"Sir, are you aware the speed limit for school buses is fifty-five?"

"No, I did not know this."

"License and registration," she said, following procedure.

She took her time looking things over.

The registration was current and seemed to be in order. The bus was registered to something down in Billings called "Sunrise Land Holdings, dba SLH Transportation." She couldn't imagine why a land company was driving high school kids around, but she had seen stranger things.

The driver was from up north in Chinook. Probably a part-time gig. He was not a professional bus driver, but his license was good for buses.

"Okay, sir, I'm not going to cite you today. Instead, I'm gonna write you up a warning this time. But you'd better slow down and 'arrive alive.' These vehicles are not equipped with seat belts. Do you understand?"

"Yes."

"Okay, here's your warning," she said, handing him a scrap of paper from the ticket book. "You don't have to appear in court or pay a fine, but this remains on your record for six months. Do you understand?"

"Yes," he said, studying the warning. He had turned pale. He looked like he'd just been handed six months in the county lockup.

As she started walking back to her car, the girls in the back of the bus were still jumping around and waving at her and banging on the window. She just gave them a big wave and got into her Durango. By the time she got her ticket book put away, the bus was a quarter mile down the road toward Billings and driving much more slowly.

Jamie smiled, proud to have done a good deed for the day.

CHAPTER
TEN

JIM HAMMER BEGAN his Monday with an early morning phone call to his old friend Tim Tommis in Silver Spring, Maryland.

Tommis had been the communications genius on the team Hammer had led in Afghanistan, a man who could conjure comms and data and intel out of the ether in ways appearing like magic to even the most brilliant nerds. He had lost the use of his legs to a 7.62mm round in the base of his spine on the way out, but every member of the team pitched in to take turns carrying him across the Hindu Kush to safety.

Tommis had barely skipped a beat in his career. He left the US Army on a medical discharge, along with a basket of medals and commendations, and then reinvented himself as the go-to black magician for numerous —the exact number is safe with him—freelance covert operators and old friends, like Hammer.

"I got your message," Hammer said. "How's things?"

"Oh just another jolly day inside the Beltway. Gridlock on I-95 at Exit 160 and worse on East Capitol Street at 295. As always, the worst gridlock is inside that big domed building on the Hill. Usual fun and games here. How is it out there in the Wild West?"

"Wild."

"Sounds fun"

"What do you have for me?"

"Okay, let me cough up my notes."

Hammer could hear the sound of Tommis scooting from workstation to workstation in his wheelchair on highly polished hardwood flooring. His friend inhabited a warren of electronic gear with more computer screens than a Bangalore call center.

"Okay, here's what I've got. As your assessor friend learned, your Sunrise Land Holdings was formed two years ago and it's owned by the Hambledon Global Advocacy Group. Like the brochure you sent me says, Hambledon is an international NGO with offices in London and McLean, Virginia. The American office in McLean is run by a Brit named Westley Carker. He's the one who recruited the guy your friend met, Tom R. Brach. They set up Sunrise, based it in Billings, and Brach became the managing director."

"What's Brach's story?"

"He was actually in real estate over around the Chesapeake Bay area for a number of years, mainly doing high-end second homes. Before Hambledon recruited him, he worked for a couple of lobbyists. He's a typical Beltway opportunist. He's reinvented himself as a real Billings community pillar. He joined the local real estate organization and the Rotary. He got a seat on the board of a performing arts center. Some of his minions in the Billings office are a guy named Tony Stayton, who went to Oregon State, and a small-time realtor named Kally Stefano. She's a local girl from out there."

"What else did you find on Hambledon?"

"The American office in McLean is in a really fancy office park. Lots of glass. Seem to be well-funded, but they've only been in the States for about four years. The London office is a storefront in Chelsea. They position themselves along with NGOs like Oxfam or Save the Children, or like World Vision, but most people have never heard of them. As you've seen, the brochure says *nothing*. It's just a generic piece of fluff…looks like they just bought some 'smiling children around the world' stock photos."

"What do they actually do?"

"They claim to have do-gooder projects in two dozen countries. Let me read the buzzwords…child protection, climate justice, economic empowerment, educational empowerment, gender empowerment, the list goes on and on."

"I get the idea."

"What did your lady friend say they were doing out there in the Wild West?"

"She said Brach talked about beautiful pristine open spaces."

"How lovely. Where do I send my donation check?" Tommis asked sarcastically. "Let me keep digging. I should have more in a day or so."

"Thanks a million, Tim."

"Just doin' what I love, buddy."

———

Lauren Stahling always walked to work. Even on the days when a winter storm dropped and drifted three feet of snow onto the landscape, they plowed the streets early and she could walk in the street. The walk gave her twenty minutes to think about the piles on her desk and to organize her day.

Weather excepted, it was always the same view, the same buildings, the same trees, and more or less the same cars. It was familiar, constant, and normal, a comfortable place to anchor her reality as she organized each day in the back of her mind.

This Monday morning, she was thinking about how much the past week had changed things for Logan County and how little most people knew about what was going on. They knew Steve Coe had been shot, and he was getting better. They knew Kyle Fahr had been thwarted in his attempt to arrest the perp, but most people assumed the feds would do the right thing and justice would eventually be done.

Almost no one had ever heard of, much less thought about, Sunrise Land Holdings, and *nobody* knew the runway out at the old Tredquist place was receiving visits from unmarked airliners. Only the people around the county courthouse saw the look on the county attorney's face when the attorney general told him to back off, and to forget Steve Coe had ever been shot.

As the county courthouse came into view around the last big hedge, the view was suddenly no longer familiar, constant, or normal.

At the sheriff's office, on the side of the building opposite the main entrance, she could see a group of people milling about who seemed agitated. Walking over to get a better look, she saw *why* they were unsettled.

A black Escalade was parked at an angle, as though it had driven up in a hurry and the driver had ignored the marked parking spaces. A man in a black suit with a black overcoat and a blond buzz cut was standing apart from the crowd as though he was guarding the scene. Lauren couldn't tell whether he was armed.

Her first thought was to walk straight into the sheriff's office and ask what was going on. She was a county officer, and she had every legal right to do this. So she did.

She made it as far as the door when the man in the black overcoat stepped briskly toward her to bar her way.

"Federal agent," he announced, flashing his badge and federal ID. "Nobody goes in here."

"I'm the Logan County Assessor," she said angrily. "My office is in this building."

"*Nobody* goes in here."

Lauren Stahling turned from angry to furious. She could see this guy was an officious twenty-something with a boundless sense of self-importance. He was also potentially dangerous, but this was a public building in *her* town and she was mad.

"As I said, I'm the Logan County Assessor, and I am going to my office."

By now, all eyes of the group of about a dozen onlookers were on her. She thought she heard someone start to clap.

"*Nobody* goes in here," he repeated, placing himself directly in the doorway.

"Let me show you my card," Lauren said, pausing to reach for her purse to get her business card.

Her hand had just barely taken hold of her purse when she found herself staring at the muzzle of a Glock 19M.

"Don't do it," he demanded heavy-handedly. "*Drop it!*"

Lauren let go of her purse, which fell to the sidewalk, and raised her hands.

She could hear the crowd start to hiss.

"What the hell is going on?" came a booming voice from inside the sheriff's office.

Moments later, an older man with a thin mustache, also in a black suit and topcoat emerged. He saw his fellow agent aiming his Glock at a well-dressed woman with her hands raised.

"What's going on, Kr) uegher?"

"I'm the Logan County Assessor," Lauren repeated furiously. "My office is in this building."

"She was going for a gun," Agent Aron Kruegher told his boss.

"I was going for my business card!" Lauren said loud and firmly. "And I told you that!"

Special Agent Vincent Milino reached down, picked up Lauren's purse and started rifling through it.

"There's no gun, Kruegher," he told the younger man with the blond buzz cut as he thrust the purse at Lauren. "Holster your weapon. I got what we came for. Let's roll."

In a matter of mere seconds, the two men had bundled themselves into the Escalade and were driving away at high speed.

Lauren and the onlookers were left staring at one another with expressions begging the question "*what just happened?*"

Lauren just looked around and shrugged. There was light applause for one of their own who had stood up to an armed bully.

She turned and entered the building at last. In the center of the room was the main counter, which was, as is the case with police stations everywhere, situated behind bulletproof glass. Even so, the clerk behind the desk had a terrified look on her face. The two large metal doors on either side stood wide open. Deputy Jamie Manderson stood just inside one, a confused look on her face.

It was now Lauren's turn to ask what had just happened.

Jamie began to reel off a bewildering tale.

"It's usually quiet around here in the morning, especially on Mondays, and I thought it would be today," she began. "We had just opened when those two came in here. They flashed their badges and said they were federal agents. Of course they were. Who else dresses like that?"

At this point, Sheriff Kyle Fahr pulled up in his sheriff's department Durango and dashed to where Jamie was standing with Lauren.

"You're late," Jamie told him. Her tone was a little more perturbed than one normally uses to address one's boss, but she *was* upset. "You missed the fun."

"What the hell happened?" Fahr demanded. "Who's responsible for all this?"

"The feds."

"The feds?"

"Yes, Sheriff. It was your friends in the black suits and the Escalade."

"What did they want?"

"I made a routine traffic stop yesterday out on the state highway. A school bus I clocked at sixty-seven. Had to pull him over."

"I thought the speed limit was seventy," Lauren interjected.

"So did he. It's actually fifty-five for school buses carrying children."

"A school bus on a Sunday?" Fahr said skeptically.

"It wasn't a regular school district bus. It was one of those contract buses taking a bunch of high schoolers on a field trip. It was a bunch of kids from one of the reservation schools up by US 2. They probably had to be there first thing Monday morning. Going down to Billings or to Bozeman to the dinosaur museum. I didn't ask. That's their business, not mine. Mine was that they were in too big of a hurry to get there. The federal agents wanted to talk about the traffic stop."

"What about it?"

"This was the really weird thing. They wanted me to hand over the ticket. They wanted all record of the traffic stop handed over. Before you ask, they did not say *why*. Even though I just gave the guy a warning, they wanted it. They wanted to make it like it to be like it never happened. Like when some guy asks you to tear up the ticket, which is the lamest thing in the book."

"What did you tell them?" Fahr wanted to know.

"I told them *no*, of course. This was when they started getting out of control. Banging their badges on the glass and shouting 'federal agents' over and over. Telling me their authority trumps mine. I finally told them to wait until the sheriff gets in to sort it out."

"Obviously they did not wait for me."

"*Nope*. By this time, this crowd of people had started to gather around out there, so when the guy with the mustache pulled his weapon, I opened up the door. I am not going to start exchanging fire with over a traffic stop warning ticket."

"You gave it to them?"

"I'm not going to get into a shootout when there are bystanders out there bystanding."

Fahr then went behind the counter and started looking around.

"I started to give it to them and they grabbed the whole stack I had here. Lots of random stuff from last week. Don't worry. It's already backed up."

"Including the warning ticket?" Lauren asked.

"Sure," Jamie said proudly. "I even took pictures on my phone...the plates...the guy's license, and the regis- tration."

"May I?" Lauren asked, pulling her own phone out of her purse.

"Go ahead," Jamie said. "Doesn't matter now."

"Well, I guess I need to get to work," Lauren said with a wink when she'd finished. "Before I get in trouble for being late."

———

Jim Hammer would not see the cell phone photos of the sheriff's office confrontation which Lauren Stahling emailed to him until late Monday afternoon. After beginning his own day *on the grid* with Tim Tommis on Eastern Time, he was now so far *off the grid* on Mountain Time he turned off his device to save the battery.

Hammer's spot off the grid was a patch of ground on a rise overlooking the same 10,000-foot runway on the former Tredquist property where he had been early Sunday morning.

Before him sat his well-worn seven-inch tripod and his powerful Oberwerk 25x100mm CF center-focus binoculars. He had tilted the eye cups so he could glance down without having to glue his eyeballs to the cups.

Hammer may have favored retro gear in his side arms, but he went for state of the art with his optics. For portable binoculars, he carried his handy HD II, but for parking himself and watching a target for a long time, the 25x100mm CF brought him so close it was like he was at the next table in a crowded restaurant.

The airplane he had seen yesterday was gone, but there were still a few people coming and going in and around the pale-green aluminum building that was the closest to the runway of several similar structures. In addition to a lone sedan, one of the white Tundras was parked nearby.

As Hammer was spending most of the day watching and waiting for something to happen, it was certainly clear this airstrip was the central point of interest for Sunrise in whatever mischief they were transacting here at the former Tredquist place.

It was late in the day and starting to grow darker when something finally happened to interrupt the monotony. Hammer heard the hum of a vehicle approaching from the south, from the direction of the Tredquist ranch house compound. He turned his head, but not the binoculars. He could see it was the same Mercedes E-Class that had been parked at the ranch house on Friday, Tom R. Brach's E-Class. Within the field of view of Hammer's Oberwerk, Brach guided the gunmetal gray sedan to a stop near the cluster of people in front of the aluminum building and climbed out.

Moments later, everyone looked up at the sound of a pair of the Pratt & Whitney Canada PW127 turboprops approaching from the north. The ATR72 was coming back.

Hammer saw the wing lights, and then the aircraft itself. It came in low, banked slightly, lined up with the runway, and settled in. Within a few minutes, it had taxied over to where all the people waited and the pilot shut down the engines.

Unfortunately for Hammer, the cabin door was on the opposite side, so he could not get a good look at the passengers who emerged. He saw enough, little flashes of the colors of their clothing to see they were civilians lugging their own carry-ons. It was a full flight. One person, a dark-haired woman in yellow pants, wandered off, but she was promptly shooed back toward the others, who all disappeared into the metal building.

It was growing dark as Brach climbed back into the Mercedes and took off. Hammer waited another half hour, but nothing more happened. The ATR-72 departed, and they buttoned the place up for the night.

It was dark by the time Hammer reached the county road, turned on the Norton's headlight and pointed it toward Obsidian.

CHAPTER
ELEVEN

"I JUST TURNED on my phone and saw those pictures you sent this morning," Hammer said. "An Escalade in front of the sheriff's office? A traffic ticket? Somebody's driver's license? What happened?"

"Nice of you to return my call," Lauren replied, still fuming about the Monday morning run-in. "Where were you that you had your phone turned off? No, let me guess."

"Looks like the feds showed up again," he said.

She told him of the fracas at the sheriff's office, which led to the school bus story.

"That makes no sense," Hammer said.

"It made no sense to me either," Lauren said, until I connected the dots. "You can't see it in the picture I sent, because I took the pictures of the paperwork in a hurry, and the one of the warning citations is blurry. It's also a carbon copy from Jamie Manderson's ticket book...but the bus is registered to a company called SLH Transportation, which is owned by, guess who, Sunrise Land Holdings. How do you figure that?"

"What does Sunrise want with a school bus?" Hammer said.

"And why are the feds so interested in a school bus getting a warning ticket?" Lauren added. "This just confirms they're fully involved in whatever Sunrise is doing. What did you see out at the Tredquist place today?"

"I went out to watch the airport," Hammer said. "Mostly it was quiet. Just a few people coming and going at one of the buildings. Then, late in the day, Brach showed up shortly before the airplane came back."

"Are you sure it was the same one?" Lauren asked.

"I made note of the tail number."

"Of course you did," Lauren said with a chuckle. "Who was on it?"

"Civilians got off, but the door was on the opposite side, so I couldn't see much of what was going on. I wish there were some way to get inside what they're doing. They communicate with two-way radios out there because cell service is lousy."

"That's interesting," Lauren said. "I noticed the Escalade the feds were driving yesterday had a two-way radio and lots of aerials and antennae."

"I wonder what frequency they're on," Hammer said.

"Have you thought about using a police scanner to listen in?" Lauren suggested.

"That's not a bad idea," Hammer said. "They have apps on phones for that. People use them to listen to fire departments, but police departments have started scrambling their comms. You'd need a real scanner. Where can you get a police scanner in Obsidian?"

"The sheriff," Lauren replied.

————

Lauren Stahling was midway through her twenty-minute walk to work on Tuesday morning when she saw a familiar figure in a gray canvas coat walking up a side street toward the next intersection.

"Good morning, young lady," Hammer said with a grin. "Can I carry your books to school?"

She knew he was joking, but she saw his bluff and handed him the heavy tote bag with her laptop and paperwork anyway. He took it.

"Are you stalking me?"

"You mean because you're walking to work early? You said you were coming in early to talk to the sheriff about his scanner, and I figured I'd join you."

"I hope Kyle is closer to being on time than he was yesterday," she said. "I don't want to be late for work again today."

"You had an excuse," Hammer reminded her. "Besides, you're the boss."

"Oh yeah...and having a gun shoved in your face is a good excuse," she said.

"A step up from the dog eating your homework." He laughed.

———

"Good morning, Lauren," Kyle Fahr said when they strolled into the sheriff's office. "Hello, Hammer."

"You know, Kyle, what happened here yesterday raises a lot of questions, doesn't it?" Lauren said, looking around the room that had been the scene of the confrontation.

Fahr nodded cautiously, sensing correctly she was not here to make small talk. "It would seem to me you'd want to get to the bottom of what the feds are up to, after what happened to you out at the Tredquist place, and now *this*. I have a suggestion."

"Which is?" Fahr said defensively.

"Maybe, since you obviously have a police radio, you use it to scan for the channel they use to talk to Sunrise and listen in to some of their chatter out there at the Tredquist place and the airport…to see what they're saying…doing?"

"Did *he* put you up to this?" Fahr said, looking at Hammer. "*Look here*. I told you last week to back off. This is law enforcement business. I specifically told you I won't stand for civilians starting to take the law into their own hands."

"But he *isn't*," Lauren clarified. "He didn't make this suggestion…*I did*. And I'm not suggesting *I* do it…or God forbid, that *Hammer* be allowed to do it. I said *you* should do it."

"It would be illegal for me to snoop on a federal agency," he replied. "You ought to know this, Lauren. I could lose my job. Maybe even face federal charges."

"So it's okay for them to snatch an assault arrest away from *you*," Lauren said, raising her voice. "And then come into *your* space without a warrant and ransack *your* office? Have you filed a formal complaint with their field office? With Washington?"

"Not yet."

"Were you even going to do that before I just mentioned it?"

"Uh-mmmm."

"Aren't you just a little bit curious about why they were so interested in erasing all memory of a routine traffic stop that they came in here with guns drawn?"

"It's a federal case," the sheriff insisted.

"What federal case? Did they even tell you thist was a 'case' at all? Did they call you on the phone ahead of time and have a lawman-to-lawman talk about how they'd like to have *you* to make it go away?"

"I can't tell you."

"Because this didn't happen. *Did it?*"

The sheriff's expression confirmed Lauren was right.

"Okay, now that you've had your say about jurisdictions, it's my turn," Lauren said. She was perturbed and ready to pile it on. "We had a situation yesterday where these people not only trashed this place and took documents without a warrant, but one of them pulled a gun on an unarmed Logan County official...*me*...in front of a bunch of witnesses. You and I both know the names of the people who were standing around watching all this."

Fahr looked more stunned than anything else.

"I think they drew their weapons on your deputy as well," Lauren said, glaring at him. "What they do to your deputy and your office is *your* department's business, but what they do to *me* is county business, right?"

"Well..."

The sheriff was definitely flummoxed. Hammer was trying desperately to stifle a grin. He really liked the way Lauren Stahling did business.

"When I get to my office in about ten minutes, I am going to file a formal complaint with the sheriff's office, insisting *you* file a formal complaint with the feds, something you seem reluctant to do on behalf of your own department. Meanwhile, I'm going to start phoning witnesses. If you don't file a complaint today, I'm going to walk into the county attorney's office on my way home tonight and ask him to do it with the feds directly. And then I'll start making some calls *myself*!"

"Maybe it *wouldn't* hurt to take a short listen on the scanner," Fahr said after a long pause.

———

Vince Milino loosened the collar of his starched white shirt and did the same with his tie.

"It's stuffy in here," he complained.

"That's because you've been pacing for the past hour," Tom R. Brach retorted. "If this floor wasn't military-grade concrete, I'd make the usual joke about wearing a trench in it."

Brach was inside the pale-green aluminum building at the airfield sitting in a folding chair at a folding table with a paper cup of cold coffee in it. Tony Stayton, his executive assistant, was asleep in the corner on another folding chair. Nobody had gotten much sleep last night.

"We just can't have any more screw-ups," Milino said, scratching his mustache.

"It was you guys who made a mess of the sheriff's office yesterday," Brach said disparagingly. "You could have handled it with a little more finesse. I know this is Montana, but do you have to act like it's still the Wild West?"

Milino, who'd led the federal raid on Monday morning, just scowled.

"Pulling a gun on the Logan County Assessor was a really smart move," Brach added.

"Kruegher said he thought she was going for a gun," Milino said defensively. "He thought he needed to respond."

"Get real, Milino. A well-dressed woman in a business suit who had identified herself and said she was going to show him a business card?"

"Don't forget your desperate call to me a week ago when *your guy* put a bullet in a civilian," Milino shot back.

"Trespasser," Brach clarified.

"I didn't see any 'no trespassing' signs that day."

"They're up now."

"What about your bus driver who didn't know the speed limit?" Milino asked, prodding Brach.

"Who knows there's a school bus speed limit?"

"The deputy did. At least we retrieved the paperwork. I don't think the deputy is going to file a formal complaint. I think she's glad to be rid of us."

"I hope so," Brach said. "But the sheriff *did* formally complain did when you cheated him out of his assault collar. Him and the county attorney took it all the way to the state attorney general."

"We shut this down," Milino reminded him, as he stepped to the open roll-up door of the pale-green aluminum building at the airfield. "Federal jurisdiction is federal jurisdiction. And our lawyers are bigger than their lawyers."

———

As Kyle Fahr sat down at the big command center console in the back room, put his hand on the mouse and was studying the screen, Jim Hammer sat down next to him. Fahr was about to shout not to touch anything, but he quickly realized Hammer knew what he was doing.

"Be careful," was all the sheriff could think to say.

"How do you like the E4?" Hammer asked. Fahr said nothing. He realized the Special Forces vet didn't need to show off. He was just making small talk. Hammer immediately recognized the Avtec Scout E4 system. It was based on Avtec's 2K-channel EX technology but scaled for small operations that could get by with just four outgoing comm channels. It was all they needed in Logan County.

Lauren Stahling watched for a moment and finally said, "I'll let you boys get on with it. I have to go to work."

Lauren was the second to arrive at the assessor's office. She glanced at the wall clock. Only a few minutes tardy, but as Hammer had said. She was the boss.

She returned a couple of calls, delegated a few piles on her desk to her team as they filtered in, and pushed everything else aside.

Maneuvering into the state database on her laptop—best not to use her desktop computer—she started looking into SLH Transportation. As a Sunrise subsidiary, it used the same Sunrise address in Billings where Lauren had met Tom R. Brach. All the state paperwork had been filed. Two TC2000 48-passenger buses had been bought from a dealer in Colorado and registered with the Montana DMV. Everything was perfectly in order, but nothing answered the question of what a land company needed with school buses.

She looked at the Hambledon brochure on her desk and thought about her conversation with Brach. Maybe the buses were here to take children to see "beautiful pristine open spaces?" Maybe the bus Jamie pulled over on Sunday was taking children to see such places?

Yet, *nothing* answered the question of how children visiting "beautiful pristine open spaces" fit in with guns, threats, and deep, mystifying secrecy.

CHAPTER
TWELVE

JENNA TOLLIVER HAD NO SOONER HUNG up from one call than her phone chirruped with another. It was good that the state highway north to Obsidian was long and straight. It was overcast, but Wednesday morning brought none of the scattered showers which had been blowing through over the past few days.

Jenna imagined herself as the busiest woman in Logan County. She certainly had the fullest and most varied schedule. Ever since she had been student body president at Logan County High, and certainly for the past dozen or so years as Chair of the County Commissioners, she had considered herself the most important woman in the county. Somebody had to do it, Jenna insisted to herself, and she had stepped up to shoulder the burden.

She left Billings just past six this morning. She had a commission meeting at ten, an agenda meeting before that, and who knows what had piled up on her desk since she'd been gone. She and her husband, Mike Fellowes, had been in Billings for a posh party fundraiser at the five-star Yellowstone Premiere Hotel on Tuesday night. With an eye toward a role in statewide politics, she just *had to* be there and be seen. This morning, Mike had stayed on in Billings to take in a Cattlemen's Association meeting later in the day.

As she cruised north in her silver late-model Lexus LS, her mind was filled with all she had to do, and very little with any of the events that had consumed others in Logan County over the past week. She did think about Jim Hammer and about her *faux pas* of telling him she thought he was dead.

But was it actually a *faux pas* if she really believed it?

She had not thought about him in years. If he was dead, did that mean it didn't matter that she had a mad long-ago crush on him? The news of his passing, which she now knew to have been a mere rumor, had once allowed her to put this memory in a box and file it away. Now that he was "alive again," did it mean she had to take this box off the shelf?

Down the road, Jenna saw a school bus pulled off to the side of the road with its hood up.

"I've got to hang up, there's a school bus stopped at the side of the road out here," she told one of her staff assistants who had just called. "I'll be there in forty-five minutes."

Jenna pulled over onto the shoulder and lit up her flashers.

She looked both ways as she crossed, but there were no other cars to be seen.

The bus driver opened the door as she approached.

"Do you need me to call somebody?"

"No, I already did. They're on their way. Thanks."

"I see you've got kids on board," Jenna said. "I have a case of water bottles in the trunk. Left over from an event last night. You can have them for the kids if you want."

"No, it's all right. We're fine. Thanks."

"You sure?" Jenna asked, rationalizing that if you

were a bus driver broken down with a bus full of kids, why would you *not* want free water bottles?

"Yeah, positive, but thanks," the driver said, closing the door.

Shaking her head, Jenna started walking back across the state highway. Far to the south, she could see the headlights of another vehicle heading toward them and coming fast. Maybe it was the wrecker.

As she had reached the Lexus, she heard a loud scream and turned to see commotion on the bus. The bus driver was standing and struggling with some of his passengers. As Jenna watched, a girl in her late teens pushed open the door, leaped from the bus and ran across the road toward the Lexus. She stood behind the car and began pleading with Jenna. She spoke a language Jenna did not understand, but she was definitely very upset. Tears streamed down her face as she shrieked.

Jenna walked toward the girl, who ran to Jenna, grabbing her tightly. She was an Asian girl of about sixteen or seventeen with mid-length black hair. She was simply dressed in cotton trousers and a cotton top, with a light sweater and scuffed sandals. Jenna held her and spoke to her in a comforting tone, but it was clear she did not understand the words.

The other vehicle arrived and screeched to a stop. Jenna was surprised to see it was a black Escalade. She remembered the story about the Escalade full of feds that had interrupted the sheriff's arrest of the assault perp a week ago. She had been out of town for the fracas at the sheriff's office and had yet to be briefed.

Two men leaped out, and while one of them ran toward the door of the bus, the other man, a skinny guy in a suit with a blond buzz cut, walked across to where Jenna stood with the whimpering girl.

"Federal agent," the man said, holding up his ID, but not long enough for Jenna to read what it said.

"That's good," Jenna said. "I'm Jenna Tolliver, chair of the Logan County Commission. I was on my way back from Billings when I stopped to render aid to this school bus. This girl is in a panic about something. I don't know why because I don't speak her language. You need to call for an ambulance immediately and get her some care."

"Thank you for your opinion, ma'am," the man with the buzz cut said. "We'll take it from here. You can be on your way."

He grabbed the girl by her wrist and tried to pull her away from Jenna, but she only screamed louder and clung more tightly, her tears streaming down Jenna's $1,595 Max Mara Studio double-breasted pick stitch wool coat.

"She doesn't want this," Jenna said sternly. The girl's face was distorted with terror, and her voice grew hoarse. "I'm going to take her to the hospital in Obsidian myself. *Let go of her!*"

"I can't let you do this, ma'am. As I told you, we're federal agents and we *will be* taking charge of this situation. If you don't let go of this individual, I will place you under arrest for interfering with a federal agent…and attempted kidnapping."

"*Attempted kidnapping*? *You're insane.* Let me see your ID again!"

With this, he jerked the girl's wrist with such force and she lost her grip on Jenna. There was a snapping sound in her elbow.

The girl went limp and continued to scream as the man dragged her across the road toward the Escalade.

"*Stop that!*" Jenna shrieked. She wished Mike was here. She wished *Hammer* was here.

The girl's pants were torn by being dragged across the pavement, and her knee was bleeding.

"You're out of your mind," Jenna screamed, rushing toward the man. Nobody treated Jenna Tolliver like this! *Ever*. He needed to know this.

Instead, it was Jenna who was about to be taught a lesson.

The man with the buzz cut dropped the girl, swiftly threw Jenna to the ground facedown, and secured her hands behind her back with a cable tie.

"Kruegher!" the agent in charge, an older man with a mustache, shouted. "What the hell did you just do?"

"Resisting arrest," he replied proudly.

"Okay, I got the distributor cap on tight and we're ready to go. *Damn it, I wish you wouldn't have done that!* But we've gotta move. Put both of them into the trunk of the Lexus and let's get both vehicles out of here before somebody comes along."

———

Jim Hammer snapped awake, rolled over, and grabbed his phone. It was nearly a quarter to seven, and he was supposed to meet Lauren Stahling at the Shiny Rock for breakfast in forty-five minutes.

The phone continued to ring. It was Tim Tommis. It was the middle of the morning in Silver Spring.

"Tommis. Good to hear from you," Hammer answered, trying to seem awake.

"I didn't wake you, did I?" Tommis asked.

"Not at all," Hammer lied. "Wide awake for hours."

"I've got some more info on your Hambledon Global Advocacy Group. You're gonna want to hear this!"

"Okay, you've got my attention."

"Well, they're not actually based in London after all,

and not in the cutesy little village of Hambledon in Hampshire, nor *anywhere* in the UK. They do have offices there, and everywhere you look, online or elsewhere, your search always defaults to their 'rich history' in the UK, but it's an elaborate charade."

"After what I've seen, it does not in the least surprise me," Hammer said. "So where are they actually located?"

"They're actually controlled out of the seventy-third floor of the Lusail Towers in downtown Doha."

"Qatar is a long way from Chelsea. If that's the *where*, who's the *who*?"

"Again, even if you do know about the Doha connection, it's hard to peel your way into the center of the onion," Tommis said. He spoke with an eager tone of someone who had just cracked a deep secret. "There are layers inside layers. I went through all kinds of shady characters and wicked crime bosses and criminal masterminds. Like Churchill said about a riddle wrapped in a mystery inside an enigma."

"Who or what is inside *this* enigma?"

"The nucleus of this onion is a playboy sheikh named Hamad Abdallah bin-Sharia. He's part of a trillionaire oil family with tentacles in any number of legitimate and illicit schemes and scams all over the world. Private jets, big houses in France and Switzerland, and all that. It's him who is the founder and CEO of Hambledon Global. It's the sheikh's business, a fact which he disguises very, very well."

"And what is the nature of their business?" Hammer asked impatiently.

"Just like it says in the brochure you told me about. It's a charitable NGO operating on several continents, doing good works and blah-blah-blah. But like the Chelsea office, that's all just a front. Hambledon is also active in an industry with a very long, very colorful, and very *foul* history in the Middle East, and one which has always generated a *lot* of money. It's the slave trade."

"*The slave trade*?" Hammer asked with equal parts resignation and disgust. "I've seen it here and there in the places where I've worked, but it was always small-time operators."

"Hamad is anything but small-time," Tommis explained. "He specializes in buying and selling young women by the hundreds, even thousands."

"So much for the Hambledon mission statement with its 'child protection' and 'gender empowerment.'" Hammer said. "I sensed a scam, but duplicity on this scale really turns my stomach."

"This is who you're dealing with. I'll have more later," Tommis said. "Good luck."

———

Hammer arrived at the café first and told Kristen to wait on the coffee for Lauren. They did not wait long. Lauren was dressed nicely in a dark skirt and a long-sleeved, collared dress shirt under a long slate-gray fall coat. Hammer wore his uniform jeans and flannel shirt, but today's shirt was black and gray plaid and looked new.

"You look a little glum today," Lauren said cheerfully. "Did you not sleep well?"

"I didn't wake up well," he said. "I woke up to a call from Tim Tommis."

"Your intel wizard, right? What did he have to say?"

"You want the good news or bad news first?" Hammer offered.

"I'll take the good, I guess."

"The good news is Hambledon Global is *not* in the drug trade."

"Something tells me I'm *really* not going to like the bad news," she said hesitantly.

"No way to ease into this. They're in the *slave* trade."

Hammer paused for a moment while she processed this news and then continued.

"They're not based in the UK either. They're out of Doha in Qatar. The kingpin is a jet-set playboy named Hamad bin-Sharia. As Tommis described him, his forte is trafficking young women. We're talking about industrial quantities of sex slaves."

"Oh my god, how creepy!" Lauren whispered. "How awful. How revolting. Most disgusting is how the public face of this outfit says they promote doing good things for women and *children* around the world when…"

"When they're actually *selling* women and children," he said, finishing her sentence.

Sorry, but I've lost my appetite," Lauren said.

Hammer just nodded.

"Wait a minute," she said, a horrified expression on her face. "The school bus, the girls who were waving to Jamie, she thought they were *school kids*. Could they have been…?"

"This could explain the civilians who I saw getting off the airplane on Monday," he added. "I saw a dark-haired girl, and then there was the Chinese girl story we were trying to figure out."

"On the bus, Jamie saw a bunch of dark-haired kids through smudged windows two feet higher than her eyes, and made the assumption they were reservation teenagers, when they were probably Asian kids."

"Could very well be the case," Hammer agreed.

"Industrial quantities of child sex slaves coming into Montana," she whispered, staring into space. "Horrendous…horrific…words fail me."

He could see her anger in her eyes. Her jaw clenched and tear,s formed in the corners of her eyes.

"I'll be right back," she said, excusing herself to go to the ladies' room.

She had not yet returned when Kyle Fahr came in, his sheriff's badge glimmering brightly on his uniform jacket. Hammer waved him over and scooted in to give him room to sit down. Anticipating his "usual," Kristen had delivered a cup of coffee and a basket of sugar substitute packets before he had even hung his Stetson on the hook at the end of the booth.

"Are you with someone?" Fahr asked, nodding to the third coffee cup. "I don't want to barge in."

"It's Stahling; she's in the head. Go ahead. Join us."

Fahr had just taken a sip of his coffee when she returned. Hammer could see she was no longer noticeably upset. Her cheeks were still pink but no longer hot pink.

"The sheriff's joining us," Hammer announced.

"So I see," Lauren asked, shaking off the shock of the earlier revelation. "How did it go with the scanner yesterday?"

"*Shhh*," Fahr hushed in a whispery voice. "I feel like a conspirator in a damned *spy movie*."

"Is that a good thing or a bad thing?" Lauren asked with a forced smile.

"It's something I'm not used to," he said, glancing at her and then at Hammer. "I'm sure you probably did a lot of this in Special Forces, Hammer."

"What have you heard on the radio?" Hammer asked, ignoring what Fahr had said about being in a spy movie. "Any names, dates, places?"

"I haven't been listening full time, but I've written down a few things. They talk in code, but if you know what's going on already, you can figure it out. They talk about a 'client,' which sounds like Sunrise. They also talk about 'client packages.' Do you know what that might be?"

"What's *your* guess?" Hammer asked.

"If they're using code words, it's probably illegal. Maybe drugs? Do you think they're running drugs with the help of the feds, and Steve Coe got in the way?"

"With their interest in the airfield, this is what Lauren and I *were* thinking," Hammer said.

It was true. They *had been* thinking this, but Hammer was not quite ready to share the fact that this thinking had changed in the past hour.

Suddenly, the conversation was interrupted as a young woman whom Lauren recognized came into the café. Lauren waved, and she approached the booth. She knew the young woman as a staffer in the County Commissioners' office.

"Have you guys seen Jenna Tolliver?"

"No," Lauren said, "but we've only been here fifteen minutes or so."

"Who are you looking for?" Kristen asked, having caught only part of the conversation.

"Jenna Tolliver."

"I haven't seen her in here at all this morning, what time were you supposed to meet her?"

"Actually, she was supposed to be at the county court-house a while ago. She and Mike were at a fundraiser in Billings last night and on she was on her way back. She's late. We thought maybe she stopped here, or maybe somebody here knew something."

"I was on the phone with her over an hour ago," the young woman continued. "She was on the road, and said she'd be here in about forty-five minutes. Then she said she had to hang up. She was pulling over to check on a vehicle in trouble. Now I can't reach her."

"Bad cell service?" Hammer asked.

"It's good out there on the state highway," Lauren said. "One place in the county with no dead zones."

"I could call it in to the highway patrol," Fahr suggested, "although there are usually no highway patrol cars on that stretch. They're mostly more than a hundred miles from here on the interstate or on much busier state highways."

"Just out of curiosity," Hammer asked. "Did she say what *kind* of vehicle was pulled over?"

"It was a school bus."

Hammer and Lauren looked at one another with raised eyebrows.

"This could be a problem," Hammer said, getting to his feet. "We need to go find her."

"*What?*" Fahr asked, confused.

"We'll fill you in later," Hammer replied. "Jenna may be in trouble. Let's hope not, but in the meantime, we need to get to her, and *fast*. Come on Kyle, you're the only one at this table who has a car."

"What is…" Fahr started to ask.

"I hope I'm wrong, but this may have a lot to do with the 'client's packages,'" Hammer said as he and Fahr made for the door.

"You're not going without *me*," Lauren Stahling said firmly as she grabbed a wad of bills from her purse and dropped them on the table for Kristen.

"Lights and siren?" Hammer suggested coolly as Fahr hit the highway and headed toward Billings. He did not have to suggest twice. The sheriff floored the accelerator and buried the red needle, obviously enjoying the exhilaration of a high-speed dash.

"Jenna drives a late-model silver Lexus," Lauren said calmly from the back seat.

Fahr got Deputy Manderson on the radio and told her

to call the DMV for a plate number for a Lexus registered to Jenna Tolliver or Mike Fellowes and call the highway patrol to put out an APB. Hammer took the mike and suggested Jamie Manderson keep an ear to the scanner for more about "client packages."

There were few cars on the road, but as the Durango's 475-hp, 391.6-cubic-inch V8 hemi ate up the miles, there was no Lexus in sight, and no pulled-over vehicles.

"I think we've more than covered the distance that would have been forty-five minutes for Jenna driving at near the speed limit," Hammer said glumly, when they reached the intersection with State Route 200, a main east–west highway.

"I think we've lost them," Fahr said sadly, looking at the roads which led off in several directions. "I think we'd better head back to Obsidian and let the highway patrol handle the search for the Lexus. Our time might be better spent with the scanner. I shouldn't be saying this as an 'officer of the law,' but thanks to you people, I'm glad we have a way to snoop on the Escalade people."

"This may be nothing, but about fifteen or so minutes back, I saw something," Lauren said. "Not worth mentioning as we passed, but it might be worth stopping on the way back. There was a place where it looked like multiple vehicles had pulled off recently on both sides of the highway."

"Good catch," Hammer said as they pulled up on the place ten minutes later. "Let's take a look."

There were certainly recent tracks in the slightly muddy ground.

"I think I see what happened," Hammer said after they had each scrutinized the tracks for a minute or two.

"You can see that a big vehicle with dual tires, a school bus maybe, pulled over going slow," he said, pointing to the tracks on the southbound side. "Then another vehicle, either an SUV or a pickup, pulled up behind it. Its tracks overlap the large vehicle tracks, so it arrived after."

"Could it have been an Escalade?" Lauren asked.

"Yup."

"On the northbound side, " Hammer continued, crossing the two-lane highway. "There was a passenger car stopped across from the large vehicle."

"Could this have been the Lexus?" Fahr asked.

"I'll bet it was," Lauren said as she stooped to pick up a piece of dark-colored paper.

"Take a look at this," she said, holding the paper up for the men to see. "This is a paper napkin, and it has the logo of the Yellowstone Premiere Hotel in Billings. Jenna was there last night. This might have fallen out of her pocket."

CHAPTER
THIRTEEN

"OKAY, HAMMER," the sheriff said as everyone walked back toward the Durango. "Now would be a good time for you to make good on your promise to fill me in on whatever it was made you so agitated back at the diner. What got the two of you so worked up about a *school bus*? Am I right to guess this is tied in to Jamie's school bus traffic stop and all this commotion?"

"You would be guessing right," Hammer said. "For the ride back, I'll take the rear seat and let your fellow county official fill you in on our thinking about school buses and such, but mainly on what we're *sure* is going on out there on the Tredquist place?"

Hammer was counting on the anger and emotion Lauren had displayed back at the café to underscore her explanation of the facts and deductions. He was not disappointed. It was admittedly sexist to count on a woman to add effective highlights to an account of a sex trafficking cartel, but it worked as he'd hoped.

She exploded into graphic descriptions of the role being played by the landing strip and the school bus in the slave trade—emphasizing it as the *sex slave* trade. She furiously described its victims as teenagers enduring the most terrible kind of abuse.

The only words Fahr managed to slide in edgewise were phrases like "no shit" or "that's atrocious."

She then explained what Hammer had learned about Sunrise Land Holdings, and about its nefarious parent company. Without naming names, she colorfully described it as being run by a "rich sex-fiend sheikh." She was especially bitter in her references to the cartel being "under the protection of government agents who were paid to look the other way." Fahr had seen his share of official corruption in Denver, and he could relate.

By the time Fahr pulled the Dodge Durango off the state highway and into Obsidian, his face was as furrowed with anger as Lauren's had been.

"Could you take me to my place?" Lauren asked. "I need to change my clothes before I go back to the courthouse."

"Me too," Hammer said. "Could you drop me at my Aunt Charlotte's?" Hammer asked. "I need to pick up some gear. I'll drive myself to the courthouse, and I'll pick Lauren up on the way."

Fahr was almost to the courthouse when his cell phone rang.

"Sheriff, it's Jamie. Are you on your way back?"

"Yeah, I'm just parking. I was with Hammer and Lauren Stahling. They're coming there too. What's up?"

"Bad news, I'm afraid," the deputy said.

"*What is it*? Something happened to Jenna Tolliver?"

"No, I just heard from the highway patrol. The feds are 'assuming jurisdiction.' State and local law enforcement are no longer welcome in this matter. Isn't that a damned disgrace."

"*Yes, it is!* Which feds? What agency?"

"That's the bad news. It's the ATF again. It's our friends in the black Escalades."

"*Oh shit*," Fahr said angrily. "I'll be right in."

As he put his phone back into his inside jacket pocket, Fahr just stared out the dirty-around-the-edges windshield into a gray afternoon which mimicked his mood. He felt irate and he felt beaten. He felt like a spayed dog.

————

Lauren Stahling greeted Hammer with a cell phone to her ear and a duffel bag in her other hand. She had traded her skirt and stylish coat for a pair of jeans and a well-worn heavy jacket.

"That was Jessica Edredin on the phone," she said as she climbed into the blue Chevy pickup. "She wanted to know whether there's any news on Jenna Tolliver. I had to tell her we didn't know very much. Mark is climbing the walls. She said you should call him."

Hammer did so immediately.

"Mark, it's Hammer. Stahling suggested I phone you."

"Hammer, we're just about to come apart over Jenna Tolliver going missing. Is it the same bunch out at the Tredquist place? Remember, I told you that if you get around to planning to take those guys down, I want to be part of it."

"Well," Hammer said. "It's time. Let's meet down at the sheriff's office."

"Just say when."

"*Now.*"

"*You got it*! Oh, and you know, Steve Coe has been saying we ought to get the championship team back together again."

"Don't you just love a reunion tour?" Hammer said with a laugh.

––––––

Deputy Jamie Manderson greeted the sheriff's Dodge Durango with an expression of relief and an air of despondency.

"What are we going to do?"

"Keep listening to the feds' radio channel," Fahr said.

"Holly and Veronica have been taking turns," the deputy said, referring to the two sheriff's office 911 operators, who had both been "read in" on the situation. "If anything sounding like it might mention Jenna comes across the line, they'll alert me."

As he gazed at the street through the heavy glass doors, Fahr watched Hammer's pickup pull in.

"A few days ago, we had a one-sided conversation," Fahr said, taking Hammer aside as Jamie greeted Lauren. "I was afraid you were going to take matters into your own hands. Damn it, I was afraid you were going to infringe on *my* turf. I told you Logan County isn't South America or Afghanistan, and I told you special operations have no place here."

"You did say that," Hammer acknowledged with a nod.

"I just wanted to tell you, and I hate to admit it, but times have changed. My whole outlook has changed. Special operations *do have* a place here. It's like this human trafficking cartel has *declared war* on Logan County. The slave traders and their friends in the black Escalades think they *own* this county. There's nobody to push back. This needs to stop. I'm deputizing you to take matters into your own hands, *Captain* Hammer. All I ask is that you keep me in the loop."

"Well, the first thing on this loop will be to deputize a few more volunteers," Hammer told him.

At that moment, a screeching of tires on the street

outside announced the arrival of Jessica Edredin's Chevy Trailblazer. Mark was out of the vehicle before Jessica had even set the brake. Steve Coe and Erin O'Malley climbed out of the back and followed them in. Steve wore his left arm in a sling, but he walked with a pep in his step. After nine days of convalescing, he was obviously relieved to be doing something proactive against those who had injured him.

They all spoke at once, with Jenna Tolliver's whereabouts being at the top of everyone's list of concerns. Someone asked whether her husband, Mike Fellowes, was home. Coe said he'd spoken with him by phone. He explained he had stayed in Billings for the Cattlemen's Association meeting and was remaining in Billings to speak with the police about the hunt for Jenna.

Eyes turned to Lauren, who had started telling the four new arrivals, as well as Deputy Manderson, about what they'd found on the road.

When everyone had heard her account, she started passing around the napkin, now in a sheriff's evidence bag, which Jenna had dropped. Handling something the missing woman had handled just as she went missing brought sober expressions to the faces in the room.

Lauren then repeated in detail all which she'd told the sheriff about the school buses and the airfield. When she told of the part they were planning to "make Logan County a hub in the international sex slave trade," the room was silent.

When she explained why Sunrise Land Holdings had purchased the Tredquist place for this purpose, there were expressions of stunned disbelief.

"What can we do?" Jessica demanded.

Her husband's expression, as he exchanged glances with Hammer, told what he *wanted* to do.

"There is not much more my office *can* do," the sheriff

said. "The feds have taken jurisdiction of the search for Jenna, and as we've learned, they're part of this whole thing. They're getting paid to look the other way and keep local law enforcement out of it."

"I asked what *we* can do," Jessica said angrily. "Frankly, I'm not interested in what the sheriff's office *cannot* do."

Hammer decided it was his turn.

"We're on our own," he began, letting this fact sink in.

"The state can't do anything. The sheriff can't do anything, and the feds are against us. No cavalry will come riding over the hill. If something's going to be done, it's down to *us*."

"Speaking for myself, and I think I speak for everyone in this room, something's *got to* be done, right?" Jessica said.

There was a buzz of agreement throughout the room.

"Tell us what *you* would do," Jessica continued, looking at Hammer. "Tell us what you and your Special Forces people would do. Please tell us what *we* can do to save Jenna and get these slave traders out of Logan County, to shut them down for *good*."

"The sheriff deputized me to take care of this, and I asked him to deputize all of us," Hammer said to another round of nods.

"The way he put it was that a human trafficking cartel has 'declared war' on Logan County," Hammer continued. "I agree, and if you agree, we'll treat it as a *war*. It's a lot like the old range wars fought all across the West a hundred and fifty years ago. You got honest people fighting corrupt people, some of whom happen to wear badges. We all remember the story of Henry Plummer from fourth grade Montana History, right?"

Most of them recalled the story of the sheriff of

Bannock, who had a lucrative side job as a bandit back in the 1860s.

"It's why Montana had Vigilantes all through the 1860s and beyond," Jessica pointed out. "I'm in, and I know Mark is in. Are all of you ready for this?"

Everyone nodded in agreement.

"This will be potentially dangerous. Once we get started, we can't go back. Once we poke this beast, they'll try to *kill* us and we'll have to be ready to *kill* them. People will get hurt. It's our job to make sure it's them, not us. If anyone is uncomfortable with this, now's the time."

"Are you sure?" Hammer asked after a moment of silence.

Again, nobody spoke.

"I assume the sheriff's office has flak jackets or some kind of vests for everybody," Hammer said. His purpose was twofold, one practical and the other to underscore the seriousness of what was about to happen.

There were gulps all around. Only the sheriff spoke.

"We do have vests to go around, and I will deputize you all. For what it's worth, this might give us some legal cover down the road. But like Jessica asked, *what do we do*? So what's your plan, Hammer?"

"Okay, I'm going to lay it out," Hammer said after a pause. "In looking at this situation we're about to tackle, there's good news and bad news. The bad news, like I mentioned, is the feds and the Sunset people will all be working *against* us. The good news is we have the advantage of them not knowing that there is a 'we' who are working against *them*. At least until the first shot is fired."

After letting this statement sink in, he continued.

"Our two objectives are that we need to find and extract Jenna, and we need to shut down the airport. Those two things in this order of priority."

"Do we know where Jenna is?" Erin asked.

"Not yet," Hammer said. "But we are pretty sure they took her south, the direction the bus was going. The tracks show that the northbound car, almost certainly Jenna's, turned around and headed south, probably driven by one of them."

"And we're listening to them," the sheriff interjected. "You did *not* hear this officially from the sheriff's office, but we've hacked into their radio communications and have been monitoring what they're saying from the back room here since yesterday. Because of all the fuss the highway patrol made about Jenna, they know *who* she is, and they're bound to say something about her soon."

"We can't just sit around and wait," Erin said. "What would it take to deal with what's going on at the airport now?"

"We can't just go in there guns blazing, can we?" Fahr asked.

"I've been thinking about exactly that," Hammer said.

He noticed Lauren Stahling grinning a wry "of course you have" grin. She'd been waiting for this.

"The operation will begin with the sheriff," Hammer said. "He will drive into the big warehouse area at the airport. He will be polite, but purposeful, exercising his legally authorized duty in this county. He'll say there's been a noise complaint about a large number of people coming and going, and he needs to look around."

"I can do this," Fahr said. "I find myself chasing complaints like this a lot."

"It's unlikely they will take aggressive action at the sight of the sheriff's car," Hammer continued. "They'll want to see what he has to say. Odds are, they will *all* want to hear it, so everyone out there will show himself. I've had eyes on the place, so I have an idea of the lay of the land and how many are there. Sheriff Fahr will then be sufficiently intrusive as to make them show their hand. He will either see evidence of people detained against their will, or not."

"What if he doesn't?" Jessica asked.

"If Kyle is satisfied this is *not* a human trafficking site, then we all back off to square one."

"What if the opposite is true?" Lauren asked. "What if there *are* slaves there, and the Sunset people *do* pull their guns on the sheriff?"

"If they draw their weapons, they will have committed to starting a war that I intend for us to *win*," Hammer said. "I will be across the runway with my Barrett Mk22 sniper rifle and an ATN HD scope…and I *will be* shooting to kill."

You could have heard a pin drop.

"Mark will be riding with the sheriff," Hammer said. "The sheriff will get you a deputy's badge and a jacket. Bring your own SIG and holster, and also your AR-15. Mark's a combat infantryman. He served with the 305th in Afghanistan. You still know what to do, right?"

"Like riding a bicycle," Edredin said calmly.

"They'll be drawing their weapons in order to exercise deadly force," Hammer said. "Our job is to strike back immediately and in kind, okay?"

Fahr nodded, but nobody said anything. It was clear they all found the prospect of a shootout to be a sobering possibility.

"If that's what it takes," Mark said.

"Where will the rest of us be?" Deputy Jamie Manderson asked.

"My idea is the sheriff will go in with high beams, being as obvious as possible," Hammer replied. "You and Steve will be in a second sheriff's department Durango as backup, following the sheriff, but with lights out and hold and stand by just out of sight of the airport buildings."

"I can't hold a rifle," Steve Coe interjected. "But I got a SIG and a couple of extra mags."

"We've got lots more firepower here in this office if it's needed," Jamie added.

"What do we do with the girls they're holding out there?" Erin interjected.

"Try not to let them get hit by any stray bullets," Jessica said.

"I mean…um…after all that?" Erin clarified.

"I know someone who works with the big runaway and domestic violence abuse center up in Chinook," Jessica replied. "I didn't want to contact any state government agencies, for reasons I think are obvious."

"As a government employee myself, I'm embarrassed to have to agree this was a good call," Lauren interjected. "Have you spoken with her lately, Jess?"

"I did, but in a sort of vague, hypothetical way. If I give her a call, I think she read through the lines, and they'll be able to send someone at pretty much a moment's notice…lots of someones with vans."

"Excellent," Hammer said. "You and Erin can drive out behind Jamie and stand by alongside her."

"Okay, it sounds like we're all still in," Hammer continued a moment later. "I should add this will be a covert operation, like I used to run in all sorts of 'undisclosed places.' It's get in, do the job, get out, and *never* talk about it again. Except for Kyle and Jamie, who are officially with the sheriff's department, none of us were ever there. Now is the time for anyone not comfortable with the plan to back out, or for us to pull the plug."

There were nods and thumbs up all around.

Hammer picked up a box he had carried in from his truck earlier.

"Here's a bunch of burner phones," Hammer said. "Everybody grab one. I've marked each one with the first two letters of your first names and programmed all the numbers into each phone. I got these back east for another gig that never materialized, so they all have 757 area codes."

Nobody asked when Hammer had the time to do all this. It was clear he'd put a lot of thought into his plan.

"One more thing, if we get a call from Holly or Veronica saying there is a fix on Jenna's location, a call at *any point* before we engage the 'enemy,' we'll abort the whole airport thing and rendezvous back here. Okay?"

Again, everyone nodded.

"Okay, let's roll and keep our burner phones close," Hammer said. "Everybody, get your weapons and check your gear. We'll meet back here in twenty minutes and get going. I'm going to head over now and get my Norton, and my 'hunting' rifle."

"I'm going upstairs to the assessor's office and tell my staff I'm taking a few days off for hunting season," Lauren said.

As she started to leave the room, she turned back and looked at Hammer

"One more question. Do you still have that extra helmet you used to let me wear on the back of your Norton in high school?"

CHAPTER
FOURTEEN

VINCE MILINO BREATHED EASIER when the massive roll-up door rolled down with a tooth-jarring *clang*. On this cold, bleak Wednesday afternoon in October, he was climbing out of his Escalade in a cavernous excavation equipment garage located about thirty miles north and west of Billings.

After a decade as a DC cop, Milino had been a federal agent for a more than twenty years, a few with the FBI but most of them with the ATF—but today, he was working his surreptitious, but lucrative, side-gig for Hambledon Global. Through the years, as he had worked his way up through the ranks, Milino's skill and cleverness, and especially his *loyalty*, had gotten him noticed.

As in most organizations and bureaucracies—especially those involved with secrecy and the dark world of classified operations—the hierarchy which Milino found himself climbing was not so simple as the steps in a ladder, but more like the tangled roots of a thorn tree. Deep within the intertwined snarl there were sinews whose activities were often unknown or unseen by the forward-facing part of the bureau. Milino's loyalty to one such a sinew had given him a parallel career within the shadows, and it had been well rewarded.

Meanwhile, just as the Hambledon Global Advocacy Group faced forward into the sunlight with the bright smile of a kind and generous philanthropy, its dark side operated in the shadows with the aid of agencies within governments who could make inconvenient truths go away.

That's what Milino did for Tom R. Brach. He was on speed dial to step in to smooth any rough spots that appeared in the road as Brach moved Hambledon's product. The sheriff's attempt to arrest the man who shot Steve Coe was such a rough spot. Jenna Tolliver innocently trying to aid a frightened teenager was another.

As his eyes adjusted to the dim light inside the equipment garage, he saw Brach was not here to meet them. Tony Stayton, Brach's factotum, was there instead, and wearing one of his gaudy orange ties. Four men in Sunrise Land Holdings ball caps headed toward the school bus, while Stayton walked over to the Escalade. Aron Kruegher had brought up the rear of their convoy in Jenna Tolliver's Lexus.

"Where's Brach?" Milino asked as he climbed out of his big black Cadillac.

"He's back at the office. He sent me," Stayton said. "I see you've got the silver Lexus. Every cop in this part of the state was chasing this car until you called for the ATF to take over. How did you manage to get it back here without getting seen?"

"We took back roads. It pays to study your maps ahead of time. Who *is* this woman who everybody's so hot to find?"

"You met her," Stayton said. "*Didn't you?*"

"Let's just say we weren't formally introduced," Milino said.

"She's head of some kind of county commission up there in Logan County. You really know how to pick 'em! The cops put out an APB on her. When she starts to talk, you're..."

"She won't be talking any time soon," Milino said.

"You didn't *kill* her...*did you*?"

"She's in the trunk, along with one of your Korean guests. Both of them were still alive last I looked."

"What exactly happened up there?" Stayton asked. "How did you end up with a politician in the trunk of a car?"

"One goddamn fuckup after another," Milino said angrily. "This idiot you hired to drive the bus had a loose distributor cap. Something I was able to fix in thirty seconds. He pulls over and pops the hood. He was afraid the 'guests' would escape if he got out of the bus, so he called Nuemeyer. The politician woman saw it as she was driving by. She stopped to help. If he hadn't popped the hood, she wouldn't have stopped, but she did, and while she was standing there, one of your Korean girls escaped. Grabbed onto the politician and wouldn't let go. Kruegher got 'em apart, but she grabbed him, so he knocked her down and cuffed her."

"*Oh, shit*," Stayton said.

"At that point, we couldn't *leave* her, and we obviously couldn't leave the Lexus on the side of the road."

"What are you going to do?"

"What are *we* going to do," Milino corrected him.

"What are *we* going to do?" Stayton repeated.

"Hide the Lexus in here somewhere," Milino said. "With the APB, we gotta get rid of it. Wipe it down and cover it with tarps or a load of gravel, or whatever. Bury it somewhere. Get rid of the plates. Get rid of the VINs. Then, you need to get your guests out of the bus and moved along. There should be no trace of them if this place ever gets raided."

"We got somebody coming tomorrow for the first batch, but what are you going to do?" Stayton asked.

"Now that the ATF Billings Office is taking over the manhunt," Milino said. "We're going to announce that a silver Lexus was spotted on the interstate south of Billings and headed toward Wyoming, so crossing state lines makes it a federal case."

"You're making this up," Stayton said.

"You got a better idea?"

"I thought it was the FBI, and not ATF, who handled kidnappings," Stayton said.

"Normally, that's true," Milino said with a wry grin. "But we're telling Washington that we're linking this to an ongoing gun-running case involving the Gonzalves gang down in Jalisco. The FBI knows about this investigation and they'll be glad to have us take the lead on anything connected to Gonzalves."

"Was there a silver Lexus spotted on the interstate?"

"No, but this buys us time," Milino told Stayton. "We don't have to share any more details with anybody. Not with the FBI. Not with the highway patrol in either state. We got this contained for now, so this gives you time to get rid of the Lexus, *and* your product."

"Kruegher," Milino said, calling across the equipment garage to the younger agent with the buzz cut. "I'm putting you in charge of the two women in the trunk. Get them out of there before the car gets dumped. I've got to go into Billings and meet the husband and tell him how our agency is doing all we can."

"What do you want done with them?"

"The politician may be useful somewhere down the line, but make sure you duct tape her eyes so she can't see anybody. I don't care what you do with the Korean.

You broke her damned arm, so she's going to need attention. Figure it out."

When Milino's Escalade had gone and the roll-up door rolled down again, Stayton walked over to where Aron Kruegher was standing next to the Lexus.

"Nice car," Kruegher said. "Top of the line. Fancy wood trim inside. Fifty grand or more. Wish I had one myself. Shame we have junk it."

"Yeah," Stayton replied. "But Molino's right, we can't have it found. But we're right next to a gravel pit and there's an end loader outside, so after we get rid of the plates and VINs, we can bury it in a corner of the pit so it probably won't be found for years."

———

Jenna Tolliver had lost track of time.

She had been in near total darkness in the well-insulated trunk of her high-end luxury sedan for some interval between three hours and forever She had felt it riding smoothly on highways, and roughly on gravel roads, but she had no idea where the car was. She had been thrown into the trunk, landing in an uncomfortable pretzel-twist of position facing toward the front of the vehicle. When she tried to move, the cable tie dug painfully into the flesh of her wrist.

As she lay there in the timeless darkness, her mood alternated between anger, despair and bewilderment. *What had just happened?*

Had she been kidnapped or arrested? Who were these people? Who were the men in suits with federal IDs?

Who was the Asian teenager who lay behind Jenna with her head at Jenna's feet? Throughout the ride, she had been sobbing and making sounds like she was gasping for air. Jenna tried to speak to her, hoping to share some comforting words, but the duct tape was tight across Jenna's mouth.

At last, they had come to a stop. Jenna could hear voices, but words were impossible to make out through the high-grade insulation of the trunk. Jenna tried to kick the side to make a sound, but this yielded just a dull thud.

Suddenly, the trunk lid opened. The bright light from overhead halogen fixtures stung Jenna's eyes, momentarily blinding her. She felt the teenager being dragged roughly from the trunk. As her eyes adjusted to the light, Jenna glimpsed the face of the man with the blond buzz cut who had thrown her into the trunk all those hours ago. That was the last thing she saw before duct tape was stretched across her eyes, thrusting her back into a world of darkness.

Jenna felt herself being lifted from the carpeted trunk and thrown onto a concrete floor. After the soft upholstery of the trunk, it was jarringly hard and cold against her cheek. Squirming to try to relieve her stiffness, she was rewarded with a painful kick in her lower back that brought tears to her taped eyes. Unable to scream, she merely groaned.

As she lay there, she heard the voices of a large number of people, teenage girls, she guessed, murmuring in low, frightened voices. They were thirty or forty feet away and speaking a language Jenna didn't know.

Moments later, she heard the scraping sound of the girl from the trunk being dragged across the concrete and heard her moaning. She recognized the voice of the man with the buzz cut.

"This is the bitch who tried to get away from us," he said assertively, apparently addressing the other teenagers. "She didn't get so far, *did she*?"

If the other girls could not understand his words, they certainly understood his tone.

Aron Kruegher, the man with the buzz cut, jerked the girl to her feet and addressed her forcefully.

"You're not going to do that again, are you?" he demanded. "Do you think we need you to be an example?"

"Cool it, Kruegher," another of the men in the room said cautiously. "I think they got the idea."

"Did they?" Kruegher shouted. "We gotta make sure!"

There was the loud snap of a clenched fist striking the flesh of a cheek, as the same man who had recklessly pulled his gun on Lauren Stahling two days earlier clobbered this defenseless woman. Because her hands were still bound with cable ties, the girl had no way to break her fall as she lost her balance and toppled over.

Jenna heard a loud *crack*, like the sound of a melon being dropped onto a kitchen floor. The silence which followed was at last broken by the voice of another man speaking.

"What did you just do, Kruegher? She's not moving!"

There was the scratching sound of shoes on concrete as other men approached the fallen girl.

"She's not breathing! Fuck! There's blood all over. Kruegher, you *killed* her."

Jenna heard the murmuring of the other teenagers across the room as it spiraled into wails and screams.

"Let this be a lesson!" Kruegher shouted at the other girls. "You don't screw with us!"

Jenna felt panic and desperation. Mainly, she felt helpless and *so very* vulnerable. *Was she next*?

———

An hour after leaving Kruegher to deal with the bound and gagged Jenna Tolliver, then in her own car trunk at the gravel pit, Vince Molino was sitting across a cherry wood laminate desk from Jenna's husband on the top floor of a six-story building in downtown Billings.

"I'm glad federal law enforcement is taking an interest in this case," Mike Fellowes said, "but why is the Montana highway patrol no longer involved in looking for the Lexus?"

"To your point," Milino replied, presenting himself a compassionate ally, sympathizing with Fellowes's plight. "We've had at least one sighting of the Lexus, southbound on Interstate 90, heading toward Sheridan. It has probably crossed the state line by now. This makes it a *federal* responsibility. This agency is taking the lead in the matter now."

"I hope you are doing all you can to bring her home," Fellowes insisted. "Have you got the FBI involved? Don't they do kidnappings?"

"I assure you we are," Milino said sympathetically. "The ATF, instead of the FBI, is taking the lead on this because we have an indication this may be related to an ongoing matter in which the ATF has an interest, so we have double the reasons not to drop the ball. You and your wife are in good hands."

An hour ago, Milino was working his side job. Now, he was the forward-facing face of his bureau. Even so, he was crafting an illusion. Fabrications are often wound around kernels of truth, and in this case there really *had been* a silver Lexus spotted on the interstate toward Wyoming. From there, the outlaw bureaucracy within the ATF bureaucracy had gotten creative.

Milino smiled a compassionate smile. He was actually enjoying the spinning of his web around the Montana cowboy who one day earlier had been a big shot stockman sitting on the top of the world with his politician wife.

"Do you recall your wife ever mentioning an organization down in Jalisco, Mexico run by a family called Gonzalves?" Milino asked, further building the foundation of the false narrative.

"*What*?"

"I'm just curious as to whether you might be aware of this."

"*No*. Neither my wife nor I know anybody in Jalisco, Mexico," Fellowes insisted. "We've never even been to Mexico."

"Are you sure you know all of your wife's associates?" At the heart of the illusionist's craft is the art of misdirection. Of course, the ATF really *was* investigating the gun-running Gonzalves Cartel. There was always a kernel of truth in any illusion. To link this investigation to Jenna's disappearance would misdirect law enforcement in two states, as well as anyone in whom the worried husband might confide. He loved seeing the cowboy squirm.

"What is this all about?"

"I'm afraid I can say no more," Milino said cryptically, his voice firm but sympathetic.

———

Tom R. Brach and Kally Stefano arrived early, parked Brach's Chevy Suburban in the ample parking lot, and made their way into the Rimrock Steakhouse on the edge of downtown Billings.

"We have reservations. Table for five. The name is Brach."

"Oh yes, Mr. Brach," the *maître d'* responded, recognizing the name of a regular. "Of course. May we take your overcoats? Oscar, please show our guests to Table Nine."

They were dressed to the "nines." Brach wore a dark navy pinstripe suit and a cobalt power tie, while Kally sparkled in a cerulean blue, V-necked, sequined cocktail dress with a provocatively short skirt.

As strikingly beautiful as she was, Kally was more than just an accessory for Brach's arm. As his personal assistant, she worked hard and earned her generous salary in the social and professional networks of Montana's largest city. He had joined the Rotary and all the realtor clubs, but she made sure they remembered him at every turn. When he landed a seat on the board of the new performing arts center, she would make sure his name got top billing on the programs.

And of course, in her role as the pretty PA, she was always at his side for important client meetings such as the one tonight involving three gentlemen from Minnesota.

"Davis," Brach said, rising to greet a large man in a dark-gray suit who was obviously the leader of the trio.

"Kally, this is Davis Carlsruud, he's in electronics."

"Pleased to meet you, Mr. Carlsruud," Kally said with an engaging smile.

"Call me Dave, please," the man said, taking Kally's hand and squeezing it suggestively. "The pleasure is all mine. Actually we build the conduits that make their electronic factories possible. These gentlemen are Dr. Michael Thoresensen and Roger Smusio. We're here in Montana to discuss opportunities for investment with Sunrise Land Holdings."

Carlsruud was clearly the type to be smitten by attractive young women.

"Will you be staying long?" Kally asked. "We'd be

happy to arrange a visit to our new property up in Logan County."

"Unfortunately, this is just a quick visit for my colleagues to meet Tom, *and yourself*, face-to-face."

Brach let Carlsruud order the wine, knowing that the hefty gentleman fancied himself a connoisseur. He even had some land investments near Napa—and he told Kally all about this. When he generously invited her to come out to see "his vineyards," she readily accepted, though it was clear the invitation was just a polite gesture.

For her part, she feigned interest in the other gentlemen at the table, asking Dr. Thoresensen for details of his clinical psychology practice.

When the steaks had been ordered—Kally opted for the salmon—the conversation turned to the noble mission of Sunrise. Brach was pleased when Kally more than did her part explaining the "joys of smiling children" experiencing the "beautiful pristine open spaces" that were part of the narrative. The Minnesota men hung on every word, but Brach wondered whether their eyes might be more interested in taking in the beautiful open spaces of her generous cleavage.

As he watched Kally enthusiastically outlining investment packages, his mind turned to how naïve she was. What would she think if she ever came within sight of the warehouses and the cages full of teenagers who never smiled? But Kally, who always smiled, would never learn about these things. It was not her place at Sunrise to have any inkling of the company's dark side.

When Kally excused herself to go to the ladies' room, the men got down to the real purpose of the meeting.

"As I've told you before, she knows nothing about this," Brach said, nodding at Kally as she disappeared into the foyer where the restrooms were. "It's best to have some deniability. She knows only about the sunny side of Sunrise."

"She does an excellent job of selling the bucolic part," Thoresensen said. "I'm almost ready to invest in some pristine places."

"I was going to ask if *she's* for sale." Smusio snickered. The others all cast him a dirty look.

"Let's get down to business," Carlsruud said. "Are our packages ready for pickup?"

"They will be ready at seven tomorrow morning as we agreed," Brach said. "Here are written directions so you won't need to turn on your phones or have to use GPS."

"Good. Our drivers arrived this afternoon with the vans. We'll convoy out to your holding facility, inspect the merchandise, make the necessary wire transfers, and be on our way."

"Perfect," Brach said. "Tony Stayton will be out there to meet you. I can escort you myself."

"That's okay," Carlsruud said with a wink. "I know Tony. We'll be in good hands. You and PA can sleep in and order some room service."

CHAPTER
FIFTEEN

SHERIFF KYLE FAHR glanced across the front seat of the Durango at Mark Edredin. Fahr knew he had done this before. He had climbed into Humvees and driven into gunfights, and Fahr knew he had done it many times.

Fahr had done it in a Crown Vic a few times down in Denver, but in most cases, the shooting was avoided. They say some number far below a tenth of one percent of American cops ever use their guns except at the range. Most think about it a lot, but the occasion never comes. Tonight might be the exception for Kyle Fahr.

It took nearly an hour on the county road to circle to the remote northern edge of the former Tredquist place where there was the gravel road leading to the old Air Force airfield. The road was so hard to see in the twilight Fahr almost missed the turn. Following his lead, both Jamie Manderson and Jessica Edredin made the turn, and one by one they extinguished their headlights. There was still enough light to see where they were going if they kept their eyes glued to the red constellation of taillights on the rear of Fahr's Durango. At the first glimpse of the lights of the buildings at the airfield, they both slowed to a crawl and coasted to a stop, side by side, about a quarter mile from the buildings. They had the hardest job of the night—waiting helplessly for everything to go down.

Fahr drove the Durango around to the east side of the main building, a large warehouse with its big roll-up door open to the runway. Inside, the lights glowed brightly, and there were a few people milling around. As Fahr came to a stop about sixty feet from the door, two men with sidearms approached about half the distance and stood facing the Durango. Fahr and Edredin took it as a good sign they encountered no perimeter guards farther out. The Sunrise people had clearly not been expecting visitors.

A middle-aged man in a new-appearing black fleece jacket came out the building and approached the sheriff's vehicle.

"Good evening, Sheriff," he said as Fahr climbed out. "I'm Jason Nuemeyer. I'm the manager here for Sunrise Land Holdings, who owns this property. To what do we owe the pleasure of your visit this evening?"

The two men had never met, but Nuemeyer had been watching from inside the old Tredquist ranch house when the sheriff had tried to arrest Kenny Lathrope for shooting Steve Coe nine days earlier.

Tonight, Nuemeyer was carrying a holstered sidearm, but like the other two men, he made no threatening gesture. One of the two other men standing farther back held a rifle, but he made no threatening move.

"I'm Kyle Fahr, I'm the Logan County Sheriff," he said, introducing himself and extending his hand. Doing this was a force of habit when introducing himself, but Fahr figured it wouldn't hurt to put Nuemeyer at ease— or at least to try.

Probably also out of a force of habit, Nuemeyer shook the sheriff's hand, but there was no cordiality in his eyes. He was on edge, and nearly everything in his body language, and that of everyone the sheriff could see, was the same.

"I'm sorry to bother you this evening," Fahr said, immediately regretting the use of the term "sorry"— because you should *never* apologize for doing your duty. "But we've had some complaints."

"What kind of complaints?"

"Well, noise complaints, actually. You know, in the cold night air out here, noise travels pretty far."

"What kind of *noise*?" Nuemeyer asked, obviously perturbed.

"Folks driving past on the county road have said they have heard people screaming out here."

"Probably coyotes," Nuemeyer said.

Fahr could tell by his pronunciation of the word "coyote" with three, rather than two syllables, that he was not from Montana.

"I won't discount it," Fahr said. "But we have to check it out. Part of the job. I'm sure you understand."

"Of course," Nuemeyer said, his voice still tense. "Now that we've handled this, we'll let you be on your way."

"Well, as long as we're here, I'm sure you wouldn't mind if we took a little look around. You know, just so we can check all the boxes."

Nuemeyer exchanged furtive glances with the others standing nearby—Fahr counted five, including Nuemeyer.

"Okay, but if you wouldn't mind making it quick, we're trying to close up for the night."

"What is it exactly that you folks do out here?" Fahr asked in a "making conversation" sort of tone.

"The mission of Sunrise is preservation of pristine open spaces," Nuemeyer said, as if quoting from a brochure, which in fact he was. "You know, making this available to people to experience."

"We did notice the 'no trespassing' signs," Fahr said, citing the intimidating signage while trying not to seem sarcastic.

"We're not open for business just yet," Nuemeyer explained, as Fahr walked slowly toward the vast open doorway and the illuminated room beyond. Edredin stepped out of the Durango but stayed back. He had met Nuemeyer before and did not want to be close enough to be recognized. He left the door open and his AR-15 within easy reach.

Stepping across the threshold from the asphalt tarmac to the concrete floor of the warehouse building, Fahr made a point of putting the Sunrise crew on edge by eating up time looking around and studying the details of the building. Inside, and off to one corner, there was an area set off behind a large canvas tarp that was hung like the curtain on a theatrical stage.

"What's behind the curtain?" Fahr asked.

"Oh, just crates of supplies," Nuemeyer replied defensively.

"Would you mind showing me?" Fahr suggested calmly.

"That would involve moving a lot of stuff and lifting all the framing stacked on the scaffolding."

"Hmmm," Fahr said thoughtfully. "Are you saying you *won't* raise the curtain?"

"It would be complicated," Nuemeyer said.

"Couldn't you just do just thet corner on the right, and get it over with?" Fahr asked. "I'll take a quick look, check this off on my report, and get out of your hair."

"I truly can't do it," Nuemeyer said. He was really starting to sweat.

"Here," Fahr said. "I think if you just pull this rope here…"

"*No, don't,*" Nuemeyer shouted desperately.

But Fahr gave the rope a firm tug with both her hands, and the tarp fell away.

He was quite unprepared for what they now beheld.

There were a half dozen forty-eight-inch, metal-wire dog crates stacked two high, with scuff marks on the concrete indicating there had been more next to them, but which had been moved. Inside four of the crates were nearly naked human beings—bound and gagged teenage girls.

For a moment, nobody said anything.

"No wonder people heard screams," Fahr said caustically. "What the hell is going on here? Enjoying pristine open spaces?"

"I'm sorry you had to see this," Nuemeyer said, putting his hand on his holster. "I wish you would've taken the hint and left well enough alone. I'm afraid we can no longer just let you drive away."

One of the men raised his rifle and pointed it directly at Fahr.

The other man fumbled with his holster, and two more reached for theirs.

As Fahr went for his own gun, he knew his reaction time was fatally too slow.

———

From a distance of about 1,200 yards, Lauren Stahling had been watching the five men in the building with the roll-up door for more than half an hour before the sheriff's Durango rolled in. She couldn't hear what anyone was saying, but with Hammer's Oberwerk 25x100mm CF center-focus binoculars, she could read the body language like she was standing next to the men.

She and Hammer had ridden the Norton most of the way to this vantage point and had walked the last fifty yards.

As soon as they were situated, Hammer had unpacked his "hunting" rifle, his Barrett Mk22 MRAD. He attached the bipod, carefully sighted his ATN X-Sight 4K 5-20x Ultra HD day and night vision scope, and slotted in a magazine with ten .338 Norma Magnum rounds. He laid out three more mags on his rifle case within easy reach.

Like Lauren, he had been studying the comings and goings inside the building well before the Durango arrived. He easily recognized Jason Nuemeyer and several of the others from his visit to the Tredquist ranch house with Edredin several days before.

Through his scope, he had a good field of view of everything going on as Fahr approached Nuemeyer. Like Lauren, he had an "almost like being there" view of the body language. When the sheriff stepped across the threshold, he knew it was time to slide his finger into the trigger guard.

When the first man raised his rifle, Hammer squeezed.

Fahr was momentarily stunned as he watched this man's skull ripped apart in a blinding *whoosh* that sent bloody bone fragments flying across the room.

Before this shower of scraps had fully come to rest, a second man's head was severed by a crashing, sloshing explosion.

Though he was startled and distracted, Nuemeyer already had his hand on own sidearm.

Lauren glanced over at her companion after the

second human head exploded within the building. With the AML 338 suppressor on the muzzle, and with the smoothness of the Mk22's bolt, it was like watching a silent movie.

The five puffs of sound, which came in rapid succession, seemed unconnected to what she was seeing. Hammer's right hand moved from trigger to bolt with the effortless precision of a concert pianist, completing each cycle in less than a second.

When she glanced back to look through the glass of the Oberwerk CF, she saw five bodies on the ground—and two standing. Mark Edredin was out of the Durango now, holding his AR-15 and surveying the scene with amazement. He was ready to fire, but there were no targets left at which to fire.

It had all happened so fast. It was over in six seconds.

Lauren heard Hammer change magazines and watched as he quietly scrutinized the scene, adjusting the scope to a wider field of view.

————

"Every kill shot was a headshot," Edredin observed as he and Fahr inspected the fallen bodies.

"Hammer has a good eye," Fahr said in understatement.

"Of course he does." Edredin laughed, as though there was never a doubt.

Within moments, the other two vehicles had rolled up.

"Let's take a look around," Edredin said as soon as Steve Coe and Jamie Manderson were out of the second Durango. "Let's make sure there's no other hostiles lurking around."

As the three of them, plus the sheriff, moved out

cautiously to search the building and its perimeter, Jessica had gone to work with her bolt cutters, while Erin retrieved some blankets and a few water bottles from the Trailblazer.

"Hang on, ladies," Jessica said, trying to convey a reassuring tone. "Help will be on the way soon. I've already called some people who'll be able to give you shelter."

Within a few minutes, all of the captives had been released from the humiliation of the dog crates and were clustered together on the fallen tarp.

As the others declared the warehouse clear and moved out to reconnoiter the perimeter, Hammer and Lauren rolled up on the Norton. She got off to start helping Jessica and Erin while Hammer unholstered his M1911 and rode his bike around to the rear of the warehouse to aid in the hunt for more of the Sunrise crew.

As they searched, the only thing that materialized was not a sight, but a sound—the murmuring of voices coming from a low building behind the big warehouse. Hammer carefully circled this building on his bike, but as with the first structure, the perimeter was clear.

The building, which appeared to be an old barracks, was padlocked, but Edredin kicked in the door with his boot. Fahr's high-powered Maglite revealed the source of the voices.

"Holy shit!" Coe said, aghast.

The others were speechless.

There was a row of metal cots, with more teenagers—at least a dozen more—anchored to them with bicycle chains. All of these girls were clothed, although they had no shoes.

Mark Edredin was on the phone to his wife.

"We're in the bunkhouse out back. When you have a chance, bring us the bolt cutters."

About twenty minutes later, when most of the captives had been freed and all of them consolidated into the warmer bunkhouse, Hammer excused himself with the cryptic words, "Don't worry if you hear a few gunshots from the front of the warehouse."

They did not worry, but they could not help wondering.

When Hammer returned a little while later, he handed the sheriff two evidence bags, each containing an automatic pistol.

"Stahling grabbed a couple of extras when she bagged the hotel napkin, and I put them to use," Hammer told the sheriff. "These weapons have the fingerprints of two men. If you want to jot this down in your notebook, I'll give you their names."

"Who are they?" Kyle Fahr asked curiously as he retrieved his pocket notebook and a ballpoint pen from the breast pocket of his jacket.

"They're Sunrise employees who went missing a few days ago. Their names are Brad Shannin and Kenny Lathrope. Sunrise believes they went AWOL. Apparently, they 'came back' tonight, because 9mm rounds from their weapons were fired into the five men who died here tonight. As you know, there were other bullets fired as well, but *these* rounds are connected to *these* weapons and *these* suspects in tonight's shooting, who are still at large."

"Oh…" Fahr said, gradually processing what Hammer was telling him. "I think I understand."

"If you check the back corner of the parking lot at the picnic area out on the county road, you'll find a locked vehicle, a Toyota Tundra registered to Sunrise, with these gentlemen's prints all over it," Hammer continued. "It would seem the perps in tonight's shooting dumped the company pickup and left the state in another vehicle. You might want to put out a BOLO."

"Yeah, I could do this," Fahr said.

Just as Vince Milino had been misdirecting the official search for Jenna Tolliver by erroneously entwining it with an unrelated gun-running gang investigation, Hammer was practicing the art of misdirection to create the cover story for their successful covert operation against Milino's own outlaw associates. In the craft of the illusionist, there is always an element of fact.

"And coincidentally," Hammer said. "If you look at the bullet retrieved from Steve Coe's shoulder, you'll find it really *did* come from Lathrope's gun."

CHAPTER
SIXTEEN

JENNA TOLLIVER COULDN'T STOP SHAKING. It was partly the icy cold of the concrete floor where she lay, but mostly it was the fear of being murdered—or *worse*.

After Aaron Kruegher had killed the young woman by slamming her onto the concrete floor, Jenna was sure she would be next. Her only consolation was that all of the other men in the room had begun scolding Kruegher, rebuking him for what he had done. However, when talk turned to "what we should do with *the bitch*," she knew they meant *her*.

Finally, they came for her, lifting her off the cold floor and cutting the cable ties which bound her ankles so she could walk. Her shoes were long gone and she was blindfolded with opaque duct tape, so she had no idea where she was stepping. The pavement was cold, and there were sharp pieces of gravel that hurt her feet. It was difficult going as they pushed and shoved her, and she had no idea where they were going. She hoped it would not be into another car trunk.

At last, they came to the door to a room and she was

pushed through. Jenna could tell by the sound it was a smaller room, without the echo of the cavernous equipment garage where she had been. There was actually a carpet on the floor. She thought it must be some kind of office. As she was pushed, she braced herself for hitting the floor, but instead she landed in a vinyl upholstered chair.

"Don't go anywhere," a voice laughed after her ankles were cable tied to the chair. She heard the door slam.

Jenna took a deep breath. The room stank vaguely of mildew, and it was still cold, although at least she was no longer lying on concrete. She heard voices beyond the door, but she didn't think there was anyone else in the room.

Time passed. She tried to work the cable ties to get them off her wrists, but they were too tight and they cut her, so she gave up. After a while, she remembered a movie where someone managed to get his bound wrists in front of him by getting them around his feet. Struggling like a contortionist, she tried this but only managed to clumsily fall off the chair and onto the floor.

When she had caught her breath, Jenna figured out her intended maneuver was more easily accomplished when lying down. After several tries, Jenna found herself in a sitting position with her hands in her lap. She immediately, though carefully, pulled the duct tape from her eyes and her mouth. The adhesive was powerful, and her skin stung, but she felt the triumph of being free of the tape.

The room was unlit, but there were enough cracks in the flimsy walls of the office to allow a little bit of light to seep in from the big room where the vehicles were parked. There was a desk and a file cabinet and assorted other junk in the room. By the dust which had accumulated on the desk, it appeared the office did not get much use.

On the desk were stacks of papers bearing the letterhead of Sunrise Land Holdings. She had heard of them. They were some kind of charity. Could it be this charity had been somehow taken over by this gang of human traffickers?

Jenna opened one desk drawer after another, hoping she would find something to cut the cable ties binding her hands. Rummaging around beneath stacks of papers in one of the bottom drawers, her fingers fell upon the cold steel of an old pair of scissors. This was so "too good to be true" that at first her mind insisted it must be some kind of a trap, rather than mere sloppy oversight on the part of her captors.

The scissors may have seemed at first like the solution to her problem, but she soon realized with her hands bound, she could not get the proper leverage at the right angle to use them. Several times, they fell to the floor, and she began to worry she was making too much noise. *Would she be heard*?

It took what seemed like an hour for her to finally cut through the hard nylon. Her wrists and fingers were bleeding painfully, but her hands were free! Soon she had also freed her ankles.

However, Jenna herself was *not* free!

She was still stuck in the small room. The door was unlocked—it locked from the inside—but it opened outward and they had pushed something heavy against it. Just to be spiteful, she locked the door from the inside.

There was a glass window high on the wall opposite the door, but it was more like a vent than an actual window. Again, it took some trial and error, but Jenna found she could easily reach the window by climbing onto the desk and then stepping onto the handles of the file cabinet, which became like a ladder.

She was still wearing her Max Mara wool coat, and she knew she could not make it through the opening wearing it. As she peeled it off, she saw it was torn and filthy from being on the ground. It was stained with her own blood and that of the girl with whom she'd shared the trunk.

The frame of the small window was mostly rotten, so the challenge was not so much getting it open but preventing the crash of breaking glass when the window fell—either inward or outward.

She could now smell the cold clear outside air, so it was painful to have to retreat into the room, but she decided the best thing to do was to retrieve her coat from the floor, toss it out first and let the glass fall onto it so it would make less noise.

With the opening clear of both glass and frame, Jenna pushed her head and shoulders through the narrow opening but realized this meant she could be dropping ten feet or more *head first*.

She extracted herself and pushed her legs through. When most of her body was outside, she let go, hoping not to land with her feet on the window glass. In this, she was successful, but she scratched her legs and almost twisted an ankle.

Jenna smoothed her skirt and looked into the night sky. The stars were out and it was cold, probably below freezing. Here she was, shivering in her lightweight red party dress with short sleeves, and no shoes. But she did have her battered, but warm, coat—and she was free!

She started walking over the rough gravel, each step an ordeal. She did not know where she was, nor which way was which. The only thing governing her direction was to get as far away as possible from the building where she had been. The moon had not risen, so at first, she picked her way by starlight alone.

As the moon rose, she could tell she was walking westward, but since she did not know where she was, this was not useful information. She crossed a gravel road but decided not to take it. If they discovered her missing, they'd use the roads to search for her.

She walked and she walked, using the movement of the moon across the sky to judge time and direction, until she could walk no more. The wind was picking up. The soles of her feet felt torn to shreds, so she sat down in the shelter of a rock outcropping to rest. She wanted to cry, but she was too exhausted. Before she could stop herself, Jenna Tolliver fell asleep.

———

Through the years, Lauren Stahling had occasionally indulged herself in the guilty pleasure of a romantic fantasy of waking up next to Jim Hammer for the first time.

But she had never imagined it would be like this. They were not *in* her own queen size bed, but on top of it, and they were both fully clothed. They each were wearing their coats, and Hammer still had his boots on. They both smelled of stale sweat.

It had been a most unromantic night, and one short on sleep.

By the time the people from the shelter had arrived it was nearly midnight, and it took time for all of the young women to be cleaned up a little bit, and first aid to be rendered. For the most part, they were in reasonably good shape physically, except for the chafing of their restraints and the occasional bruise rendered in a "disciplinary" way by their captors. Psychologically, they were as one would expect of young people who knew they'd been sold into slavery.

Hammer, who spoke a little bit of several languages, had determined they were all or mostly Korean, and had been able to tell them they were among friends. The look in their eyes told that they were not yet ready to believe this.

This morning's wake-up call came in on Hammer's burner phone, but Lauren answered it.

"Is Hammer there?" Kyle Fahr asked, only partially surprised to hear a female voice.

The bright red numerals on the bedside clock calmly whispered, "4:04."

"Yeah, he's right here. I'm putting this thing on speaker."

"I'm at the station. I spent the night. Jamie is on her way back up at the airport with the coroner to consolidate the scene. Meanwhile, I wanted you to know we just got the communication intercept on the radio that we've been waiting for."

"*What did they say*?" Lauren asked eagerly.

"They said 'the politician escaped.' They were extremely flustered."

"That can only mean they were holding Jenna, and she managed to get away. She's the only 'politician' who could have escaped, right? But they're obviously looking for her, and she's obviously in danger."

"The silver lining is we have a GPS fix," Fahr said. "I'll text it to you right now. It's northwest of Billings."

"Text it to Mark too," Lauren said. "He'll be furious if he gets left out, and so will Jess."

"I can do this," Fahr said. "But I'm afraid the six of you will be on your own as soon as you cross the county line. As you know, Jamie and I can't join you outside

Logan County. That's outside our jurisdiction, but personally, we'll both be rooting for you."

"Thank you," Lauren said. "And on behalf of all of us, thanks for everything you two did last night. I know we were pushing the limits of what you can *officially* do."

"No problem," he said. "I've replayed it in my head a dozen times through the night, and I can't think of another way to have done what was accomplished up there. Good luck with getting Jenna out of that mess down there."

"Thanks."

Hammer's eyes were still closed, but his brain was processing what he was hearing.

"Wake up, sleepyhead," Lauren said, poking him. "We've got to move. I made coffee last night. I'll heat it in the microwave and put it into a thermos for the road while you get yourself up."

Hammer watched as she reached into her closet and took out a well-worn leather gun belt with her father's old Colt .44 revolver. This brought back memories for Hammer. He had long ago gone shooting with her and this same pistol. With a wink, she strapped it on and went to heat the coffee. He smiled. It was hunting season, and she was getting herself ready to go hunting.

———

Jenna Tolliver awoke to a thin silver line across the eastern horizon, and the moon dipping low in the west. Her whole body was swathed in an enveloping numbness of cold, but as her mind came awake, it began processing prickles of pain that became blinding lightning bolts.

Her feet! *Oh, her poor bare feet!* The pain of lacerations

subjected to hours—she had no way of knowing how many—of freezing cold had taken a toll.

She was thankful for the wool of her Max Mara coat. It was no longer a thing of style and prestige, but a filthy thing of welcome *warmth*. She bundled herself into a ball and wrapped her bloody feet in the coat. She stared longingly at the horizon praying for sunrise. The irony of this word "sunrise" being the name of the organization which had imprisoned her was bitterly noted.

In the frail light of the promising dawn, she saw that the place where she had stopped in the darkness was only about fifteen feet from the edge of a steep cliff, with a hundred-foot drop. If she had stepped closer last night, she might have seen this precipice in the light of the new moon—but maybe not.

Lucky me, she thought, though the thought of "being out of my misery" flickered momentarily in the back of her mind.

In the distance, from across a rise over which she had stumbled in last night's darkness, she heard faint voices. If they hadn't already, they would discover she was gone, and they would come looking for her. Her teeth began to chatter so uncontrollably she feared the sound would attract her captors.

They were shouting now. They were on the hunt. She tried to make herself seem small. Her red dress stuck out like a sore thumb, but at least her coat blended into the rocky, frosty landscape.

What had she been thinking? If she had *not* escaped, she would at least be inside out of the wind, and her feet would not have been cut to ribbons. What would they do to her if they caught her?

Should she shout out and surrender? Should she trade the icy, rocky outcrop for the vinyl chair and the cable ties?

Hell no!

———

Tony Stayton had been sound asleep when one of the Sunrise guards had nudged him, whispering the menacing phrase, "We got a problem."

As he swam through the cobwebs tangling his path into the conscious world, Stayton's mind spun.

"What problem?"

"The woman is gone."

"*Gone?*"

"Kruegher discovered it. Nahlwerk was on guard, but he nodded off. He woke up when he heard Kruegher on the radio telling Milino 'the politician' had escaped."

"*Damn it!*" Stayton said. "He's not supposed to use words like that on the radio."

"Who's gonna hear us? It's a secure channel, isn't it?"

"Where's Kruegher now?" Stayton asked, straightening his orange tie.

"He's out looking."

"In the dark?"

"Yeah. He's mad as fuck!"

"He's a monster when he's mad," Stayton said, obviously worried. "You saw him kill the Korean kid last night."

"Yeah…"

"Listen, we gotta get this under control, immediately," Stayton demanded. "Sunrise has customers arriving here this morning and we can't have Kruegher screw things up, and I'm happy not to have to explain that woman to them."

"Yessir," the man said apologetically.

"You and Nahlwerk go out there and find Kruegher. As much as I'm happy not to have him around, we can't have him screw up this transaction. Get him back here and get him calmed down. That woman can't have gone far with bare feet on rocks and gravel, and there's nowhere she can go. We can deal with her later."

As much as Sunrise relied on the rogue ATF agents to get them out of the occasional jam, Stayton resented having to deal with a loose cannon like Kruegher when he wasn't needed. Even his own people were wary of him. Stayton surmised that when Milino went back to Billings, he left Kruegher behind to keep him out of the way—and Milino hadn't even seen Kruegher *murder* the Korean girl!

By this time, with all of the commotion, everyone was awake, so Stayton decided it wouldn't hurt to start getting his "first batch of Koreans" ready for the Minnesota customers. With two men out looking for the loose cannon, Stayton put the two remaining Sunrise men to work.

"Take those nine that we picked yesterday," Stayton shouted. "Clean 'em up and make them presentable, and don't let any of *them* get away."

"Now that we have Wi-Fi again, I put the GPS coordinates into Google Earth," Lauren said, staring at her laptop while Hammer drove. "The location is a gravel pit north and west of Billings. I'll take a screenshot in case we lose connection."

"What does it look like?"

"Pretty remote, like the airport was. I guess this is their distribution center, where customers pick up their slaves. Assuming they wouldn't want to leave the school bus out in the open, there's only one building nearly big enough for them to use to hide vehicles, and cages like we saw up north."

"I wish we had real-time imagery like we had in the Army," Hammer lamented, glancing over at the laptop as she held it up. "Sometimes I miss my old job, but only *sometimes*."

"You can't always get what you want," she said. "But we'll have our actual eyes on the actual thing soon enough."

"How do we approach?"

"There's a long, straight paved county road going due west off this highway. Taking that, we can avoid getting mixed up in Billings traffic. Then we can drop down to the gravel pit on an unimproved gravel road running for about a dozen miles. There's a direct road leading south from the gravel pit toward Billings so if anybody is going and coming from down there, they won't see us on the gravel road. Perfect back door."

"Great," Hammer said. "You should tell Mark or Jessica, or whoever's driving."

"It was Jessica who suggested the same idea a couple of minutes ago," Lauren said, holding up her burner phone. "They have the same coordinates. We've been texting."

"Where are they now?" Hammer asked.

"Only about ten or fifteen minutes back."

"Are you having fun yet?" Hammer asked after they had made the turn onto the other road.

"Sorry?" Lauren replied, startled.

"Last week when you invited yourself onto my last trip to Billings, you said you wanted to go because you didn't want *me* having all the fun. And here we are again."

"Oh yeah, I *did* say that, didn't I?" Lauren laughed. "It was very impulsive of me, wasn't it?"

"Was it?"

"Yes, it was. That's not something the county assessor of two weeks ago, or two years or so ago, would have done. The problem is this friend of mine from long ago showed up with this big blur of intrigue and excitement swirling around him, and the old me couldn't resist being part of the fun."

"He must be a bad influence."

"My mother hinted you were a bad influence back in the day, too," she said.

"Oh, did she?"

"I always insisted you were a *friend*, not a boyfriend," Lauren said, as Hammer nodded, recalling this as being the case. "But we sure did have some good times back then."

"That we did," Hammer said with a smile. "We *were* good friends; I remember the plots and thrills. Remember yearbook class, and the school paper, and some of those things you wrote?"

"Like it was yesterday, or maybe the week before yesterday," Lauren said. "I remember sharing schemes and scandals with you the way I could never do with my girlfriends, and *certainly* not with my boyfriends."

"And here we are, back at it."

"I can't believe it," Lauren said. "I told my staff, my team, I'm taking time off to go hunting. They all looked at me like I was crazy. Maybe I am. A few hours later, I calmly watched the captain of the basketball team shoot the heads off five people, and next was helping free a couple dozen girls from cages."

"And here you are on another road trip with a guy you haven't seen in twenty years."

"I think we were best friends back then," Lauren said thoughtfully.

"Yeah, I suppose we were. It sure felt like it."

"Until I destroyed it," Lauren said sorrowfully. "I shattered the unique thing we had."

"What do you mean?" Hammer asked.

"*That night*," Lauren said argumentatively. "That dreadful, *wonderful* night when I told you I had feelings for you and I wanted *more* than what we already had!"

"I thought it was *good*," he said. "But I always thought it was *me* who blew it. The next day, when you gave me 'the talk' about you going to college and me going into the Army, you were right. We *were* headed in opposite directions."

"And so we did," she said. "But *last night*...when I was back on the back of your Norton."

CHAPTER
SEVENTEEN

IT WAS STILL DARK when Aron Kruegher came back fuming from his fruitless search for the runaway Jenna Tolliver.

"She can't have got far," Tony Stayton said, trying to be reassuring. "She's barefoot and dressed like she's going to a cocktail party. The terrain is impossible and we're at least twenty miles from anywhere. If anything, worry she doesn't freeze to death out there. It will be light soon. She'll be easy to find."

Kruegher nodded but said nothing.

Stayton turned to the Nahlwerk and the other man who had coaxed Kruegher back to the warehouse and ordered them to come back out into the cold.

"Find some high ground and start keeping an eye on the road leading into this place from Billings," he said. "Take a short-range radio and buzz me the minute you see the Minnesota men coming this way."

"What about cops?" Nahlwerk asked.

"What cops?" Stayton laughed. "The state and county cops are off the case and our federal friends have everything contained. Just let me know when the customers show up."

"Boss," someone shouted from across the room as Nahlwerk and the other man went out. "We got a couple of these Korean gooks ready to show you."

Stayton and Kruegher walked over to the corner of the equipment garage where the cages were stacked, and where there was a bathroom and showers. The latter had been installed for the use of the gravel pit workers and were proving useful today.

Three school-age girls, dressed in uniforms as though they were on their way to school, were seated on folding chairs staring stoically into space. The sight gave Stayton a queasy feeling. As he watched, two more girls were brought out, freshly scrubbed and with their hair brushed. They looked so normal. They might have been girls in the mall in Leesburg, seven miles from his house in Virginia, hanging out, skipping school or doing whatever teenagers do these days. But instead, they were about to be sold into slavery, embarking on a dreadful road of no return. Their sad expressions showed they knew it.

What had he gotten himself into? He asked himself. The answer was both calculated in dollar signs and the knowledge he had started down his own road of no return.

Kruegher could not resist a bit of touching of the "merchandise," but Stayton just turned away. Business was business. It was not the time for groping.

────────

"It's just across that rise a quarter mile up ahead," Lauren said in a low voice. The tension of anticipation made a whisper seem appropriate.

They were, however, close enough Hammer doused his headlights and slowed the pickup to a crawl. In the gathering light of predawn, it was light enough to see pretty well.

When they were close enough on the unimproved gravel road, about a dozen miles south of the paved county road, Hammer made a U-turn and parked heading out. He grabbed his Oberwerk HD II binoculars and the two of them walked about a hundred feet to the crest of the rise.

The equipment garage was clearly visible, and tantalizingly close. The cuts and mounds and gullies of the gravel pit spread out beyond for a considerable distance. As they'd seen on Google Earth, a well-maintained gravel road snaked away from the building in the opposite direction, heading south toward Billings. There were various vehicles around, mainly the kind which would be associated with a gravel pit. There were several end loaders and bulldozers, a grader and several dump trucks. No one was at work.

There was a light breeze blowing. It was cold, but the sound of the wind would mask a certain amount of the sound they were making.

The only activity was inside the building. Light was visible in most of the windows, which was to be expected of the large open space where the lights were on. There was a large roll-up door on the left side that was big enough to admit a large truck—or a school bus—and a smaller one on the side nearest to Hammer and Lauren.

After a few minutes, Hammer handed his binoculars to Lauren and went to the truck, returning with his Mk22 sniper rifle. As he had at the other warehouse the night before, he carefully attached the bipod, sighted the scope, slotted in a ten-round magazine, and laid out three more.

Unlike the previous night, when he'd had a clear,

unobstructed view of the broad doorway, Hammer had an ideal perspective on neither door, although this vantage point offered the best possible view of both doors simultaneously.

As they watched, both doors were rolled up, first big one, revealing part of the school bus. When the smaller one went up, they could look inside and see a row of chairs with the girls cable tied to them.

"Count the bad guys milling around," Hammer whispered to Lauren. "I'll do the same. Since we don't have a clear view inside the building, and they're all moving around, if we both count, we can cross-check each another."

With his ATN X-Sight 4K rifle scope, he had as good a view as Lauren did with the HD II binoculars.

"Unless there are some who are not moving around that we can't see, I count six," she said after several minutes.

He nodded, adding there were two in suits, one of them their friend in the orange tie.

"And I'll not soon forget the one with the buzz cut," she said disapprovingly. "No sign of Jenna, though."

"Hopefully they haven't recaptured her yet," he said. "We'll have to neutralize the Sunrise bunch before we start our own search, so we better do it quick."

As they watched, two of the other four men, both carrying automatic rifles, left the building and stepped out into the cool air of dawn. They raised their collars, but not their guns. Hammer expected them to scan their surrounding for potential trouble. That's what he and his men would have done on a similar operation. He expected their eyes to fall on his and Lauren's hiding spot, and he braced himself to take a shot if necessary. But they did not bother looking up the hill.

Instead, they just started walking down the gravel

road leading toward Billings. Whoever was in charge down there had decided to have sentries covering only the road leading into the gravel pit from the south. These men were a quarter of a mile away when they finally sat down to make themselves comfortable.

Hammer shook his head. With almost reckless over-confidence, the two had set themselves up in a place where they would miss *everything* that happened on the ridge where he and Lauren were!

Looking behind them on the opposite approaches to the ridge, Hammer could see Jessica Edredin's Chevy Trailblazer had arrived. She made a U-turn and parked about thirty yards from Hammer's pickup. The four of them were walking carefully and quietly. All four were hunters, and they knew the drill for approaching wild game.

Hammer and Lauren came down to meet them at the blue pickup.

"Where's Jenna?" Jessica asked. "Any idea?"

"There's an equipment garage just across the ridge," Hammer said. "We can see Korean captives in there, but we can't see Jenna."

"If she *did* get away, we can't tell whether they've recaptured her," Lauren answered.

"We need to get in there quick and take down the Sunset crew as quick as possible," Hammer said.

"What are we up against?" Mark Edredin asked.

"Based on what we've seen, there are at least four inside the building and two more posted down the road to Billings."

"What's the plan?" Steve Coe asked.

"I'll use my rifle to take out the two sentries, but we need to use a frontal approach with the garage, like we did last night," Hammer explained.

He then directed them to a canvas tarp he had laid out

on the tailgate of his truck. He unfolded it, displaying two Glock pistols he'd collected at the airfield, along with several magazines.

"More misdirection," Steve Coe said with a satisfied smile as he looked at the weapons. "Just like you did last night."

"I'm glad to see both you and Mark are wearing gloves," Hammer said.

"It's cold," Mark Edredin said, smiling.

As Mark and Steve each took his personal sidearm out of his holster and substituted one of the Glocks, Jessica noticed Hammer was looking at the holster on her hip.

"Heavy-duty garden shears," she said with a smile. "For cable ties. Erin and I both brought them, along with the bolt cutters. The shears will cut through heavy-gauge wire too."

"And we've got the number of a women's shelter here in Stillwater County," Erin said helpfully. "We're ready to make the call. This is almost getting routine."

"Not Billings?" Mark asked.

"We figured it was best not to cross county lines," Erin said. "Just in case."

"Let's get this over with," Jessica said firmly. "What do we do next, Hammer?"

"We'll all move in closer, and you'll cover me as I go into the building alone, like the sheriff did last night."

"I've been thinking too," Lauren interjected, interrupting Hammer. "I'm thinking that going in there alone is *women's work*."

Everyone, including Hammer, looked startled. Jessica was the first to smile and nod. She got it. She knew what Lauren was thinking.

"I may be totally off base," Lauren said. "Please hear me out. What Steve said about misdirection obviously plays into this. If Hammer goes in like he just said, they may not expect him, but they're programmed to react defensively to a big guy who looks like he just stepped out of an action movie, right? They're programmed to draw weapons and open fire. *But* they're not expecting an apparently unarmed woman to walk in there, to misdirect their instincts, and to act, well…*disarmingly*."

Hammer got it now.

"And what's more, the guy with the orange tie who I met at the Sunrise office is down there. When I met him, I was wearing my hair up like I am now. He'll recognize me. I can buy you guys time to size up the situation and, do what needs doing."

————

"I think it's getting light enough for me to find a barefoot politician in a bright red dress, don't you?" Aron Kruegher said, sliding a fresh magazine into his ATF-issue Glock 19M.

"Probably," Tony Stayton said. He was relieved to have Kruegher make an exit. His continuous pacing for the past hour was getting on Stayton's nerves. "Try to wait to bring her back until we're done with the Minnesota people. It might be awkward."

"Okay. I can do this."

"And one more thing," Stayton said as Kruegher was walking away. "Try not to kill her. Milino said she might be useful."

"Oh go to hell," Kruegher spat back.

As tired as Stayton was of his pacing, Kruegher was furious at the nagging blame he was getting from the Sunrise people for killing the Korean girl last night.

"Milino also wants you idiots to get rid of the Lexus. Do you think you can handle this?" Kruegher said as a parting shot.

Stayton just rolled his eyes and said, "Good luck."

"This won't be hard," Kruegher said. "I'll just pick up the trail from below the window she punched out in the office where *you* put her. You know, the room where *you* put her? The room she *escaped from*?"

When the ATF man was out of sight on the other side of the building, starting his hunt for the missing politician, Stayton breathed a sigh of relief. It was his turn to start pacing, though. He was anxious to make the transaction, get rid of the Lexus, and get out of this place.

"When are those Minnesota guys supposed to get here?" one of the Sunrise men asked.

Stayton looked at his watch. The Minnesota men were not late—exactly.

"Soon," Stayton said. "Brach gave me a half hour window. We still have more than twenty minutes."

"Maybe you should call Nahlwerk? Ask whether he's seen any headlights in the distance coming up the road?"

"Relax," Stayton cautioned the man, even though he himself was anything but relaxed. "He'll call when he sees them."

What Stayton and his men did not know was Nahlwerk would *never* call. He would never see headlights.

The last thing Nahlwerk *did* see was something he least expected. The head of the man next to him had simply exploded in an astonishing blur. The only sound had been the melon-on-the-garage-floor sound of something comprised mainly of water coming apart suddenly and violently.

Thanks to the AML 338 suppressor on the muzzle of Hammer's hunting rifle, there were no other sounds to consider.

Nahlwerk had very little time to contemplate what he'd seen.

Less than two seconds later—probably closer to one second—a soft, unjacketed .338 round clipped him on the bone just behind his left ear. His radio, the one with which he was supposed to stay in touch with Stayton, tumbled uselessly to the ground, and Nahlwerk's seated body crumpled anticlimactically.

———

"*What*! *Who are you*? Where'd you come from?"

As with Nahlwerk, Stayton was suddenly experiencing the unexpected.

An attractive woman had just walked through the big roll-up door.

Who *was she* and what was she doing here? His first instinct was that he was seeing things.

With her relaxed smile and fashionable lipstick, she was obviously not a threat—but her abrupt presence was a mystery demanding explanation.

"Are *you* with the Minnesota people? Stayton asked.

"Not exactly, Mr. Stayton," she said, her mind whirring. This was the first she had heard of "Minnesota" people and she had to quickly integrate them into the tale she was planning to spin.

"Let's just say I came on ahead of the…um…Minnesota people to meet with you."

"Wait a minute," Stayton said. "I know you from somewhere, don't I? Don't tell me."

Lauren just smiled a smile of the most contrived sweetness she could muster.

"Yes, Mr. Stayton," she said. "We met last Wednesday in Tom R. Brach's office on the eighteenth floor of the First Interstate Bank building."

It all came back to Stayton in a crash.

"I'm Lauren Stahling, I'm the county assessor up in Logan County."

She was just as striking in jeans and a battered canvas coat as she was in a blazer and pencil skirt. Maybe even more so.

"When are the Minnesota people coming?" he asked.

"Soon. You can count on it," Lauren answered, thinking on her feet.

"How can you help *you*?

"Thanks for asking." Lauren smiled. "I'd like to continue the conversation we had on the eighteenth floor, mainly the one I had with Mr. Brach. We talked of the open spaces of Logan County, the *remote* open spaces."

As Lauren unspooled her narrative, Stayton and the other Sunrise men were focused entirely on her, and not on Hammer, Edredin, and Coe, the erstwhile Logan High dream team, as they crept close to the building.

"We talked about the mission of Sunrise Land Holdings to preserve those open spaces, and of making this available to people to enjoy," Lauren continued, rolling off an ornate storyline cribbed from the Hambledon brochure and from her own wickedly mischievous imagination. Finally, as she saw her team was on the floor, she turned a screw.

"Did those girls sitting back there come here to enjoy the big skies of our Big Sky Country?"

Stayton recoiled. The Stahling woman had touched a nerve. He heard the sarcasm in her voice.

He glanced around the vast room.

Ahead of him was a calm, confident professional woman asking questions which, from her, were more than slightly embarrassing.

"Well, um…"

Behind him were nine young women, degraded and abused, crippled by humiliation to the point where they could not comprehend the type of self-assurance which flowed with such ease from the woman with the effortless smile.

"Would you mind asking one of them to step over here so we could ask her about how she is enjoying the pristine open spaces?" Lauren asked, nodding toward the seated girls. "Or maybe ask *all of them* to come over here?"

This was too much. She was starting to run circles around him in front of his men.

"Do you speak Korean, Mr. Stayton?" Lauren asked.

He was steaming. That was the last straw.

He needed to take control of the situation, and he had the trump card. The SIG P228 in his pocket would intimidate the smug grin from those pretty lips.

As Stayton began to make his move, a tall man emerged from the darkness as though in a wisp of vapor.

Stayton saw the man's gun appear so quickly, his own attempt to raise his SIG felt like slow motion.

He saw the muzzle of the man's gun, a handgun so much larger than the SIG, pointed directly at his eyes. Then it flicked slightly, as if the man had changed his mind and decided to shoot something else.

He had.

The massive destructive bulk of the .45ACP round smashed into Stayton's right shoulder, vaporizing both muscle and bone, and turning his lateral thoracic artery into pulp. The second round, bulldozing its way into the inside of Stayton's left leg, left his femoral artery spewing a ghastly torrent of blood.

In the case of Nahlwerk and the other sentry down the road, business was business for Jim Hammer. These were each a quick, efficiant kill. With Stayton, the inevitable end would not come so quickly. When you threaten deadly violence against a woman about whom a man cares, as Stayton had with Lauren back in Obsidian, a man like Hammer is unlikely to respond with the generosity of delivering an immediate death.

The other three Sunrise men in the equipment garage had followed Stayton's lead when he went for his gun, but having been distracted by Lauren Stahling's intricate misdirection, their reaction time was fatally slow.

The other two men from the long-ago dream team appeared out of the darkness on either side of Hammer and opened fire immediately, taking out each target with a single shot. Edredin and Coe were both hunters, raised on the need for conserving ammunition.

It was all over in seconds.

"There's a complication here," Lauren said as the three teammates approached her. "He said something about some 'Minnesota people.' They're expecting company here soon. So soon he thought at first I was them. I'm going to go out and take a look down the road. See if I can see headlights coming this way."

As she stepped across the threshold from concrete to gravel and walked away from the building, she saw a flicker of movement in the shadows, just inside the door.

It was another Sunrise man who had not shown himself earlier.

He had apparently been out of sight when the confrontation took place and stayed unseen. Now about to make his move.

His eyes were not on her. He did not assume her to be a threat as he raised his gun to shoot Hammer in the back at very close range.

He thought wrong.

For Lauren, it was a "time stood still" moment of light-speed judgment.

Should she alert Hammer?

No, she should not. He would be unable to turn,

locate the target and shoot in less time than the man could squeeze off an easy shot.

As so often happens when time stands still, memories come racing back from the depths of wherever in the mind they're stored. For Lauren, it was hunting coyotes at dusk or dawn, of quietly approaching them, of seeing the light of their beady, wily eyes, and of drawing her father's .44.

In those long-ago days, she had found if she clicked her tongue just right, the coyote would pause and look directly at her. In that moment, she took her shot.

In today's silvery dawn, she clicked again.

Wily eyes flicked toward her.

She took her shot.

When you threaten deadly violence upon a man about whom a woman cares, she feels no obligation to show you any consideration whatsoever.

In fact, when this happens, her first and only thought is simply to *kill you*.

CHAPTER
EIGHTEEN

IT WAS LIGHT OUT NOW, and a few large flakes of snow had started falling from the low clouds. Aron Kruegher was about a hundred yards from the equipment garage when he heard the sound of gunfire.

At first, he was startled in the way the sound of a not-so-distant fusillade is always startling. But on reflection, he knew it had nothing to do with him. This was Sunrise's operation. Anything going on up there was between them and the Minnesota people.

His assumption, as the shooting stopped was that Stayton and his people must have gotten into a disagreement with their customers. He knew the Minnesota people were mobsters, and mobsters sometimes get greedy. He knew from experience that there was no honor among thieves. So many times had he heard of—or seen with his own eyes—one criminal cartel cross another over guns or drugs or whatever.

It didn't matter to Kruegher. He couldn't even see the place from where he was, and they could not see him. He'd wait it out.

If the Sunrise men prevailed in the shootout, he'd go

back to them with the politician and Stayton would be pleased. If the Minnesota mob came out on top, they'd load up all the slaves and be on their way. They knew nothing of Kruegher, and they didn't know about the politician. They'd drive away not knowing.

But Kruegher had to *find her* first.

He had started at the small window through which she had escaped and had systematically zigzagged across the swath of ground leading away from this point. The snow in the air had started to stick to the ground, but it didn't matter. There was no trail to follow.

This was of little concern for Kruegher, because he knew she could not have gone far. Walking barefoot in the cold and dark over rough terrain, she would have moved very slowly. Sooner or later, he'd spot the bright red dress and she'd be cornered.

As he moved outward, he at last came to a steep cliff. Stepping carefully on the crumbly rock, he approached the edge and looked down. There was a hundred-foot drop into jagged rocks below. If she'd gotten this far in the dark and gone off the treacherous edge, there would be a red dress enclosing a blood-splattered body down there—easy to see. But it was not there. The scattering of white flakes listlessly fluttering downward was not enough to have yet covered such a thing, so he knew she was somewhere nearby.

He decided to walk along the edge and keep looking. If he did not see her, he'd just backtrack with his zigzagging. She was cornered.

After no more than five minutes, he saw a flicker of movement, and at last, a patch of red fabric.

"You didn't get very far," he said, taunting her as he approached.

Jenna Tolliver was crumpled into a crevice in the rock about ten or so feet from the edge. There was terror in her eyes, and her whole body trembled, either from fear or hypothermia, or a combination of the two. Her legs were nicked and bruised, and her face was reddened from the cold and from having duct tape ripped from it.

"You look awful," he said, teasing calmly. "I bet this was not the nicest place to spend the night."

"All right, so you've f-f-found me," she said, trying to be defiant though her voice rattled and trembled from the hypothermia. "What do you think you're going to do now?"

"You probably heard the gunfire?" he asked.

"Who were you shooting at?"

"The Sunrise boys were having a little difference of opinion with the Minnesota boys, but this doesn't have anything to do with me...or *you*."

"Who are the Minnesota boys?" Jenna asked, gritting her teeth to try to steady her shaking voice.

"They're the customers for all the fine product from the bus," he said with a smile.

"You still haven't said what you are planning to do... with m-m-me," she said, still trying to appear defiant. "Are you going to k-k-kill me like you did that girl last night?"

"My boss thinks you're too valuable for that. I've heard you're a politician. You didn't *tell me* you were a politician."

"You mean when you were manhandling me into the trunk of my car?"

"Resisting arrest." He laughed. "Politician or not, you were resisting arrest and I'm a federal agent."

"*Ooooh* give me a break," she groaned. "What's a federal agent doing in the s-s-sex trafficking business?"

"You're jumping to conclusions," he said with a laugh.

"*Bullshit!*"

She couldn't think of anything else to say.

"You're a spunky one, I'll give you that," he said. "I like them spunky, actually. How about we get to know each other a little better?"

With this, he crouched down beside her, placed his hand gently on her leg.

Staring at him through a haze of exhaustion, and shaking like a leaf, she knew she was helpless to do anything as he answered with his touches, her question about what happened to her next.

———

The dust from the shootout with the Sunrise men had barely settled in the big equipment garage. Jessica Edredin, Erin O'Malley, and the dream team were at work snipping cable ties. They had freed the nine girls who were seated in chairs and had started working on the cages when Lauren Stahling yelled to everyone from outside.

"We've got company," she shouted. "It's a Lincoln Town Car and two minivans."

"*These* must be the Minnesota people," Mark Edredin said.

Snow was in the air as the Town Car came to a gravel-spitting stop about thirty feet from the large roll-up door. The vans pulled in beside it.

The passenger-side door of the car was the first to open.

A large, imperious man with a domineering manner and a dark blue suit emerged. The fallen Sunrise men were inside and not immediately visible, but his attention was captured by the Korean girls milling around outside. Anxious to breathe fresh air and to be away from their cruel confinement, they had all wandered outside.

"You must be the gentlemen from Minnesota," Lauren said with her broad and distracting smile as she extended her hand. "I'm Lauren Stahling, Mr. Stayton said to expect you."

"Carlsruud, Davis Carlsruud," he said, taking her hand. She had sensed the tension in his expression when he first emerged from the car, but now he seemed more relaxed. All he saw was an attractive woman in a slate-gray fall coat. He did not guess there might be a gun belt was beneath this coat. Why would he?

"This is Roger Smusio and Dr. Michael Thoresensen," he said with a grin.

By now, the men in the vans had also stepped out. They all had sidearms, and two carried AR-15s. Two drivers and two men riding shotgun.

"*Very* pleased to meet you," Smusio said with a roguish grin as he sized up the woman who greeted them. Lauren immediately took him for the aspiring "lady's man" in the group. One in every crowd, she thought to herself. Even his handshake felt oily.

Thoresensen's handshake was damp with a trace of cold sweat. He was obviously nervous to be greeted by a woman while working as a human trafficker. His body language said *I'm not really a slave trader; I'm just riding along.*

"Doctor?" Lauren said, looking at him with her enchanting smile.

"Clinical psychology," he said anxiously.

"Interesting," Lauren said disarmingly, pretending she was actually interested. "I got as far as Psych 202 at the University of Washington. Graduated in Finance."

From his obscured vantage point, Hammer was admiring her theatrical prowess and the way she took charge of the situation. He remembered she had been in school plays way back when, but he recalled nothing about them. If she had been *this* good then, he probably wasn't paying attention.

"Where is Mr. Stayton this morning?" Carlsruud asked.

"I'm afraid he got called away unexpectedly," Lauren replied truthfully. "But we are *definitely* here to take care of you."

"You caught us a little off guard this morning," he said. "We weren't expecting to see the merchandise out wandering around."

By now, the nine women from the line of chairs had gathered into a cluster some distance away and were watching the proceedings with trepidation.

"We're supposed to inspect nine," he said, pointing to the girls. "I guess these must be them. When we're satisfied, which I'm sure we will be, I'll send the wire transfer to Brach. Then we'll load them into the vans and be on our way."

"Just out of curiosity, where will these ladies be going?"

"They'll be working in the service industry," Carlsruud said with a wink. "But you *know* this, don't you?"

"The servicing-of-gentlemen industry," Smusio added with a smirk.

"I understand," Lauren said, no longer smiling. "Thank you for confirming your intentions in this transaction."

"*What the fuck*?" Carlsruud shouted. "*Are you cops*?"

"No," Lauren said as she stepped behind the blade of a bulldozer.

The two Minnesota men with the AR-15s, well-trained for scenarios like this, but unprepared today, reacted first and died first. It happened so quickly the two drivers had time only to realize that they would be next. Each died with his hand on his holster.

None of the Minnesota men had seen Hammer positioning himself and his Barrett Mk22 MRAD on the top of the dump truck parked next to the roll-up door.

Smusio tried to grab one of the AR-15s, but Mark Edredin was expecting something like this and stopped him with a bullet.

Carlsruud scrambled for cover and pulled a pistol. He was trying to get a clear shot at Lauren when Steve Coe, shooting one-handed because of his sling, dropped him. His gun spun out of his raised hand and landed about two feet from Dr. Michael Thoresensen, who was crouching behind one of the vans.

"I cannot be arrested," Thoresensen shouted. "I'm an important man. I'm the chair of the Twin Cities Psychiatric Association. I'm on the board of the foundation. I only got into this as an investor. I'm not even supposed to be here today."

"We're not impressed!" Mark Edredin shouted.

The doctor lunged for the pistol, but the moment his hand closed around the grip, he was struck by bullets from two Glock pistols previously owned by Sunrise.

"I think what he had in mind was suicide by cop," Lauren said as she looked at Thoresensen. "Even though I *told him* we aren't cops."

"Death before embarrassment. How pathetic," Steve Coe said with a disgusted glance at the barely recognizable head of what had once been the chair of the Twin Cities Psychiatric Association.

———

Jenna Tolliver was living a nightmare, trembling uncontrollably and alternating between numbing pain and total numbness. She had been going in and out of consciousness for what seemed like hours and seeing things she was sure were hallucinations. There was gunfire in the near distance, and things floating past her face.

When the man with the buzz cut who'd thrown her in the trunk and duct taped her face first appeared, she thought at first she was imagining it—but he turned out to be real.

In a moment of lucidity, she's even had a conversation with him. Or maybe her fading mind was just playing tricks.

When the man removed his overcoat and began to caress her leg and speak to her in intricate, intimate metaphors, she closed her eyes and *hoped* she was just imagining it.

When he placed a hand firmly on each of her legs, she *prayed* she would wake up from the nightmare she was living.

As her eyes flickered open, Jenna saw, standing about twenty feet behind buzz-cut, a larger-than-life image she thought *recognized*.

She couldn't believe her subconscious would fabricate a hallucination of *Jim Hammer*!

But buzz-cut saw the hallucination too.

His right hand left Jenna's leg as he stood, grabbing for his Glock 19M.

He had barely begun to raise the pistol when Hammer closed the distance and firmly grabbed the man's wrist. There was a sound like the limb of a tree breaking in a storm, and the man staggered backward.

In the barely controllable flickering of her eyelids, Jenna could see the man vividly, his wrist dangling limp and his face wrenched by what must have been horrific pain.

She clenched her eyes shut for a moment, and when

she finally reopened them, the man was gone. He'd simply disappeared.

She never heard the sound of his body colliding with the rocks far below at the bottom of the cliff. The falling snow muffled it.

"Glad to s-s-see you," Jenna said as Hammer massaged her frostbitten feet and wrapped Aron Kruegher's overcoat around her bare legs.

"You're good now," he said in a reassuring voice, well-practiced from countless battlefield situations.

"Hammer, " she said, growing dizzy as he easily picked her up off the ground. "You know…I saw you in a dream last night."

"Good," he said with a smile. "I was worried last week when you said you dreamed I was dead."

"Last night…" she said. "Last night, I dreamed it was *me* who was dead."

CHAPTER
NINETEEN

"WHERE AM I?" Jenna Tolliver asked. "It's so hot in here. Where am I?"

"Glad to hear you're finally warm," Lauren Stahling said, glancing at Jenna in the passenger seat of her own Lexus.

Lauren reached over to turn the fan on her heater down a notch from full blast.

"You should be all right," Lauren said. "Hammer checked your pulse and vitals and said you were in pretty good shape, considering. You just needed to get warm. Keep those blankets wrapped around you."

"Where am I?" Jenna Tolliver repeated.

It was snowing harder now and the wipers were slapping hypnotically.

"You're in your own car," Lauren explained. "We're on the way to the hospital to get you and your feet looked at. The Billings Clinic is the best trauma facility in the state. You'll be in good hands."

"I had the craziest nightmares," Jenna said. She held up her hand and stared at it. She was no longer shaking.

"A lot of them were real," Lauren said. "But don't think about this. You're safe now. Look, those idiots even left your purse in the car."

"A silver lining," Jenna said with a laugh. "After all this crap, I'd hate to lose my *purse*."

"I saw your phone is still in there. If you got a charge, why don't you call Mike? He's probably worried sick."

"He's really gonna be *pissed*."

"Somehow, I doubt it," Lauren said with a grin.

"Hey babe," Jenna said when Mike Fellowes answered his phone.

"Hello," he said tentatively. "Who is this? How did you get this phone?"

"Who do you think it is? This is your *wife*, you numb-skull," she replied, using one of the terms of quasi-endearment she used for him.

"*Jenna*...is it really you?" Fellowes gasped, his words audible to Lauren on the speakerphone. "They said you were *kidnapped*. The police and the feds are looking all over for you. They said the Lexus was spotted in Wyoming!"

"Well it's sure not in Wyoming now!"

"Where *are* you?"

"Almost to Billings. I can see the signs. Where are *you*?"

"I'm in Billings, too."

"Can I talk to him for a second?" Lauren asked.

"Wait a minute, babe, Lauren wants to talk with you."

"Lauren? Are you with Lauren Stahling?"

"Yeah, she's driving. I'm holding the speakerphone up to her."

"Mike, this is Lauren."

"Hi...can you tell me what's going on?" Mike asked, sounding confused.

"Lauren *was* kidnapped, but she got away."

"Who? How?"

"The less said, the better," Lauren said. "I hate to sound conspiratorial, but let's just say the ATF and the cops are *not* your friends."

"Okay…"

"Can we just say Jenna got away and drove herself into Billings?" Lauren asked. "Her mind is kind of hazy, so let's just leave it at that. Forget you talked to me."

"Okay," he said. "I'll play along. That ATF guy was kind of an asshole anyway, and I don't think he was being straight with me."

"I can *guarantee* he was *not*," Lauren said.

"How is Jenna? How did her mind get hazy?"

"She was out all night after she escaped and has a touch of hypothermia, but I've got her warmed up and she's okay for now."

"I'm not shaking anymore," Jenna said, laughing. "I was a mess."

"She's got some bumps and bruises, and her feet are cut from walking barefoot after she got away. Can you meet me on Tenth Avenue North at Twenty-ninth, across from the hospital?"

"That's only a few blocks from here," he said. "I'm on my way."

———

Mike Fellowes was out of his pickup the moment he saw Lauren drive up in his wife's Lexus. Lauren stepped out and gestured for him to get into the driver's seat.

"Babe, you look…"

"Like shit?" Jenna said with a weak smile.

"Your face…"

"I was duct taped," she explained. "It looks a lot worse than it is…I hope."

"Mike," Lauren interjected, closing the door. "The ER is a block away and they have a Level One trauma center. This is the best place in four states for her to be right now. Why don't you drive your wife over there and let the ER docs take over? And forget I was here. She drove herself most of the way, and that's that."

"Okay, " Mike said as he climbed in and reached for the ignition. The car was still running, so he put it in gear.

By the time he glanced in the mirror, Lauren was nowhere to be seen.

It was like she had never been there. After what she had said earlier, he figured that's the way it needed to be.

———

In the distance, through the lightly falling snow, Lauren was watching as the Lexus pulled into the emergency entrance. The CCTV cameras caught the whole thing, but they never saw Lauren.

She continued walking the other way on Tenth Avenue, not knowing quite where she was going. She decided she would go to one of the car rental places downtown and head back to Obsidian.

As she walked, she opened her purse to check her burner phone. The only thing was a text from Hammer. She looked at the time. It had come an hour ago while she was driving.

"Can I buy you a plate of waffles?"

What the hell did this mean, she wondered, throwing the burner phone back into her purse and continuing to walk.

At the next intersection, she looked to her right. There, through the snowflakes, in all its neon splendor, was the Montana Waffle Hut. It was half a block long with its own parking lot, so it was not a mere hut, but it probably had waffles.

She jaywalked across Tenth and went in. The breakfast rush was over, so the place was mostly empty. Looking around, she did not see Hammer, so she decided to wait for him at the counter.

Lauren pulled her long coat around her. It was not because she was *that* cold, it was just that even in Montana, it was not usual practice to walk into a waffle house wearing a gun belt with a recently fired revolver.

After she ordered a cup of coffee, she noticed that three seats away, there was an attractive woman in a cerulean cocktail dress. Her blond hair was slightly on the disheveled side, so Lauren surmised she had not been home to change since she went out on the town last night.

The woman had the alert, almost jittery, expression which comes with two too many cups of coffee, and her frequent glances at the cell phone next to her cup indicated she was probably waiting for someone to come or call. Lauren could sympathize. So was she.

Wednesday night had been a long one for both of them.

Lauren smiled sympathetically when the woman glanced over.

"Expecting a call from my boss," she volunteered. Lauren was surprised she shared this information with a stranger but guessed she had been waiting for a long time and was anxious to talk.

"I'm just waiting for a friend," Lauren replied. "Guess we're in the same boat."

"Or the same waffle house counter," the woman replied with a grin.

"Exactly," Lauren said, chuckling.

"My name's Kally," the woman said in a friendly way.

"Lauren. What sort of business are you and your boss in?"

"We're with Sunrise Land Holdings, it's a nonprofit with a mandate to preserve pristine open spaces," Kally said with the smoothness one would expect from someone who was used to delivering a practiced spiel.

Lauren practically choked on her last sip of coffee.

"Excuse me," she said, dabbing her mouth and chin with a paper napkin. "I'm fighting a cough."

"It's okay," Kally Stefano commiserated. "It's that time of year."

"Thank you."

"My boss and I had an investor meeting last night at the Rimrock Steakhouse with some people from Minnesota that Tom, or I should say Mr. Brach, knows," Kally explained. She obviously was one of those people who liked to talk. "He was supposed to hear from them early this morning from one of our satellite locations, but they didn't call. We came here for breakfast, and when he couldn't get hold of them, or the Sunrise people who were supposed to meet them, he decided to drive out and check. He's coming right back."

"How long has he been gone?" Lauren asked, trying not to betray that she knew *exactly why* he could not reach any of these people.

"It's been a couple of hours," Kally said, obviously worried things were sliding out of her comfort zone. "Actually longer."

Then, looking at Lauren with a suddenly very serious, furrowed brow, expression, she said, "*I know what you're thinking.*"

"Okay, " Lauren almost choked again. How could Kally possibly know what she was *really* thinking at this moment when visions of blood, bodies, and frightened slaves filled her mind?

"Before you say anything, *yes*, I *am* sleeping with my boss. I know you noticed my evening dress, which is not exactly a daytime dress, and I *know* it's obvious we spent the night together. I *know* what you're thinking, but he and his wife are getting a divorce, and she lives back east."

"I'm not going to judge you for who you sleep with," Lauren said with a sense of relief.

"I shouldn't be telling you this, but I'm worried."

"I'm not here to judge. I'm here to listen," Lauren said. How could she not want to hear *more*?

"It's good to have someone to speak with," Kally admitted. "It's almost better to share this with a stranger, I think."

"Sure."

"Here's my card. Maybe we could get together for coffee sometime. It would be great to have someone to talk to who's not part of the Sunrise community."

"I'm afraid I don't have a card," Lauren lied.

"What do you do?"

"I've got a county government job."

"Secure, huh?"

"Yeah," Lauren said, studying Kally's card. "Hmmm. Vice president of networking? That's impressive."

"I was in sales, mainly real estate, before I met Tom… Mr. Brach. My job is to make sure he…and Sunrise…are well connected in the community and the state. He's from back east, so he's not familiar with the way things are done here."

"You're from Montana?"

"Born and bred. Billings High," Kally said proudly. "My parents moved here from La Jolla before I was born, though."

"What sorts of networking work do you do for Mr. Brach?"

"You name it. Got him into the Billings realtors' networking group, told him to join the Rotary, and him a seat on the board of the new performing arts center, you know the one?"

"Of course."

"It pays well, and then we sort of...um."

"I'm not judging you. I'm sure he's a nice man."

"He can be a little intense," Kally admitted. "He's really anxious to impress the home office back in McLean. That's in Virginia."

"And last night you were impressing investors from where did you say? Minnesota?"

"That's right," Kally Stefano confirmed. "The big man was Davis Carlsruud, he's big in lots of ways, if you know what I mean. Apparently, he's big in electronic conduits."

"Yes, I know what you mean," Lauren agreed with a smile. She did not say she had witnessed the violent death of the big man. "So he was interested in pristine open spaces? Where are these pristine open spaces your company is preserving?"

"The big one is up in Logan County, do you know where that is?"

"Yes, I do," Lauren said without adding this was the county where she had her county job. "Have you been up there to see those open spaces?"

"No, I haven't. I wanted to go, but Mr. Brach insists I should stay close to the office here in Billings. He goes up there sometimes. So does Mr. Stayton."

"Mr. Stayton?"

"Tony Stayton. He's Mr. Brach's executive assistant. He runs run day-to-day affairs in the office. He works hard, but he's not very creative. He's always wearing these bright orange ties. It's like he's still at Oregon State."

"Oh," Lauren said. This poor woman had a lot of surprises in store for her.

Suddenly, the cell phone on the counter started buzzing and chirping, catching Kally momentarily off guard.

"Oh good," she said with a tone of relief in her voice. "It's Tom."

"Where are you?" Kally said, obviously concerned. "I'm still waiting. I was starting to get a little bit worried."

"Okay."

"Uh-huh."

"*What*? Will I see you before you go?"

"That soon?"

"When will you be back?"

"Not go into the office today? *Why*?"

"Not until you tell me? Why?"

"Okay. Okay. I won't."

"Because it's all so sudden. That's why."

"Okay, but…"

"How can I *not* worry?"

"Okay."

"You know I love you, don't you?"

"*Call me*."

Lauren watched as the call ended abruptly, leaving Kally staring at her phone, a dumbfounded expression on her face.

"Bad news?" Lauren asked as a tear trickled from Kally's eye.

"He's leaving town. He didn't say where."

"When?"

"He's at the airport. The plane leaves in twenty minutes."

"At least he called to say goodbye," Lauren said sympathetically.

"He can't tell me why. He doesn't know when he'll be back. He told me not to go into the office today, or until he tells me to. He just…"

"What are you going to do?"

"I don't know," Kally said sadly after a long pause. "I guess I'll go home and change."

CHAPTER
TWENTY

CHARLOTTE HENDRICKSEN and Linda Stahling had known one another since long before Charlotte's nephew Jim, and Linda's daughter Lauren, had been in school together, but over the course of the past twenty years, as the younger generation had moved on, they had remained friends.

They were part of a social circle of women of a certain age, many of them widows, who spent their time enjoying such mundane activities as volunteering at the church and solving the world's problems at a distance— usually from the vantage point of a booth at the Black Rock Café.

Lately, however, they'd found something new to talk about. Charlotte's nephew, recently retired from the Army, was back in town with no current plans to move on, and he had been seeing a lot of Linda's daughter. If there was anything that women of a certain age enjoyed more than their social circle, it was matchmaking.

"Well, you'll never guess what Lauren told me," Linda said happily as she settled into their usual spot at the café on this cold Thursday morning.

"Give me a clue," Charlotte replied, greeting her with a twinkle in her eye.

"Oh, I can't think of one, so I'll just tell you. She said she's taking time off from work to go hunting with guess who?"

"I know James has got a whole arsenal in his room, and he's been talking about antelope season ever since he got back."

"Lauren showed me her hunting license," Linda said as they both ordered coffee and waffles.

"Well, she didn't have far to go to get it. The county building is a small place."

"I know she had a huge crush on him in high school."

"I thought they were just friends," Charlotte said.

"They were huge *friends*, but a mother can tell when it's more than that."

"It would sure be nice," Charlotte said. "I know James has had some girlfriends over the years, but he was never stationed anywhere long enough for anything to develop."

"It would be amazing. Lauren has been so lonely since her husband died. She won't admit it, carrying on like there's no problem, but a mother can tell when her daughter is lonely. I hope she can find someone."

"It would be nice if it could be James, he's pretty rough around the edges, but deep down, he's a good boy."

"They should have fun on their hunting trip," Linda said. "They're going up into the Buffalo Jaw Mountains. It's a long way from anywhere. I hope they'll be all right."

"James won't let anything bad happen to Lauren," Charlotte reassured her friend. "You can count on it."

"At least we know it will be a nice quiet time for them to be together."

"That's for sure!"

———

Lauren Stahling watched Kally Stefano walk despondently through the front door of the Montana Waffle Hut and nodded to the waitress for a refill of her coffee cup. She opened her purse and looked at her two phones—her real phone and the burner phone. Nothing from Hammer. Nothing from anyone.

She could empathize with Kally Stefano. Two women sitting at a coffee shop counter waiting for a man. Two different women from two different worlds, waiting for men from two different worlds, yet not so different at all. Two different women from two different worlds bound together by the same cruel sequence of events, and the deceitful narrative spun by Sunrise Land Holdings and its parent company back east.

Very soon, Kally would know what Lauren already knew about what had happened to Sunrise that morning, and her world would explode. At least Brach had the kindness to tell her to stay away from the office.

As Lauren closed her purse, her eye caught the television set above the counter as it flashed "Breaking News." On the screen were images of the building at the gravel pit, of women with blankets wrapped around their shoulders getting into vehicles, and body bags being loaded into vans.

"Could you turn it up," Lauren asked the waitress, who shrugged and did so. The lunch crowd had mostly moved on and there was only a half dozen or so patrons left to be disturbed by the blaring news report.

"...in rural Stillwater County, only thirty miles northwest of Billings," the reporter said. "The women's shelter in Columbus received an anonymous tip from a passerby that there was a large number of teenage girls milling around this building at a gravel pit. The Stillwater County Sheriff has confirmed there was a fatal gangland-style shootout between members of a known underworld organization from Minnesota and a Billings-based charity known as Sunrise Land Holdings. The sheriff is certain the motive involves a human trafficking operation, and the young women, who appear to be Korean, are the victims…"

Lauren shook her head. The pieces of the narrative had fallen into place. Hammer's planning several moves ahead had paid off.

"…Among the dead who have been identified are Davis Carlsruud, a prominent figure with suspected ties to organized crime in Minnesota and Anthony Stayton, an executive with Sunrise Land Holdings of Billings. Both were armed when they died…"

Suddenly, a shadow fell across the counter, and Lauren looked up.

"Sorry I'm late," Jim Hammer said.

Lauren was so glad to see this big man she wanted to give him a hug. Instead, she just squeezed his hand.

"Did you see this?" Lauren asked as the televised bulletin ended and the waitress turned down the volume.

"Yeah. There's a bunch of girls who'll eat well and not sleep in cages tonight…thanks to what we did and will never talk about. Have *you* eaten? I'm starving."

When they had gotten their waffles and relocated to a corner table, Lauren told Hammer about Kally Stefano and Tom R. Brach. He just nodded thoughtfully.

"I'm so glad to see you," she admitted after a long pause, her face growing more serious. "I wanted to say… I wanted to tell you…thanks for saving my life up there today."

"Thank you for saving *mine*," he said with a smile, setting down his fork. "I guess we make a good team."

Lauren was searching her mind for the perfect reply to the second comment, something about "making the team," when Hammer's phone rang. She could see it was Tim Tommis.

"What's up, man?" Lauren heard Hammer say as she listened in on his side of the conversation.

"Yeah, it was lively."

"News travels fast. I know in the news world if it bleeds, it leads. They devour this stuff."

"Uh-huh."

"*Really*?"

"Well, yeah. My friend out here just learned Brach is on his way back there, too."

"Uh-huh."

"You're right. See you, man."

Lauren could practically hear the grinding sound of the wheels churning in Hammer's head as he set his phone down.

"What did Tim Tommis have to say?"

"The shootout made some of the news channels," he said.

"I figured as much when I heard you quote the old maxim about how 'if it bleeds, it leads.'"

"Well, old Hamad bin-Sharia over in Qatar got the word," Hammer explained.

"Oh yeah? I'll bet he's none too pleased."

"And he's coming to the States in a few days. Surprise visit. Nobody knows yet...not even the gang at the Hambledon Global offices in McLean. At least not yet."

"But Tim Tommis knows," Lauren said, not phrasing it as a question.

"Not much he doesn't know. He's a Merlin, that guy."

"It doesn't take a lot of clairvoyance to know you're

planning to be there too," Lauren said with a knowing grin.

"You're a mind reader."

"No, I just have a memory of a Special Forces captain telling me one of several things he'd learned is taking out foot soldiers never leads to the root of any problem. He told me you've got to work your way to the top. Now the top dog is coming soon to *your* crosshairs."

"You're a quick study." Hammer chuckled.

"You're an open book," she said with a wink. "When do we leave?"

"*We?*" Hammer asked after reacting with a startled expression.

"I recall you saying *we* make a good team," she said with a wry smile. "And under present circumstances, I couldn't live with myself if I let *my* team member go off alone. What if something happened and I wasn't there to help?"

"I understand," Hammer said with a trace of a smile.

"I know you do. I know it's been your world for twenty years, a world where teams are teams and the stakes are life or death. Today, I understood all this for the first time. Whether I was ready for this or not, I've realized I'm part of this now. I killed a man this morning. I've crossed a line, but having seen all those women in cages, I have no interest in crossing back until *my team* works its way to the top and cuts the head off this beast."

Hammer nodded. Hell hath no fury like a woman scorned, and few things scorn a woman like watching men enslave women—*literally*.

He had not consciously set out to recruit her into this mad endeavor, but he was glad things had worked out this way with a person possessing her deftness and determination.

As for Lauren, she was pondering what she had just

said and asking herself why she felt more *excitement* than apprehension.

"Like I said a week and a half ago," she quipped in a lighter tone she clearly intended to break the somber mood. "I can't let *you* run off and have all the fun."

"I've got to take the pickup. There's no way I can take all my gear on an airliner, never mind that .44 of yours. How soon can you…?"

"Well, I need a shower and a good night's sleep…and so do *you*. And one more thing, I've got to stop at the mall. There's no way I'm driving all the way to McLean, Virginia on one change of underwear."

CHAPTER
TWENTY-ONE

IT WAS deep into the wee hours of Friday morning when Tom R. Brach unlocked the front door of the tiny condo he kept in a high-rise residential building a few blocks from the McLean, Virginia offices of the Hambledon Global Advocacy Group, the parent of his own Sunrise Land Holdings.

He took the condo a year and a half ago when Stacey kicked him out of their split-level ranch house in College Park, Maryland. He deliberately didn't tell his estranged wife about this place, and when Hambledon sent him to Billings to set up Sunrise, he decided not to tell them either. He figured when you're recruited into the human trafficking trade, it might be prudent to keep certain things close to your vest. He was glad he did. Today, like never before or in his wildest dreams, he *really* wanted nobody to know where he was.

The place smelled stale and stuffy as one might expect of a place which had gone unused and uninhabited for a little more than a year. The refrigerator was empty except for a box of energy bars which had a "use by" date way in the future. Brach unwrapped one, poured himself a tumbler of bourbon, and flopped down on the couch. He was beyond exhausted. Using a fake ID he kept for emergencies, he'd taken the first flight he could out of Billings, which left him with a five-hour layover in Minneapolis, and a half hour wait for a cab from Dulles Airport.

The only good news was nobody knew where he was, and nobody knew about this condo. When he told Kally Stefano he had to leave town, he didn't say where. He added that he'd be back in a matter of days, but he was *never* going back.

After he had driven out to the gravel pit and had seen sheriff's deputies and freed slaves milling around the building, he knew the Montana operations of Sunrise Land Holdings were going down in flames—and that Tom R. Brach would soon be a wanted man, or at the very least wanted for questioning. He saw the local "Breaking News" report while he was waiting for his flight in Billings, and this confirmed both his worst fears and his decision to leave town without delay.

It was time to disappear, and so he did.

Brach had thought about sending Kally back to the office to start the shredder, but he had always been careful to keep all of the potentially incriminating documents on the laptop which was always at his side. He truly liked Kally. He did not "love" her, although he had intimated as much without actually saying it, but at the same time, he did not want to see her on the spot when the cops raided the place.

What the hell had happened?

It was obvious to Brach that there had been a betrayal by Davis Carlsruud and his Minnesota goons. Those avaricious bastards! They had gotten greedy and picked a fight with Tony Stayton and the men at the gravel pit. Brach had become suspicious the night before when Carlsruud specifically asked him *not* to come to the gravel pit on Thursday morning. He wished he had done things differently.

Spinning though his weary brain were an endless roster of things he wished he had differently, but now, all he could do was pour himself another glass of bourbon.

He passed out from exhaustion before he had a chance to take his second sip.

It was early afternoon when Brach finally awoke. He was still seated on the couch. The overpowering mustiness of the condo competed with the odor of spilled whiskey. He stumbled across the room to open a window, wishing he had done this the night before. Realizing a share of the mustiness reeked from his own unwashed body, he wished he had showered the night before.

He felt a little better after his shower and he made himself a cup of coffee. The off-brand pods for the Keurig machine carried no expiration date and the coffee tasted okay. With two cups of this and another energy bar in him, he plugged his collection of cell phones and unlisted burners into chargers and checked for text messages.

There were several from Kally Stefano on his Sunrise phone. The early ones promised she'd be ready to go back to the office when he returned and wished him well. The later ones conveyed dismay and utter disbelief at what she was hearing on the news. The last one read simply,

> How could you let me get involved in something like this???

He thought she should have been glad he did keep

her out of the office when the cops came. He assumed the cops had come by now.

There was only one message from Brach's own boss, and it had come in while Brach was still in Minneapolis. Westley Carker, Hambledon Global's managing director for North America, had asked:

Is it true? Advise ASAP.

Brach had replied immediately from the airport bar, texting tersely:

Affirmative. Double crossed by customer. Am currently in transit.

This bought him some time.

After pouring another cup of coffee, Brach fired up his laptop. He always had it in his car, so he did not have to go home or to the office before he headed for the Billings airport.

The news sites still carried the bulletins from the gravel pit, but now there was more. There had been a second shootout, this one at the airfield on the former Tredquist place up in Logan County. There were more pictures of bewildered Korean teenagers being "rescued" by volunteers from a women's shelter.

There were also pictures of the ATR72 turboprop airliner used to fly the Korean girls in from the remote seaport in British Columbia. It had landed sometime after the shootout and had been seized by the "gallant" sheriff of Logan County, Montana. Kyle Fahr was on the news was telling the media he arrived after the shootout had happened and fortuitously was in the right place at the right time to intercept the slave-carrying aircraft when it landed a few hours later.

Brach was incensed. This hayseed bumpkin sheriff was basking in fifteen minutes of fame as a hero, while he was sitting in a musty apartment as a fugitive.

The only silver lining appeared to be the stories were no longer receiving top billing on any of the news sites. The media had other fish to fry. There was the ongoing scandal involving the attorney general, and the usual dreadful stories from the Middle East. Thankfully, Montana was a long way from the East Coast news desks.

What was not evident—and of course it would *not be* —was a full court press by Carker's team of influencers and PR people to coax their friends in the media to bury this story where the sun never shone.

Brach decided to check on the Sunrise website but could not get through to it. It was like it wasn't there. He flipped to the Hambledon Global website. There it was with its smiling children and sunny stock photo landscapes.

The last time he had looked, Sunrise Land Holdings had its own tab on the website's navigation bar, where it was proudly touted as a prized "subsidiary" in the mission of making those "beautiful pristine open spaces" accessible to children around the world.

Today, this tab was gone. Damage control was in full swing. There was only a short statement from Carker denouncing the "abhorrent criminal activities" of what was now characterized as an organization "at one time loosely affiliated" with Hambledon.

Brach had the eerie feeling of knowing that overnight he'd gone from managing an integral cog in a well-ordered machine, to a pariah associated with an abhorrent, unaffiliated cog.

He looked again at Carker's message. "Is it true? Advise ASAP."

Brach decided that sooner or later, he'd have to

communicate with Carker and "advise," so rather than postponing the inevitable, he started composing an email. Halfway through, he asked himself whether it was really a good idea to put anything in writing. The answer being no, he decided he'd go see Carker in person—*and unannounced*.

His boss, or the man who had been his boss twenty-four hours ago, did not know Brach "lived" a mere fifteen-minute walk from the Hambledon Global offices, and Brach wanted to keep it this way. One thing about working with Hambledon which had become second nature for Brach was subterfuge—concealing documents, creating dummy accounts, using burner phones, and all of those things he once knew only in spy movies. He was so used to this it became a routine part of his thinking.

This morning, on his way to see Carker, he would create a fake residence for himself. It was not he feared Carker so much as he trusted him only to behave in his own best interests. This was, after all, the international slave trade.

Brach threw a couple of shirts from his closet and a toothbrush into a duffel bag, grabbed a couple of expendable burner phones and some newspapers he bought in Minneapolis and walked down the street to the Marriott, where he booked a room using the name on one of his many credit cards. As far as anyone knew, this would now be his current residence in the DC area.

Less than two weeks ago, he had lived a comfortable life in Billings, respected within his social circle, and a prominent member of civic life. Now, his life had spiraled down this! At least he was still alive, when Tony Stayton and others were not.

Ten minutes after giving his hotel room a rumpled, lived-in look, Brach was using his Sunrise ID card to pass through security at the steel and glass office building on

Colshire Drive. He was surprised it still worked. He went through the metal detector, glad he'd left his SIG P228 concealed back at the condo and walked to the elevator that would take him to the posh, though tastefully decorated offices of Hambledon Global.

As he walked into reception, two workmen were touching up the paint around the place on the wall where they had just removed the Sunrise logo from its place next to that of Hambledon.

"Tom R. Brach to see Mr. Carker," he told the timid young intern at the reception desk.

"Do you have an appointment?"

"He's expecting me."

Westley Carker was product of some of the best schools in Britain and of a commercial family which had been in various enterprises since Dickensian times. He'd been eminently well connected in the business world—on both sides of the law—long before Hamad bin-Sharia picked him to be the forward face of Hambledon in America.

"He'll see you now," the receptionist said, seeming startled by how quickly her boss had demanded her to "*send him in*."

Carker remained seated after Brach entered his office. He paused for a moment before he spoke, as though in disbelief that Brach had actually come. Carker did not invite Brach to sit down, sending the message that he expected it to be a short meeting.

"I certainly didn't expect to see you here this afternoon, Mr. Brach," he said in a cordial tone. Carker was one of those people who smiled with his mouth, never his face. People who knew him recognized his sinister side. "When did you get in?"

"I took a late flight and checked into a hotel this morning. You asked me to advise you as to what happened. I decided to come in person. You can't say much in a text message."

"I admire your audacity," Carker said, his cold gray eyes a riveting presence in his fleshy, sunburned face. "Business as usual...show must go on, and all that."

"Right..."

"Tell me then, what *did* happen? The media is painting a picture of something between a Wild West gunfight and a gangland war. In your text message, you mentioned a double cross?"

"It was Carlsruud and his Minnesota thugs," Brach explained. "He's known to have underworld ties all over the upper Midwest. They got greedy and started shooting. It's obvious. The night before, he was explicit. He did *not* want me at the meetup. He wanted to deal with Stayton."

"And you *agreed* to this?"

"I *did* go out there," Brach insisted. "But by the time I got to the place, the shooting was over. Some good Samaritan had called the local women's shelter and there were Korean girls all over the place. I got out of there. I'm no good to you if I'm run in for questioning."

"Certainly not," Carker agreed.

"If you don't mind me saying, I wish your people had done a better job of vetting Carlsruud."

"We're looking into this," Carker said, obviously irritated to have Brach shift the blame back onto his plate. "But what can you tell me about our airfield in northern Montana, which was *your* responsibility? I'm sure you've seen the news about *what* happened. What can you tell me about *how* it happened?"

"We have a couple of traitors, who are probably working for Carlsruud and his people."

"*Oh?*" Carker asked, clearly intrigued.

"Two of the people who Jason Nuemeyer hired up

there, Kenny Lathrope and Brad Shannin," Brach explained. "They disappeared a week ago. Nuemeyer was looking into it."

"Lathrope? Isn't he the one who shot the hunter?"

"Right. Nuemeyer figured they decided to do a runner because of that."

"But *you* don't?"

"I did at first, but there was one news report saying their pickup truck was found near the airfield after the shootout," Brach said. "The report also said the sheriff was looking at Lathrope and Shannin as the ones who gunned down all our people up there. Fingerprints on guns found at the scene, too."

"That would be interesting," Carker said thoughtfully. "Do you believe it?"

"Damned, hot-tempered, redheaded Lathrope! Shannin follows him like a Rottweiler puppy! They were at *both* shootouts. I'm sure of it. Somebody had to have been left standing, and it was them. We can't yell at Nuemeyer for hiring him, because he's one of those who Lathrope killed."

"I see," Carker said. "This is a very troubling loose end."

"At least the news reports are dying down today," Brach said, trying to cite the positive.

"You have no idea how many newsroom arms I've had to twist, and how many favors I've had to call in to make *that* happen," Carker snarled.

"Have you talked to our ATF friends since this went down?" Brach asked. "It seems to me this is a manhunt *they* should be handling. The deputy director who Hambledon has been paying, whoever he is, has a lot of skin in this game, too."

"I can assure you he's aware of what happened out there and he's on top of this."

"Make sure he knows about Lathrope and Shannin."

"As you know, the director has Vince Milino on the ground out there. You've worked with him. You know he's not one to be trifled with. Am I right?"

"I do know Milino," Brach confirmed.

"I recall he saved Sunrise's behind when *your* man Lathrope shot the hunter, Am I not right?"

"You're right, but Milino's man Kruegher is just as reckless as Lathrope," Brach said defensively.

"We're lucky to have Milino to keep this man in check and things under control, aren't we?"

"I *hope* he'll get things under control. We are...we *need* the ATF to run damage control on this. Sunrise couldn't operate without..."

"Excuse me, Mr. Brach," Carker interrupted. "You used the words 'we' and 'Sunrise' in your comment. I assumed you understood that the entity formerly known as Sunrise Holdings is no more. Its passing association with Hambledon was a trivial connection that is now nonexistent. There is no 'we,' Mr. Brach. The bank accounts are all closed. We have all the passwords."

"*What*? How?"

"It's over, Mr. Brach, and there is nothing for you ever to have been part of. Like it never happened. I suggest you take a well-earned vacation and discuss none of this with anyone again. Ever. You are not employed by any organization remotely affiliated with Hambledon Global. You and I are done here... *permanently*."

Brach swallowed hard. He knew Carker would be angry, but he had expected all of the work he had done over the past couple of years in Montana would account for *something*. Carker had once called him *brilliant*.

Brach had expected to be chastised and then reassigned. He hadn't expected to be unambiguously disavowed. The finality in Carker's words, and his tone of voice, amounted to a door slamming on a past life.

"Have I made myself clear, *perfectly* clear?" Carker asked as Brach stood, bewildered.

"Yes."

"Then, good day, sir."

———

As Tom R. Brach left the building, he had a sense he was being followed. He glanced back but saw nothing.

Nevertheless, he couldn't shake the feeling. After making a couple of innocuous, seemingly random twists and turns as he strolled, he confirmed he was right.

He *was* being followed.

Brach calmly made his way to the Marriott and made sure the two men who were tailing him saw him board a crowded elevator. They wouldn't know which floor he went to without asking at the front desk, and he figured this would slow them down.

When he reached his room, Brach changed his coat, put on a ball cap, took the stairs to the basement, and exited through the parking garage. When he circled around to look into the lobby from across the street, the two men were still sitting in the lobby.

Why?

Were they waiting for him to come back down, or was this a coincidence, and they were just two men sitting in the lobby?

In any case, Tom R. Brach was now coming to accept the fact he was a marked man.

CHAPTER
TWENTY-TWO

IT WAS dark when Agent Vincent Milino guided the Honda Civic he had picked up the Alamo desk at Dulles Airport into the gravel parking lot in rural Fairfax County, Virginia. This place was about as far off the beaten track as one could imagine finding less than an hour's drive from the Beltway.

He checked the address. This was it—Ensign Eddie's Crab Shack, a low, almost ramshackle building where they served blue crab by the bucket and patrons drank beer straight from the bottle.

Milino pulled off his necktie and went in. It was dark inside and seemed quiet for a Friday night. He was not used to meeting his boss in places like this. As a field agent with nearly two decades of federal law enforcement service, he was accustomed to being picked up in a comfortable government car, whisked to 99 New York Avenue in Washington, shown up to the deputy director's stylish glass and laminated walnut office, and offered a Scotch.

Looking around, he finally spotted Darwin Farthers

seated at a table in the corner near the back door. The ATF Deputy Director was drinking a beer and dressed for the occasion in a faded Orioles ball cap, a plaid flannel shirt and jeans. He nodded to Milino and gestured for him to sit down.

"You're right on time, but you look like a fed," Farthers said, handing Milino an open bottle of Sam Adams.

"I *am* a fed," Milino reminded him. "And so are you. You really know how to pick a meeting spot."

"Nobody would think to look for us here. Nobody is going to eavesdrop, electronic or otherwise. We have a lot to discuss that nobody else should hear."

Milino nodded. Being summoned to Washington was like being sent to the principal's office but meeting his boss in a place like this underscored the deep, dark criminality of their association with the world of human trafficking.

"Are you hungry?" The deputy director was trying to make things artificially casual. "Let's order a basket of crab to start."

Milino, who had lost his appetite the day before, didn't say anything as the order was placed.

"I spoke to Agent Headny this morning while you were in transit," Farthers said. "It seems you have him minding the store in Billings?"

"That's right," Milino said. "I've been working with Shane Headny out there for a couple of years, but I haven't read him in on the full extent of our work with Sunrise. I've kept it vague, and he's not the curious type."

"When we talked, it was clear he was getting nervous about the media and the authorities focusing a lot of attention on the shootout between Sunrise and the Minnesota people."

"I'll call him tomorrow morning and calm him down," Milino promised.

"Headny was also wondering about Agent Kruegher," Farthers continued. "He hasn't been in contact with the Billings office since the shootout."

"Headny doesn't need to know Kruegher was there," Milino said.

"Kruegher was where?" Farthers asked, alarmed. "At the shootout? I didn't see his name on any of the sheriff's office lists of fatalities, and I was under the impression there were no survivors. Headny assumes *you* know where Kruegher is."

"I haven't been able to get hold of him either," Milino admitted. "I left him at the gravel pit equipment garage on Wednesday night to take care of the two women he threw into the trunk of the Lexus."

"That's another big difficulty for you to clean up," Farthers scolded, shaking his head. "As you are painfully aware, one of those women, the Tolliver woman, is a county official and she's semi-high-profile for a place like Montana. This is not good. At least she's no longer a missing person."

"Fortunately, Kruegher put her in a duct tape blindfold, and she didn't see much. She didn't see anyone except *maybe* him. She never saw me or Brach. I phoned the hospital. She had a bad case of hypothermia, but she's recovering from that. But they also said she was pretty delusional. She didn't remember much about what happened."

"She managed to drive herself to the hospital, though," Farthers reminded him.

"People summering trauma do this sort of thing on impulse," Milino said. "Apparently it happens more often than you think."

"I suppose, but let's hope she doesn't get back any more of her memory."

"We can always blame Sunrise," Milino said, almost flippantly. "They've got a lot to be blamed for."

"One thing we *can't* lay on them is *your* statement to the media about the Tolliver woman's Lexus being spotted in Wyoming...and *you* blaming the Gonzalves Cartel," Farthers said, continuing his rebuke. "You made us look pretty damned inept when the victim herself showed up in a missing vehicle which you said was in the next state!"

"I was trying to direct attention away from Montana so the highway patrol and all the sheriffs would stop looking for the car until we disposed of it."

"We'll have to live with it now," Farthers said. "But we still need to find Kruegher. What happened to him? If he was out there at the time of the shootout and he wasn't killed, where is he now?"

"I've tried calling him a dozen times," Milino insisted, showing his boss the call log on his phone. "It always goes to voicemail. One of the first things I'm going to when I get back to Billings is..."

"Let me stop you right there," Farthers said. "You're *not* going back to Billings."

"I beg your pardon?"

"Unfortunately for all of us, you made yourself the face of your blunder with the missing Lexus screw-up. We can't have you in Montana anymore. We'll let Headny can take care of Billings. I've already briefed him. You're permanently reassigned."

"Oh? Reassigned where?"

"Reassigned to headquarters for now. We need to keep you out of the crosshairs of the press.

"So I'm on desk duty?"

"No. You'll be under cover. Low profile. Out of sight.

You already know all about Hambledon Global, so until I have time to bring somebody else up to speed. You'll be working with Joe Foullon."

"The assistant deputy director?"

"Correct. He could use the benefit of your background on Hambledon. Hamad bin-Sharia himself is coming to town in a few days and we need to provide backup to Hambledon as they try to keep him under the radar."

"When's he coming?"

"We don't know yet. The sheikh is very paranoid about his schedule. Not even Westley Carker over at Hambledon knows. The sheikh is understandably furious about what happened to his flow of product through Montana and he's obviously interested in the 'whys' and "what nexts.'"

"Heads will roll at sunrise," Milino said.

"Have you looked at the Hambledon website?"

"No, I had to take three planes to get here, and the Wi-Fi on airplanes is terrible these days."

"Don't bother," Farthers said. "All mention of Sunrise is gone, and Hambledon has washed themselves of them. It's like the two were never under the same roof."

"I guess my old friend Tom R. Brach will have to find himself another job," Milino said.

"We've learned Brach's out of Montana too. He's *here*. He's staying at a Marriott in McLean and he had a meeting with Carker this morning. I've already asked Joe Foullon to have some of his people keeping an eye on Brach. Carker's secretary at Hambledon is one of ours. Agnes has been on the job for about a year. Part of the furniture by now. She's briefed Foullon and me on Carker's meeting with Brach this morning."

"Why did Brach come here?" Milino asked rhetorically. "If Brach is so damned clever, I can't fathom why he'd show himself at Hambledon after what happened to his operation out west. Why didn't he keep his head down? With Brach knowing all he knows about Hambledon's skeletons, I wouldn't put it past Carker to arrange an unfortunate accident for him."

Farthers did not comment.

CHAPTER
TWENTY-THREE

THE MINUTE HAND of the clock on the wall above the reception desk at the Marriott Hotel was edging toward the bottom of the four o'clock hour. The young night clerk was watching muted YouTube videos on his tablet, and the two men who had been sitting in the lobby all afternoon were dozing. They had shown the clerk their federal IDs, and he had asked no further questions. The Marriott was literally in the shadow of the Beltway, and he was used to seeing feds coming and going constantly.

They asked for nothing, and he knew to say no more.

Since midnight, a middle-aged couple in a jovial mood had passed through the lobby on their way in from a Friday night party somewhere, but otherwise the place had been deserted. Suddenly, the hushed calm was interrupted by two men in overcoats with turned-up collars who burst through the front door and strode purposefully to where the clerk was engrossed in his entertainment.

"Police officers," one of them announced, flashing an ID. "Have you seen this man?"

His companion produced a photograph.

"I work nights," the clerk said, more annoyed than apologetic. "I come on at eleven. I don't see a lot of faces. Is he a guest here? I could look him up by name."

"His name is Thomas Roland Brach," the first man said.

At the mention of this name, the two dozing federal agents perked up. They exchanged knowing glances but otherwise remained as they were.

"Okay, let me see," the man behind the desk said, tapping his keyboards, deliberately not responding to the exigency of the two in overcoats with an urgency of his own. "Brach...Brach...Brach. Okay here it is. Yes, we do have a Mr. Brach. He checked in Friday morning."

"We need his room number," the first man said.

"In the interest of the privacy of our guests, we do not reveal room numbers to third parties," the clerk said, repeating the canned phrasing. "If you'd like to contact..."

"We don't have time for this. Do I have to remind you we're police officers?"

"Let me contact my manager."

"Why don't you just give us the room number?" the second man said.

"Could I see your identification again, sir?"

He didn't like being pushed around, and he was exercising what little authority he had. He was also waiting for the two dozing federal agents to take notice.

"That's the State of Montana, and it says sheriff's office...you said police," he pointed out boldly. "Do you have jurisdiction here?"

"We're running out of patience here," the second man said, pulling back his overcoat to show off a holstered sidearm.

At the sight of the gun, the clerk capitulated. He knew

the collars were not turned up because of the cold October weather outside, but he was not prepared to die or be injured for company policy.

"He's in 636. I'll have to escort you."

"We'll find our way. Give us a passkey."

The moment the elevator door closed, the two federal agents dashed for the stairs, leaving the rattled clerk alone in the lobby.

———

The two men in overcoats tiptoed carefully down the sixth-floor hallway. They had already screwed Wolf-9SD suppressors onto the muzzles of their Beretta 92FS pistols. They were planning for a quiet visit to Tom R. Brach.

They listened carefully at the door to 636. The television was on but turned down very low. The key card passed over the lock and the green light appeared. The first man crouched low to quietly open the door, while his partner took careful aim through the widening crack.

The room smelled of microwave popcorn, but there was no movement, no sound.

The first man gently closed the door as the other entered the room, gripping his Beretta in both hands. The tension was palpable.

There was the shape of a sleeping person lumped in the bed, and there was a desire on the part of the second man to get the job done.

Thanks to the suppressor, the noise of the 9mm Parabellum round being fired was barely that of a cough.

He was ready to squeeze off a second when he felt a hand touch his wrist.

The other man then reached over to the lump in the

bed and jerked off the covers, revealing only blankets and pillows.

As the shooter looked aghast at his partner, both men realized simultaneously that in their eagerness, they had not bothered to clear the bathroom.

Luckily for them, there was nothing there but towels on the floor, a dripping shower, and a few toiletries.

"This pile in the bed didn't even look like a person," the first man said to the shooter. "Now we've blown it. Try to dig the slug out of the mattress while I look around."

"Then where the fuck *is he* at four o'clock in the morning? Who goes jogging at this hour?"

"He took his wallet then," the first man said in disgust. "There's nothing here but a couple of shirts in the closet, and a receipt from a coffee place. I'll take it and let's get out of here."

The two men stepped out of the room into a hallway which was not as deserted as they had expected.

"*Federal agents,*" came a shout. "*Put your hands where we can see them.*"

The impulsive shooter of bedclothes still had his Beretta in his hand, and he swung it into action, squeezing off several rounds in rapid succession.

The two ATF special agents promptly returned fire with their unsuppressed Glock 19Ms. The thunder in the hallway was deafening. A dozen anonymous people in nearby rooms awoke to the terror of a gunfight a few feet from where they lay.

One of the ATF men took a round in the upper arm, just to the left of his body armor, and the two men with the Berettas used his momentary distraction to dash toward the exit door and start down the stairwell on the side of the building opposite the stairs the feds had used.

The uninjured ATF agent was only seconds behind

the fleeing assassins, but they did have a head start. He descended a short distance in pursuit and fired several 9mm rounds, but with the concrete of the walls and the metal of the stairs, these were useless. He gave up the chase and dashed back to his friend who was bleeding profusely.

———

Vince Milino had not expected to start the first Saturday of his new assignment investigating a hotel shooting. He had gotten the call at five o'clock in the morning, which was three o'clock Montana time. When he arrived at the Marriott, he was both exhausted and pumped with adrenaline.

The presence of ATF agents in the confrontation had given the agency jurisdiction over the crime scene immediately, and the name Thomas Roland Brach had brought Milino rushing to the crowded sixth-floor hallway. The place was already crawling with crime scene techs.

"What do we have here?" Milino asked, climbing over the yellow tape.

"One shot fired here in the room," the tech replied without looking up from the bed. "Somebody mistook a pile of sheets and pillows for a person. Other than this unforced error, they knew what they were doing. They picked up the brass and recovered the lead from the mattress. The hallway is a different deal. We recovered 9mm brass from all over. They fired four rounds as they escaped to the north stairway. Our guys fired three from the head of the south stairs and two more as the perps were headed down the stairs."

"They didn't follow the perps?" Milino asked.

"Agent Sykes had a wounded partner. He came back to the hall to help Agent Sandoval."

"Is Sandoval all right? Looks like he lost a lot of blood."

"I don't know. I heard the EMS people talking. You'll have ask them. Sykes is still here somewhere."

Cory Sykes was in the hallway and not hard to spot. He was the only person among the swarm of techs with nothing to do.

"Sykes? I'm Agent Milino. Director Farthers has me taking the lead on this. I'm sorry about your partner."

"Thanks. I think he'll pull through. Hope so."

"You wanna walk me through what happened?"

"We were ordered by Assistant Deputy Director Foullon to tail a man named Tom R. Brach. We followed him on foot yesterday from an office building off Colshire Drive. He came here and we followed him in. Our orders were to 'follow, not approach,' so we waited. We ended up waiting for about twelve hours. We were ready to call for backup, when two guys calling themselves cops came boiling into the lobby asking the night clerk for Brach's room number."

"I take it they got it."

"They had to threaten the clerk. We followed in the stairwell while they came up on the elevator. They were in the room, and we were about to go in when they came out. We identified ourselves as federal agents and *they* opened fire."

"Did you hit either one?"

"I don't know. I pursued the suspects as they ran and got off a couple of shots in the stairwell, but my partner was badly hit, and I came back to render aid. I stand by this decision. Sandoval was bleeding out and needed a tourniquet."

Milino thought to himself he would probably have done the same thing. The guy was young, and losing a partner at any age is one of those things that stays with you.

"Did you question the clerk?"

"Yeah, I was with him downstairs when I got word that you were coming, so I left him with local police and came back up here."

Milino and Sykes went back down and quizzed the clerk, who was keyed up by the excitement of "assisting" federal agents—those were his words—but he provided very little information beyond confirming what Sykes had already told Milino.

When he phoned Farthers, all Milino could tell his boss was who the two shooters were *not*.

"They weren't police, and they weren't with any sheriff's office," Milino reported. "They wouldn't have said 'police' and then flashed 'sheriff's' ID. They would have had badges rather than printed IDs, and they wouldn't have been using turned-up collars to hide their faces."

"I'm betting they're Carker's men," Farthers said.

"I pulled the CCTV footage from the lobby and will have it for you later today," Milino promised.

"Make it *sooner*," Farthers demanded. "Get it to Foullon ASAP. And while you're at it, you and Foullon need to find Brach before Carker does."

CHAPTER
TWENTY-FOUR

IT WAS a dark and gloomy Monday night, and the rain was coming down hard when the old blue Chevy pickup with the camper shell glided into a carport in a wooded section of suburban Silver Spring, Maryland. Jim Hammer drove straight through the tarp at the back of the carport and made a hard left into a garage which was not visible from the street. Only when the door had rolled closed did the light come on in the garage.

A heavy metal door on the house side of the garage slid open, revealing a smiling, bearded man in a wheelchair.

"I see you left the light on for me," Hammer said with a grin.

"Good to see you," Tim Tommis said, rolling his chair out of the way for the two people to enter. "C'mon in."

"Tim, this is Lauren Stahling," Hammer said, introducing his companion as they stepped into the house. "Lauren, this is Tim."

"I've heard a lot about you," she said, extending her hand.

"Mostly good, I hope, as one says," Tommis replied.

Her hand was cold from the weather outside, but her smile was warm and engaging.

"Yes, indeed, but he definitely understated the extensiveness of your man cave," she said, gesturing at the open interior of the mid-century bungalow.

Servers and computer towers with winking, colored lights filled the large living room and continued into other rooms beyond. Over and among them were tables piled high with other equipment and numerous flat-screen monitors of various sizes.

"What can I say?" Tommis said with an affable shrug. "I'm a geek."

"To the umpteenth power, apparently," Lauren said, looking at the data flowing through the screens.

"How was your trip?"

"Long days, but straightforward," Hammer said. "We took Interstate 90 out of Billings, dropped down to bypass Chicago, picked up 70, took 270 out of Frederick to the Beltway, and here we are. It's good to see you. It's been too long. It's good to be *working with you* again."

"Likewise," Tommis agreed. "I'd say this calls for a drink."

"I won't disagree," Hammer said as Tommis spun his wheelchair and glided across the room to his liquor cabinet.

"Tom Bulleit's Rye." Tommis smiled as he produced an embossed bottle with a thin green label and three glasses. "Twelve years in toasted American white oak."

"Normally, I'm a Merlot kind of girl, but I guess the occasion calls for something a little more special," Lauren said, smiling. "Count me in."

"First of all, kudos to you two and all of your Montana friends," Tommis said after pouring two fingers of whiskey for each of them. "You totally...and very *spectacularly*...wrecked and ruined Hamad bin-Sharia's whole northern border scheme. It has crashed and burned."

"I'm glad to hear that," Lauren said. "We've seen just snippets on the news."

"We can thank a lot of people up in Montana for helping to bring it down," Hammer said, raising his glass.

"The sheikh is a big-time player," Tommis said with a smile. "But it looks like you kids knocked over his Montana cart in *one night*!"

"We don't care for human trafficking schemes in Montana," Lauren said emphatically as she took another sip of her whiskey. "I'll admit I had no idea what it was in the beginning. I only got involved in this because I wanted to spend some time with an old friend from high school. You know, the whole mystery of what these characters were doing on that land out there sounded like an interesting adventure, and I decided I could *use* some adventure in my otherwise ordinary life."

Tommis was amused by the body language between his two guests at the dropping of the phrase "spend some time with an old friend."

"As Hammer probably told you, at the start we guessed they were drug runners," she continued. "When we figured out it was human trafficking, the more infuriated I got. When I saw the cages, my eyes glazed over and I told this big guy here that I'm all in. We had to stop it."

"I heard from the big guy you did a pretty inspired job yourself of bewildering the bad guys."

"I'm in county government." She laughed. "I talk for a living."

"And a good job of handling a .44 in the right place at the right time to keep me from going six feet under," Hammer reminded them.

"It was a successful night," Lauren said with modest understatement, blushing slightly at his accolade. "But as my old special operations mentor once said, popping a couple of foot soldiers...his words...doesn't get you to the core of the problem. I believe he said it was a tactical solution to a strategic problem. Right?"

"This sounds like something the 'captain' would have said," Tommis agreed.

"Which basically means Hamad bin-Sharia got stung, but he didn't go away," Lauren continued. "In fact, Hammer tells me you told him that bin-Sharia is coming here to visit his friends in the pristine fields of Hambledon. Right?"

"That's right," Tommis said. "He's coming to check on his investment."

"When?" Hammer asked.

"Nobody seems to know because the sheikh doesn't announce his travel plans, but it will probably be toward the end of this week. In the meantime he continues buying and selling humans. He's made himself into one of the biggest players in the international slave trade."

"Where do they actually get their slaves?" Lauren asked.

"In his part of the world, indentured servitude is deeply entrenched, and it has been for centuries," Tommis explained. "The call it 'kafala.' It's a sponsorship scheme in which workers, mainly from Africa or East Asia, agree to pay huge sums to the bosses in order to get jobs. The bosses hang onto their passports until the employment contracts get paid off. In some of the Emirates and Gulf States, ninety percent of the manual labor force, from domestics to construction workers, come in under kafala."

"Are they actually slaves, or just low-wage workers?" Lauren asked.

"They show up in the Gulf States, get their passports confiscated by their new bosses, and they're stuck," Tommis said. "I'd say when you're stuck in a situation like *that*, you're a slave. The sheikhs over there get the same kind of 'loyalty' from their pathetic personnel pool which was once upon a time guaranteed by leg irons. Of course, this isn't to say that they don't *still* use leg irons."

"Or cable ties," Lauren quipped. "Are you sure it's '*kafala*' and not 'Kafka?'"

"Good point. Kafka could have written their playbook." Hammer laughed. "But *kafala* is just the tip of it, just the routine everyday part of it. It doesn't include the huge market in sex slaves, like what we've seen firsthand in the past week."

"What you saw last week was part of bin-Sharia's plan to branch out into this country on a large scale," Tommis continued. "A couple of years ago, he brought in Westley Carker from his London headquarters to set up the Hambledon office here in McLean. Then Carker hired Tom R. Brach to set up the Billings office. It was Brach who found the land with the old Air Force auxiliary field."

"The old Tredquist place," Lauren clarified.

"Quite clever, if you think about it," Tommis said. "A remote airfield near a remote part of Canada?"

"Believe me, we've been thinking of little else for the past week or so," Lauren said.

"Those girls were shipped across the Pacific from Korea in container ships, landed at a remote port in British Columbia and flown across the border," Tommis continued. "The poor kids were the most vulnerable possible, mainly orphaned street urchins picked up in the bad side of Korean cities and promised a good life in America."

"They sure got lied to," Lauren said. "You should have seen their faces."

"As we have," Hammer said glumly.

"And all under the protection of federal agents," Lauren added. "So what can you do when you can't just call the cops?"

"You do what you did in Montana," Tommis said. "You have to just do what needs doing. Sometimes, you have to go off the books to deal with these people the old-fashioned way. Like our team did in Afghanistan. As Hammer probably told you, there was a huge operation run by Taliban warlords under the paid protection of double-dealing NGOs and crooked Pentagon bureaucrats. Opium has flowed out of that place for centuries, and it still flows today and it will tomorrow, but those specific characters will never push another single ounce of the black stuff ever again."

"Yeah, Hammer did tell me a little bit about what you guys did off the books over there," Lauren said.

"As you know, we're here now because we decided enough was enough *again*," Hammer said. "We're here now because the sheikh is coming *here*."

"As you would say, we're finally getting to the core of the problem," Lauren said with a smile. "I guess it's time for a *strategic* solution to *this* strategic problem. Right?"

Hammer just laughed.

"I should also tell you bin-Sharia is not coming alone," Tommis interjected. "He's bringing a friend."

"You have our attention," Hammer replied.

Tommis pulled his chair in between a couple of screens and began twirling a trackball with his left hand as his right hand scampered across two keyboards.

"It may have been Brach who set up the Montana part of this scheme you upended, but the guy who filled the pipeline with slaves was a French mercenary turned slaver named Maxime Evrémonde."

"Who's he?"

"The sheikh started working with him about a year ago. He's a cruel, nasty piece of work. He started out with the Commandement des Opérations Spéciales, the French Special Forces, running sanctioned operations in Africa. When he got out, he went into *unsanctioned* operations. He dabbled in moving drugs and blood diamonds into Europe and the Gulf States, but found there was more money in moving people."

"Oh, lovely," Lauren said sarcastically.

"I'll show you," Tommis said, wheeling a few feet to another screen.

Here, he pulled up a pair of headshots he'd downloaded from some country's passport agency. Lauren studied the two faces. Hamad bin-Sharia and Maxime Evrémonde side by side. It was a study in compare and contrast. Both men were around fifty. The sheikh had a fleshy face, a thin mustache, and an insipid smile. Evrémonde had a hard, chiseled face with a hard, chiseled expression. The scars—she assumed they were battle scars—were like places where the chisel had slipped during the chiseling. His eyes radiated cruelty.

"The sheikh is the *Sheikh*," Tommis said. "But Evrémonde is the *Devil*."

"Well, I guess we'll have to add him to the list," Hammer said boldly. "We'll just stand by to learn when these characters are due to set foot on American terra firma."

"While you're waiting, I have other news," Tommis said. "I've learned that some of your old friends from Montana are showing up here in the DC area, too. Vince Milino of the ATF here, and for some reason, Tom R.

Brach is back. On Friday afternoon, he showed up at the Hambledon offices in McLean and got fired."

"We knew he left Montana," Lauren said. "I had a chance meeting with Kally Stefano while I was waiting for my date at the Waffle Shack in Billings. He texted her he was leaving town, but he didn't tell her where he was going. She seemed genuinely confused, acted like she had no idea about the trafficking."

"She probably doesn't," Tommis explained. "All indications are Brach is using her as part of the cover story for Sunrise being in the 'pristine open spaces' business. The police took her in for questioning but let her go. No evidence she was involved. Actually, no evidence of anything. The police searched the Sunrise office in downtown Billings and apparently found nothing of substance. Of course, the ATF was on the case pretty quickly. Their job was, and is, to keep the heat off Sunrise and Hambledon so they nudged local authorities out of the way."

"While we were on the road, we watched the Sunrise website disappear, and Hambledon disown their relationship with Sunrise on their own site," Hammer said. "It sounds like Brach is definitely a man without a home."

"But there's more," Tommis said. "To complicate matters, somebody tried to kill Brach in his hotel room very early Saturday morning."

"*Who did*?" Hammer asked. "Was it the ATF?"

"Here's the complicated part. There *were* ATF men tailing Brach at the time, and they were sitting in the lobby when the shooters arrived. The shooters claimed to be cops, actually, sheriff's office people from Montana. The ATF guys followed them upstairs, and they had a little firefight in the hallway. One of the ATF men got hit and is still critical."

"Montana sheriff?" Lauren asked. "Which county?"

"It was all bogus," Tommis explained. "Milino, bless his heart, figured all this out because they used fake IDs instead of badges."

"Okay, you said somebody *tried to kill* Brach in his hotel room," Hammer interjected. "What happened to him in this firefight?"

"It turns out he wasn't there," Tommis said. "It was the old pillows under the bedclothes ploy. It was his room, but he wasn't there."

"How do you know all this?" Lauren asked.

"I've got Milino on tape telling ATF Deputy Director Darwin Farthers all about it. It's queued up for you here if you want to listen."

With this, Tommis darted across the room to another computer about twenty feet away. The floor throughout the entire space was uninterrupted smooth, polished laminate, which facilitated wheelchair movement to any of the numerous machines in a matter of seconds.

They heard Milino's voice telling Farthers about the absence of badges, the turned-up collars, and the CCTV footage from the lobby. They heard Farthers demand Milino "find Brach before Carker does."

"I won't ask how you got this," Hammer said, grinning.

"Please don't," Tommis replied with a wink. "Don't ask if Santa is real; just enjoy your new toys."

"Does Santa know what happened to Brach?" Lauren asked.

"Not just yet," Tommis admitted.

"I think I might have an idea," Hammer said thoughtfully.

CHAPTER
TWENTY-FIVE

JUST TWENTY-ONE MILES around the DC Beltway from where Tim Tommis was pouring two fingers of Tom Bulleit's Rye for his guests on that Monday night, Tom R. Brach was watching the rivulets of rain running down the window of his condo.

Two weeks ago, Brach had been the fairest of Westley Carker's fair-haired boys. Then Lathrope had shot the hunter and things started to unravel. It got worse. On Brach's first day back in McLean, they fired him, disowned him, and tried to *kill* him.

As had been the case when Brach had stumbled into his condo on Friday morning, nobody knew where he was, but now they knew he was in town. Nobody knew about this place, and as long as he stayed put, he was safe, but he had been sitting here all weekend.

He didn't like staying put. He was starting to feel like a trapped rat whose time was running out.

He could see the Marriott from the condo, not well, but he could see it.

As he watched the rainwater-blurred image of the

place, his mind was replaying the events which had taken place there on Saturday morning.

He had awakened to the sight of the flashing red and blue lights of emergency vehicles over there. He couldn't make out what was happening, and he should have stayed put, but curiosity got the best of him. Dressed in a stocking cap and nondescript overcoat, he had approached cautiously.

"What's going on?" Brach asked. He picked an EMT rather than a cop, fearing a cop might get suspicious.

"Somebody tried to shoot some guy up on the sixth floor," the woman said. "They ended up trading shots with the feds. One of the feds was hit pretty bad."

"Looks like the feds are really swarming this morning," Brach observed.

"Yeah. Local cops are pissed about that, but I guess local cops are always pissed when the feds take over jurisdiction and send them home."

"Was the guy on the sixth floor hurt?" Brach asked.

"Somebody said the room was empty."

"Did they catch the ones who shot the fed?"

"I guess they got away. Why are *you* interested?"

"Oh, just curious about the commotion."

Brach walked away shaken.

Sixth floor. Empty room.

This had been meant for him. He bought some junk food at a convenience store and sneaked back into his condo.

For the past three days, he'd been afraid to move, cornered by apprehension. A trapped rat whose time was running out.

As he watched the rain, he racked his brain for what to do.

Where could he turn?

Suddenly, it came to him.

Why hadn't he thought of this earlier?

He once had an aunt, who he had visited as a kid at her place up in the hills near the Weymouth Woods Nature Preserve in Moore County, North Carolina. His cousin had the place now, and once, a couple of years back, he had invited Brach to come visit. At the time, this was the farthest thing from his mind—but *now*?

Brach flipped open his laptop and went to the Amtrak route site. Just as he remembered, the family place was only a few miles from the train station in Southern Pines, and Amtrak still stopped there. The train, which continued south to Columbia and Savannah, departed from Union Station in Washington at 7:23 a.m. He could make this using public transportation—and still have a chance to get some sleep.

He shoveled his things into the roller bag he kept at the condo, set the clock radio alarm, and dozed off.

Tom R. Brach had a new lease on life. He had a *plan*!

———

He went to sleep contented but awoke in the arms of a nightmare.

The clock read 4:22 a.m., and Tom R. Brach could feel the roughness of his SIG P228 against his cheek. He'd had a dream in which he had put the pistol under his pillow with the safety off.

It wasn't a dream. When he lifted the gun, the safety *was* off.

He could have accidentally blown his brains out in his sleep with his own SIG.

As he lay there in the dark, his head still clouded by fright and despair, he wondered whether this might have been *not* a bad thing. Who would miss him?

He had spent a lot of hours over the past few days

thinking about his soon-to-be-ex-wife who hated him, and about his teenage daughter who was at that age where she hated everyone and everything. They were only forty miles from where he lay, but they might as well be ten thousand miles away.

His daughter was about the same age as all those Korean girls in the cages, a reality which was one not lost on him, but one he tried not to think about if he could help it. If he had any sort of moral compass at all, he thought, this ought to bother him, but after he bit his lower lip until it bled, he was able to push this out of his mind.

Who would miss him? Carker had not only fired him, he has explicitly disowned him. Then Carker had him followed. Why? There was only one thing he could think of, and that's why he put the SIG under his pillow.

Gradually, as he remembered his plan, Brach relaxed. He did have something to live for. He had a *new lease on life.*

It was so quiet in the predawn darkness of Monday morning that the ring of one of Brach's burner phones startled him.

"Who the hell can this be?" Brach asked out loud as he stumbled into the kitchen imagining a spam call. Burner phones were as susceptible to this scourge as were real phones. The clock on the microwave read 4:38 a.m.

Picking up the phone, he was stunned to see a *real* name on the caller ID.

Kenny Lathrope!

Brach felt himself turn pale and clammy.

Kenny Lathrope. The redheaded fool who shot the hunter in the reckless blunder that had set the dominoes tumbling.

Brach thumbed the icon and put the phone to his ear.

"Lathrope?"

"Yeah," the voice said in a gruff whisper which was barely audible because of the traffic noise in the background. "Brad's here too. Where are you?"

"*What*?"

Brach felt himself panic.

"I'm not in Billings," Brach said, hesitating to say more.

"Neither are we."

"What happened at the airfield? Where have you been?"

"Came cross country to get back at Hambledon."

"*What*? Where are you now?"

"Meet us...Morgan Boulevard Metro Station, parking lot...one o'clock this afternoon," the voice whispered before the line went dead.

Brach sat down, realizing he was hyperventilating.

Lathrope. Appearing out of thin air. A meetup?

What did he mean by *"get back* at Hambledon?" Revenge?

He knew it was crazy, but Brach decided he should meet with the crazy redhead. He had to know what Lathrope meant by "getting back" at Hambledon. If it was revenge, Brach thought he might even want *in on it*. They had tried to kill him, so he would take satisfaction in striking back.

He took his SIG P228 from the nightstand and proceeded to field strip and clean it. He wanted to be ready.

Just a few days ago Lathrope had been instrumental in toppling Brach's grandest creation, and now, just *maybe*, the two men were on the *same side*.

There would be another 7:23 to Southern Pines tomorrow.

———

Jim Hammer laid Kenny Lathrope's cell phone on the table as it warbled through its powering down ritual. Tommis had given him an almost magical algorithm that could outwit the password protection of any device, so he was able to access Lathrope's as easily as if he was the late Kenny himself. Hammer was playing the game two moves ahead and crossing his fingers Brach would take the bait.

The architect of Hambledon's imploded Montana project had been wronged, and revenge is a powerful, but distracting, motivator. Hammer knew this from firsthand experience, and he himself was susceptible to this curse. He had constantly thought about revenge as he conducted his own war against the monolith that had stood behind Brach's creation. But vengeance, simple vengeance, could not be his sole motivator, because this distraction is what clouds your judgment. At this moment, though, Hammer was betting it *had* just clouded Brach's.

Hammer turned off the street noise audio Tommis had queued up for him, and suddenly, he was enveloped by silence, and by the dark stillness of the house of twinkling, colored diodes.

Hammer stood and walked softly back into Tommis's guest room. He looked at the long, smooth female body in the cool silver light of the moon, a body more perfect, he mused, than you'd find in Renaissance sculpture. As he listened to her quiet, rhythmic breathing he pulled up the blanket to cover her, and he thought about the Best Western in Sioux City. It was there, last week, when two old friends had become lovers. No words had been spoken, but things were articulated, and in this conversation, there had been harmony in all senses of the word.

Maybe it was the cognizance that life is short, having been brought into focus when each of them used deadly force to save the life of the other. Maybe it was the reality of their being alone against the world, on a crusade of their own making, two determined people righting a wrong while writing their own rules.

Or maybe it was just the mere acceptance of what they already knew—that the fire had been burning there all along.

CHAPTER
TWENTY-SIX

STACEY BRACH WHEELED her Honda CR-V smoothly into the driveway of her split-level ranch house in suburban College Park, Maryland, like she had done on innumerable Tuesday mornings over the past few years, climbed out and slammed the door. Driving her daughter to school, such a joy when Kindrid was seven, had become torture at seventeen. How can one person so young find so much in her world to despise?

Of course, Stacey had her own set of problems. Heading the list was a husband who kept putting off signing the divorce papers. Now there had been a mention on cable news about his being a person of interest in a sex trafficking ring out in Montana. The story went away the next day. She hoped none of her friends had seen it.

At least her clerical job at the Department of Agriculture had moved from a cubicle on Independence Avenue in downtown Washington to work from home, so she did not have to deal with coworkers face-to-face.

She had just started to turn her key in the front door lock, when a silver Lexus LS pulled into her driveway.

Two men in suits and black overcoats got out and began walking toward her.

"Are you Mrs. Brach?"

"That depends," she answered cautiously. "Who are you?"

"We're with the Hambledon Global Advocacy Group," one of the men said, showing her a company ID with the same format as the one she had once seen belonging to her husband.

"Okay," she said. "That's the company my soon-to-be ex-husband works for, but I'm guessing you probably know this. What do you want?"

"We're looking for him," the second man said. "When was the last time you were in contact?"

"It's been months. He's been living in Montana for the last couple of years, but you probably know that. I have not laid eyes on him since he's been out there. Why are you asking?"

She *knew* why, it just seemed like the thing to ask.

"He hasn't contacted you in the last several days?"

"You mean since this business about the trafficking hit the news? No, like I said, I haven't heard him in months. And no, I know absolutely nothing about any trafficking.

"Are you aware he's here in the DC area now?"

"*Absolutely not.*"

"Are you in contact with anyone in this area with whom he might contact?"

"*Absolutely not,*" she repeated, feeling feisty. "Why don't you go ask around at your *own* office in McLean?"

With this, the two men looked at one another, thanked Stacey for her time, and climbed back into the Lexus. They had not bothered to mention they had tracked him to the McLean Marriott, where they had tried unsuccessfully to *kill him*.

Stacey went into the house and tossed her coat and

purse onto the sofa. She poured herself a cup of cold coffee knowing this was the last thing she should do to calm down and shoved it in the microwave.

She had just retrieved it when a when a black Escalade with tinted windows pulled into the space in the driveway recently vacated by the Lexus.

Again, it was two men in suits and dark overcoats. She opened the front door as they made their way up the walk.

"Stacey Brach...Mrs. Stacey Brach?" the first man said, flashing a badge. "I'm Federal Agent Vincent Milino and this is Agent Cory Sykes."

"Yes, I am, and before you ask, my husband is not here, and I have not seen him in two years. Like I told your friends fifteen minutes ago, I know nothing about human trafficking, and I am as outraged the next person about this whole ugly business."

"What friends?"

"Those two men who just left. They were from Hambledon Global. That's the NGO my soon-to-be-ex-husband works for. They said he's back in the area. I thought he was still in Montana, where he's been for two years."

"Has he tried to contact you?"

"Like I told the two from Hambledon, I haven't spoken to him in months and I have not seen him in two years."

"If you do hear from him, could you give us a call?" Milino asked, handing her his card. "And let us know if you hear from Hambledon again, or if anyone else contacts you."

"If *you* see him, tell him to sign the damned divorce papers," she said, shaking her head. "This is beyond belief. First them, now you, and who knows who's next. Everybody'd looking for him. Suddenly, the bastard is the most popular person in Prince George's County. But I'll tell you one place that he's *not* wanted, and that's here at this house."

The irate woman who slammed the door then became the frightened woman who went weak in the knee and abandoned the coffee cup in favor of the bottle of chardonnay in the refrigerator.

"*Oh shit*!"

She sat in the living room, sipping her wine and staring at the space in the driveway next to her CR-V as though expecting the arrival of a third car.

Stacey poured a second glass and picked up her phone. She had not dialed this number in a very long time. She half—or more than half—expected Tom R. Brach *not* to pick up.

"Hello," he answered. "Stacey?"

"That's right. *Where are you*? I've had federal agents here looking for you, and people from your work. Why? What have you done? *No*! Don't tell me. I don't want to know."

"What did you tell them?"

"The truth. I told them I haven't seen you in two years."

"Good."

"They said you are back here in the area. Is this true?"

"Passing through."

"Well, can you please pass through here long enough to sign the divorce papers. Please and thank you."

"Yes, I will. For sure."

"You know where to send them, or have you lost my lawyer's address? No, never mind, just send them here. You haven't forgotten this address, have you?"

"No."

She pushed the end-call button. She'd had enough of Tom R. Brach for one lifetime.

———

"Good morning, Hambledon Global, how may I direct your call?" Agnes Wickfield asked as she answered the phone at the NGO's North American headquarters.

"I need to speak with Mr. Carker," the gravelly voice on the line replied.

"Who may I say is?"

"It's Kenny Lathrope," the voice whispered. It was hard to hear it over the traffic noise. "Tell him it's Kenny Lathrope. I work for Mr. Brach in Montana."

Jim Hammer was sure Carker did not know Lathrope's voice, but he was taking no chances. He was getting good use from the cell phone he had retrieved at the scene of Lathrope's demise. The hot-headed redhead was playing a useful role in his afterlife.

"A Mr. Lathrope for you," Agnes said when Carker picked up. "He says he works with Mr. Brach."

"Put him through *at once*!"

Although they had never met, Carker knew the name of the man who had shot "that hunter" out in Montana, and he knew Lathrope as a loose end who had successfully stepped off the grid.

"Mr. Lathrope, so good of you to call," Carker said, turning on the charm. "What can I do for you this morning? How's the weather out there in Montana?"

"I'm not out there these days. I'm here in Virginia. I know you've heard a lot of shit about what went down, but there's a lot you still need to know. I'm setting up a meeting. Mr. Brach is coming and you should be there too."

Carker was floored. He had just learned of the dead-end visit by his men to Brach's wife in College Park, and thought he was at an impasse with finding Brach. Now this! Tom R. Brach was practically falling into his lap, with Lathrope himself as a bonus.

"This sounds first rate, Mr. Lathrope," Carker purred in his deliberately posh British accent. "When and where shall we meet Mr. Brach?"

"Brach is meeting me at the Morgan Boulevard Metro Station parking lot at one o'clock today."

"Very good, sir. I'm looking forward to hearing what you have to say."

Carker never took public transit in any form, but he was sure his men could find a metro station parking lot. At least he *hoped* they were capable of such a pedestrian task—after their failed friendly fire fiasco at the Marriott.

———

Having surreptitiously noted the details of the call, Agnes Wickfield went on break. She left the building and phoned the unlisted burner phone number of ATF Deputy Director Darwin Farthers.

She may or may not have known that Farthers referred to her as "part of the furniture" at Hambledon, but she greatly relished her role as his "inside woman" at the NGO Farthers was paid to protect. She felt like a spy in a James Bond movie and this gave the forty-something cat lady a sense of purpose and excitement.

"Mr. Carker just took a call from a man named Lathrope. It seems they're going to be meeting Mr. Brach this afternoon at the Morgan Metro Station in Maryland. I hope this is useful information."

"Agnes, you have no idea," Farthers replied.

CHAPTER
TWENTY-SEVEN

IT WAS A GLOOMY, drizzly Tuesday afternoon as Tom R. Brach stepped off his car at the Morgan Boulevard Station. The second-to-last station on both the Blue and Silver lines of the Washington Metro, it is surrounded mainly by open space and parking lots. It can be busy on pro football game days because it's the closest station to Northwest Stadium, but at non-peak hours on other days, it can be almost deserted.

Jim Hammer picked it for "Lathrope's" rendezvous because of all this, and because Brach could take the Silver Line directly from McLean. Hammer intended this as one more incentive for Brach, who might have been reluctant to come if it meant being seen changing trains at a busy station in downtown Washington.

Brach nervously pulled his ball cap down over his face, even though it had already been tugged as low as it would go. He patted the SIG P228 he carried in his over-coat pocket "just in case," and went to look for Lathrope.

There were two men walking toward the Park & Ride lot in the distance, but neither had flaming red hair. The nearby lot had quite a few cars, but he could not see into most of them. Where was Lathrope? When would he show himself? Was he in the lot, or was he taking a train?

Brach knew he was early—the clock in the station had read 12:42 when he passed it. But he'd rather be waiting for a while than have Lathrope arrive first. He decided to keep moving. A man loitering attracts more attention than someone who seems to know what he's doing—but as Brach was admitting to himself at this moment, he really *didn't* know what he was doing.

Brach knew he could have been most of the way to North Carolina by now. He almost regretted the extreme curiosity which caused him to change his plan. What had persuaded him to take a meeting with this dangerously impulsive man?

As he circled to the back side of the nearest parking lot, he heard a car door open.

He looked, not immediately recognizing the man who was climbing out of the car.

It was not Lathrope, but he recognized the man as one of Carker's goons. Thoughts spun through Brach's mind.

Where's Lathrope?

Lathrope isn't here, you idiot.

This is a trap!

Because of the awkward length of the Beretta 92FS with its silencer attached, it took a moment for the man to get his weapon out from beneath his coat. This gave Brach time to duck behind a car before he heard the muffled cough of two rounds being fired. The headlight of the car he was behind shattered.

As he pulled his own weapon, Brach heard the gravel-on-pavement sound of the man moving into position for a third shot.

Brach had never been in a gunfight in his life, but instinct told him to keep moving. Scooting in a crouching position, he scrambled into the space behind the next row of cars.

As he did, he heard the door of another car open and he felt the droplets of safety glass on the bill of his cap as a second shooter attacked him from the opposite direction.

Maybe it was still instinct. Maybe it was just exasperation demanding he seize control of the situation, but Brach popped up from behind the car that sheltered him and squeezed off a shot at the second attacker.

Maybe it was all those boring nights in Billings filled with visits to the shooting range. Maybe it was dumb luck.

Brach's 9mm slug impacted the man's jaw, ghoulishly splitting it into two blood-splashed halves.

As Brach turned, he saw the other man coming for him and raising his gun.

It seemed like slow motion.

Brach swung his SIG around to aim it even as he saw the Beretta aimed toward him.

He felt the pistol buck in his hand at the same moment that a round ripped into his shoulder.

The brachial artery running down into the front of your bicep from the auxiliary artery in your shoulder carries a lot of blood, so if it is ruptured, blood loss is catastrophic. Just before the darkness descended, Tom R. Brach felt the numbing pain and the damp warmth of the blood pooling next to his left ear.

————

Squinting through his high-powered binoculars and through the misty light drizzle, Vince Milino had carefully studied the faces of the two men who arrived at the metro station around 12:20 p.m. It came as no surprise that these were the faces of the same people who had appeared on the CCTV footage from the Marriott which he had seen on Saturday.

He handed the glasses to Sykes, who confirmed them as the two who had shot Sandoval. The agents had no doubt these two were the Hambledon men who'd paid a visit to Stacey Brach that morning. They emerged from separate vehicles, conferred briefly, and then returned to their cars.

The two feds watched and waited as Tom R. Brach finally emerged from the station building and started to scan the parking lot for Kenny Lathrope. Milino and Sykes had seen no sign of him but assumed he would show himself now that Brach had shown up.

Instead, it was the Hambledon foot soldiers who appeared, one and then the other, obviously overly eager to make good on reversing their disappointment at the Marriott.

Milino thought to himself that if it had been him, he would have waited to see whether Lathrope showed up, but he decided eliminating Brach was the overriding assignment for the two Hambledon men.

As the shooting started, Sykes readied his Glock 19M. Milino eased the Escalade into drive but kept his foot on the brake. They watched with amazement as Brach managed to score hits on both of the hit men before he fell.

Some people who had been coming out of the station were pointing and shouting, but they were some distance from the action, and all three of the shooters had fallen among the parked cars and were not visible.

With the blue lights in the Escalade's grill now winking, Milino raced forward, screeching to a stop near where Brach had fallen. He and Sykes approached the three bodies, methodically confirming each was lifeless.

———

Jim Hammer lowered his Oberwerk HD II binoculars as a Summerfield, Maryland police car arrived, sirens howling. He had planned things several moves ahead and they had all come together as he'd hoped. Tom R. Brach had been found and eliminated, and nobody was aware Jim Hammer and his team were in the game.

Alerted by calls from bystanders, Metro Transit Police were next on the scene, but the two feds had already secured the scene and called for a federal crime scene team. As had been the case for Sheriff Kyle Fahr in Logan County, Montana, two weeks earlier, local law enforcement was jurisdictionally out of luck.

Hammer slid the safety on his Colt .45 into the "on" position and started the blue Chevy pickup. He had places to be and things to do. There was more than just late autumn mist in the air.

———

"I didn't even have to get out of my truck," Hammer said with grim satisfaction as he poured himself a cup of coffee. An hour after watching Tom R. Brach's demise, he was back in Tim Tommis's kitchen. "My only disappointment was that Carker sent surrogates and didn't come himself."

"We've already heard about it from Agent Milino," Lauren Stahling said. "He was telling it all to Deputy Director Fathers. Over the speaker, it sounded like he was right *here*. I always thought wiretaps were scratchy and hard to hear."

"This is a landline phone tap," Tommis clarified. "It's all hard-wired, solid-state audio. Undetectable because it goes through their own phone server."

"They're still going on and on about Kenny Lathrope, though," Lauren added. "Milino said the Hambledon people didn't wait for him to show up before they started shooting, but Milino and the other guy spent some time looking for him in empty cars in the parking lot. They never found him. I wonder why not."

"Who knows?" Hammer teased.

"Sorry to interrupt," said Tommis, who was looking at another screen about ten feet away. "I think I finally have confirmation of the sheikh's ETA. According to my tap on the ATF, their spy inside Hambledon says they think he's coming in late on Thursday. He's planning to meet Carker that evening at a house somewhere in the country down in Fairfax County. Evrémonde will be there too."

"So will I," Hammer said coolly.

"At last, he gets his chance for the *strategic* solution to the problem at hand," Lauren with a smile.

"What more can you tell me about this guy before I step into the ring?" Hammer asked.

"The big thing is he's a paranoid," Tommis said. "Nobody knows his exact schedule. That's why I said they *think* he's coming on Thursday night. Everything is last minute and subject to change. I don't know where the secret house in the country is, but I'm working on it. If you get close to him, be aware his bodyguards are sadists, the kill-for-thrill types like we've met before."

"So we have."

"Another possibly useful fact about his paranoia is he doesn't keep any of his data on encrypted servers in guarded compounds somewhere. He keeps his entire operation, all of his business stuff on a multi-terabyte hard drive that's installed in a laptop he carries with him at *all times*. So, if you get a chance to put a bullet in his head, save a couple of rounds for the laptop."

"This is good to know," Hammer said.

"I've also learned that him and Evrémonde and Carker will also have a friend from high places at the table for this meeting. Somebody from the Capitol will be on board."

"*The* Capitol," Lauren said with surprise. "You mean…"

"Yup. The one up there on Capitol Hill," Tommis said. "*That* Capitol. You've seen the Hambledon brochures. Politicians love being associated with the kind of stuff. Who does not like a charming, environmentally friendly NGO? Their big secret sponsor is Senator Austin Olconian, the chairman of the Senate Natural Resources and Environment Committee. He's been instrumental in keeping the work the ATF does for Hambledon out of the prying eyes of congressional oversight."

"I'm sure that's useful," Hammer said sarcastically.

"Olconian is also one of the sheikh's customers," Tommis added. "He fancies himself as a ladies' man, and I hear he has a weakness for 'captive' ladies."

"That sucks big time," Lauren said with disgust. "*Really* big time."

"Well, it *is* very big time, but like they say, follow the money," Tommis continued with a shrug. "It's just like with drugs and guns. They complain about it but write legislation through one door of their offices up on the Hill and reap 'campaign contributions' through the other door."

"I know," Lauren admitted.

"Most people don't like to think about it, much less talk about it. That's why the Jeffrey Epsteins of the world and all their friends in high places go on and on and almost never seem to get called to answer for their mischief. But if they do get called to question, they don't get a chance to answer."

"Do you have audio from the senator?" Hammer asked.

"Sorry to say, but Santa has no flies on the walls up there. I do have information Olconian is sending his chief of staff to see Carker tomorrow. This guy is an ambitious go-getter named Chad Marltyn."

"Excuse me?" Lauren said, looking startled. "Did you say Chad Marltyn? Marltyn with a 'y'?"

"That's the one. Do you know the name?"

"I knew someone by that name at the University of Washington a long time ago."

"How many Chad Marltyns can there be?" Tommis asked. "He's about your age, I think. A young guy on his way up."

"Thanks for calling me 'young,' but this guy was from Washington state and Olconian is not a senator from Washington."

"I hate to be a breaker of stereotypes," Tommis said. "But a huge slice of congressional staffers have never been to the state that their person represents before they were hired."

"Do you have a picture of this guy?"

"Sure do."

"That's him," Lauren said when Tommis produced a headshot. "This is the Chad I knew with twenty years less hair and more puffiness. It doesn't surprise me he's here now doing this. He was really into student government and political stuff."

"Small world," Hammer mused. "How well did you know him?"

"We went out a few times. You're not jealous, are you?"

"No," Hammer said, albeit hesitantly.

"I know what you're thinking," Lauren said.

"What are we thinking?" Tommis asked.

"You're thinking that because I *knew* him, I could use this to be the fly on the wall up there."

"Well, this *could* be helpful," Tommis said. "We have the ATF bugged, but they'll be arm's-length from the sheikh meeting. Only Carker and Olconian will be meeting with the sheikh and Evrémonde. It would be good to have someone inside at the senator's office in the run-up to the meeting."

"You don't have to do this," Hammer said.

"Yes, I do," Lauren said. "Anything to help make things go the way we want them to. I can make contact with him. I can be a fly on that wall. It feels more than a little bit creepy, but I'm here to help take down a creepier monster. *I can do this.*"

CHAPTER
TWENTY-EIGHT

"THANKS FOR MEETING ME OUT HERE," Assistant Deputy Director Joe Foullon said, climbing out of his Lincoln Town Car. It was early Wednesday morning and he was meeting Vince Milino at a deserted turn-out on Route 28 near Marshalton, Virginia, an hour and a half south of Washington.

"Of course," Milino said, staring into the gloomy low clouds hanging over rural Fauquier County. "It seems I've been spending most of my time in the field this week."

"And doing battle with our colleagues at Hambledon, I see."

"Continuing to clean up their messes is more to the point," Milino clarified. "Like securing that fiasco at the metro station yesterday, when three of theirs shot each other."

"Among them, the man who shot Agent Sandoval, apparently," Foullon added.

"Yes, Agent Sykes confirmed that," Milino said. "Also on the KIA list was Tom R. Brach, the man who set up a disastrous scheme to import 'product' into Montana by air."

"Tying up a loose end," Foullon said. "I'm glad that *we* didn't have to do that."

"Agreed," Milino said thoughtfully.

"See that," Foullon said, nodding at a Cessna 182 buzzing low overhead. "He's on final approach to Marshalton Airport, which is just beyond those trees. It's a general aviation field that's getting more use since they extended the runway to 7,500 feet. They put in refueling capacity for business jets. They're too far from DC to attract a lot of business jet traffic, but Hamad bin-Sharia's people have picked it precisely because it *is* out of the way. His Gulfstream will be flying in here Thursday evening. Carker, and Senator Olconian's people will meet them. Red carpet, you know."

"And you want me here to babysit them," Milino said, stating his understanding of the ATF role in the arrival of one of the world's preeminent human traffickers.

"They know you and your people will *be there* but stand back unless they need you. Officially, you're not even there. Just stand by in case of trouble."

"Do you expect trouble?"

"There is always the unforeseen, but this is all very tightly controlled, so nobody around here knows about what's going on. The airport will be advised only that it's an oil tycoon's Gulfstream. Carker is keeping this visit very close to his vest. Inside the ATF pipeline, only you, me and Farthers know about the sheikh coming. Whoever you bring with you that night will not know where you're going until you get here. Those are the *only* people who need to know. *Nobody else* knows a thing about this."

This was not exactly true.

As the two ATF vehicles pulled back onto Route 28

and headed north with the Town Car in the lead, they paid no attention to the aging, nondescript blue pickup that had stopped near a small bridge. The scruffy-looking man in the ball cap would have looked like a fisherman trying his luck in the little stream called Licking Run—*if* Milino had noticed him, but he did not.

Jim Hammer put his Oberwerk HD II binoculars back into their case on the seat of his Chevy and headed north a discreet distance behind the others. As they passed though Manassas, they struggled their way through some road construction and congestion and finally made a right on Braddock Road. As they headed east toward the DC Beltway, Hammer was making mental notes of intersections and other features which may or may not be important later.

It was a case of an experienced federal agent used to spotting a tall, versus a special operations man who knew how to make himself invisible. Hammer won. It didn't hurt that it was now raining.

In a heavily wooded area west of Ravensworth, Virginia, the two ATF cars slowed and made a left onto a narrow gravel road. The blue pickup didn't even slow. Around the next bend, Hammer turned into the vacant parking lot of a large rural church and opened the laptop Tim Tommis had given him this morning.

He immediately logged into the link Tommis had set up by hacking into a site providing real-time, high-rez, global satellite imagery using Geographic Information Systems data from geostationary and polar-orbiting NOAA and commercial satellites. This gave Tommis, and now Hammer, a live satellite view of anywhere. It was like the DOD satellite systems Hammer and Tommis used in Afghanistan and elsewhere, but somewhat better —thanks to Tommis's tweaking.

The screen immediately centered on Hammer's position, but he easily scrolled back to the side road. He spotted the two ATF vehicles and zoomed in as they slowed to a stop between a white two-story house and a nearby barn. The two men got out, and Hammer watched as Foullon showed Milino around the immediate area of the two buildings.

On the Geographic Information Systems feed, Hammer saw the road into the house from Braddock Road, and he saw a country road about a quarter mile parallel. What most interested him was a barely distinguishable dirt road off the country road that was like a back door to the Ravensworth house.

When they walked to the house and went in, he switched to infrared and followed their heat signatures. This was so much easier in a wood-frame structure than in those damned caves in Afghanistan where the satellites had to look through a lot of rock. He watched the heat signature imagery flare slightly at one end of the building as they apparently turned on the furnace.

The house was deserted except for the two of them, but Hammer could imagine what it would be like on Thursday night.

———

Chad Marltyn left the McLean Metro Station and made his way to the coffee shop on Colshire Drive where the senator had instructed him to meet Westley Carker, the managing director of Hambledon Global operations in North America. When he had met Carker previously, it had been in the Hambledon offices. He wondered why he was asked to meet in a coffee shop, but he knew the reason was above his pay grade.

However, he reassured himself that there wasn't very much that *was* above his pay grade. The only person in his office at a higher grade was the senator himself. In the decade he had been in Washington, he had actively climbed the ladder from a nothing gofer to being chief of staff to a Senate Committee Chairman. He had ridden his poly-sci degree from the University of Washington through several campaigns in several states before latching on to the coattails of Austin Olconian. It had been a wild, but exhilarating ride, but he'd enjoyed every politically charged moment of it.

He bought a black coffee and took a corner table away from the windows as the senator had instructed him. Carker strode in about four minutes later, bought a small green tea and joined him.

"Good to see you, Mr. Marltyn," Carker said cheerfully in his congenial upper-class British accent.

"And good to see you, sir," Marltyn said, taking the older man's proffered hand. "The senator sends his regards as always."

"We'll be seeing one another a time or two in the next several days, which is why I asked Austin to send you out to see me today. I'm sorry for the cloak-and-dagger, but we'll be meeting with people who are cautiously protective of their privacy, and we must respect this."

"Certainly. Does this have anything to do with what happened with that subsidiary of Hambledon out in Montana?"

"Oh…no…no…no," Carker said, almost defensively. "Oh that terrible, tragic disarray out there. Shocking. I should tell you Sunrise Land Holdings were *never* a Hambledon subsidiary. We were working with them on ideas for some land they acquired out there. We had no idea of their organized crime connection in Minnesota or any of the rest of it. We are stunned and *appalled*. We've issued a press release."

"I'm sorry it happened," Marltyn said. He was, but

only because of what a negative Hambledon association might do to the senator's reputation. It was not he was unaware of Hambledon's dark side, the human trafficking side, the side you *never* talked about, he just did not want to read about it in *The Washington Post*.

"The man who was behind Sunrise, this Tom R. Brach fellow, was killed in a mugging attempt at a subway station in Maryland yesterday," Carker said in a confiding tone. "If there's any silver lining, it's this man's divorce had not been concluded, and his wife will be the beneficiary of a sizable life insurance payout."

"A Hambledon policy?"

"Well...um..."

"Going back to the gathering you were describing."

"Oh yes," Carker continued. "I will be meeting a gentleman named Hamad Abdallah bin-Sharia. As you may know, Mr. bin-Sharia is the founder and CEO of the Hambledon organization. We'll greet him at a suburban Virginian airport Thursday evening. The senator wants his chief of staff to be there at the airport. You will accompany us to the meeting which will follow in a secluded antebellum house at an undisclosed location in rural Virginia. 'Watch for the wooden duck,' they tell me. The senator will join us there."

"I see."

"Mr. bin-Sharia rarely comes to the States, and when he does, he craves a low profile. This meeting is strictly need-to-know, and you are one of but a few people who know. Please keep it this way. *Understood*?"

"Of course," Marltyn replied. He was no stranger to secret meetings and to the worlds of self-important people who lived their lives surreptitiously. He imagined this meeting would dip into Hambledon's dark side, the human trafficking side, but he knew it was not to be discussed ahead of time, or *ever*.

"I'll send a Hambledon car for you tomorrow after-noon at half four. Clear your schedule for the next several days, and plan on not getting much sleep on Thursday night."

———

Marltyn was back on Capitol Hill in time to check in at his office in the Hart Senate Office Building, return a few calls and make it to Espresso Kestrel on Maryland Avenue for his afternoon double-shot soy-milk cappuc-cino. He was too young to be a creature of habit, he told himself, but he *had* become addicted to the routine.

Indeed, it was this very routine made the chance meeting he was about to have not a coincidence at all.

He was in the midst of returning some emails when he happened to glance up and notice a woman coming through the door. She was the kind of woman who was more than easy on the eye. She was one who invites the eye to linger. Her long brown hair tumbled across her shoulders, and her eyes radi-ated a confident brilliance. She was stylish, but in an understated way, with an attractive slate-gray fall coat over a teal-blue sweater dress and knee-high black boots.

It was her expression which caught his attention, but it was her face, thirty-something, yet timeless, that made him do a double take.

Wait a minute! I *know* this woman!

As he stared at her in profile, ordering a cup of coffee so calmly and assuredly, it dawned on him.

Could it be?

I know this woman!

As she turned, he caught her eye.

At first, her first expression was the one women

always have when they catch a man staring, but then it softened.

"Lauren...Lauren Stahling," he said, standing.

"It can't be," she said. "Chad, is it really you? What are you doing *here*?"

"I work here," he said. "Actually not *here*-here as in the Kestrel, but here on Capitol Hill. Come join me. Please sit down."

"What do you do on Capitol Hill if you don't serve coffee?" she asked with a lighthearted grin, playing him. She remembered teasing him long ago, back when they were more than merely friends. She remembered liking him, and now, here he was. In many ways he was the same old Chad, but picturing him as an accomplice to human traffickers certainly took the "same old" out of the equation.

"I work for Senator Austin Olconian," he said. "I'm his chief of staff."

"I always knew you had an interest in politics," she said, letting a smile conceal other thoughts. "I guess you found your way to the center of it. How long have you been doing this?"

"I've been with the senator for about ten years, " Marltyn began, before going into a long description of what he did for the senator. It took him several minutes before he realized he had not asked about her.

"I went back to Montana with my accounting degree and got a job in the county assessor's office," she answered, deliberately downplaying her job to make it seem less worth remembering. He did not ask which county.

"What is Lauren Stahling doing in Washington?" Marltyn finally got around to asking.

"First of all, I use my married name now, even though I'm not still married, so it's Lauren Ransdell," she said.

She had picked a surname that had never been hers, but one she could use if she managed to get Marltyn to introduce her to the senator. "I came here for the Eastern Association of Professional Assessors Conference at the Hilton."

She flashed a badge and lanyard with the assumed name which she had in her purse.

Lauren had discovered this conference on the internet the day before as she was scrambling to build a backstory for why she was in DC. She had quickly late-registered online and had just dropped by the hotel's convention room long enough to pick up her badge, a few brochures and a free canvas tote bag. If anyone checked up on her, they would learn Lauren Ransdell was in fact a registered attendee.

Having established her reason for being in town, she moved into the real reason for this "accidental" rendezvous with her old acquaintance.

"So you really work with Senator Olconian," she said, feigning interest in the man whose office she hoped to visit. "Being from Montana, I've actually been following his work with the Senate Committee on Natural Resources and the Environment on public-private partnerships in land use. His work making it possible for nonprofits to take over large parcels of land shows a lot of promise in getting the right kinds of stakeholders involved in stewardship."

She had also been looking into the senator's background and mastering the buzzwords—from "stakeholders" to "stewardship"—which popped up in his press releases.

"I'm impressed," Marltyn said, raising an eyebrow. "You seem to know a great deal about the senator's work."

"Oh, it's just an interest of mine. Wish we had more

time to talk about it. You look busy and I have to get back for an end-of-the-day breakout session."

"Yeah, um...maybe we could continue this over dinner. What do you say? Do you have plans?"

"Oh darn," Lauren said, putting on a disappointed expression while surreptitiously playing hard to get. "I wish I could, but I've got to meet some people. It would be great to catch up though."

"What about tomorrow during the day," Marltyn said, happily coming up with a good idea to prevent this woman, who represented pleasant memories from his past, from slipping through his fingers. "I know the senator's schedule is open from about noon on. You could come to our offices and I could introduce you to him. I'm sure he'd be pleased to speak with someone as well-informed as yourself."

"This would probably work," Lauren said with a smile, trying not to appear too eager, even as she congratulated herself on her success. "Then you and I could hook up later to talk about old times."

CHAPTER
TWENTY-NINE

"GOOD MORNING, SIR," the driver said, snapping to attention with military precision as he opened door of the black Mercedes S-Class under the portico at the Hay-Adams on Sixteenth Street Northwest. A luxury car and a top tier luxury hotel. Maxime Evrémonde was used to traveling in style.

Beneath his expensive camel-colored overcoat and manicured nails, however, there lay a hard and untamed rogue. His career had started with dug-out canoes, sleeping without a tent in disease and vermin-infested African jungles, and slicing peoples' throats with a 200-millimeter blade. Like many fellow veterans of the Commandement des Opérations Spéciales, the French Special Forces, he had moved easily from uniform into a career as a soldier of fortune. He soon found this dark world of mercenary adventure to be a gateway to lucrative business opportunities. Some went for drugs or blood diamonds, but for Maxime Evrémonde, it was the profitable market in buying and selling *people*. A fifty-kilo "liver donor" was worth as much or more in Doha or Dubai as many kilos of unrefined opiates.

Though he maintained a luxurious apartment in the Seventh Arrondissement in Paris, Evrémonde now spent much of his time among the elite of the Gulf States. His skill at sourcing and selling human beings as commodities had made him a whispered household word throughout the region. This had brought him to the attention of Hamad Abdallah bin-Sharia, and to the place he was headed on this drizzly Thursday morning.

Rain was falling when S-Class glided smoothly into the passenger zone in front of the steel and glass office block on Colshire Drive in McLean. The driver had the door open and the umbrella deployed before Evrémonde had put his cell phone into his overcoat pocket.

"I'll call you," he said with just a trace of a French accent.

The driver nodded.

Agnes Wickfield was waiting in the lobby and she whisked Hambledon Global's VIP guest around the security turnstiles. Maxime Evrémonde should never have to experience the degradation of going through a metal detector.

They took a private elevator directly to Hambledon's inner sanctum, where Westley Carker was waiting in his office.

"Thank you, Agnes," was his way of saying "close the door on your way out."

She was used to a career as a factotum, being seen but not heard. She didn't mind. She enjoyed just being in a world of intriguing characters and mysterious doings.

"Good flight, I trust," Carker said, extending his hand.

"Fifteen hours on Qatar Airways, but it was nonstop and the champagne was acceptable."

"I thought you might come in with Mr. bin-Sharia tonight on the Gulfstream."

"I wanted to come in ahead of the sheikh to discuss matters with you," Evrémonde said, taking a seat.

"Everything's ready for his visit," Carker said. "You and I will be meeting him at the Marshalton Airport tonight at 1900. Olconian's chief of staff will be there. Transport will be a bulletproof Mercedes G63. Armor level BR6, which will stop assault rifle bullets. We'll have the sheikh's favorite Macallan forty-year Scotch in the car."

"This should put his mind at ease," Evrémonde said. He had always thought the sheikh went way overboard with security, but it was *his* money, and *his* obsessive paranoia.

"We'll take him directly to the safe house near Ravensworth where we'll meet the senator. Nobody knows about this. The house was built back in the 1850s and used as a CIA safe house in the 1950s. They used to debrief defectors and hostiles there. There will be two protection levels beyond whomever the sheikh brings. My people will be on site, and the ATF gentlemen are on call. If all goes well, you'll never see them."

"*Très bien*," the Frenchman said without smiling. He was pleased, but not overly impressed. "Monsieur bin-Sharia has grand hopes for America. There are potential customers in the tens of thousands. What are your strategic plans?"

"We are in the final stages of setting up on some formerly public land in New Mexico that was made available to us through one of Senator Olconian's public-private initiatives. I'll be flying down next week to get things started and to peruse the existing infrastructure."

"I hope you are planning safeguards to prevent a repeat of what happened last week in Montana," Evrémonde grumbled. "That was a disaster for you, and nearly a disaster for the sheikh. I hope you will be containing the press, and the sheikh will not be tainted by a continuing public relations fiasco."

"Fortunately, the local police are treating it as an open-and-shut case of rival gang hostility. The national press are treating it as 'Wild West' violence."

"How quaint," Evrémonde mused. "Apparently no one survived to tell the tale. Correct?"

"Mr. Tom R. Brach, who might have spilled the whole backstory on the affair, will not be talking. As you may have heard, he was killed during an attempted mugging yesterday."

"I do hear Washington is a dangerous place," Evrémonde said with a nod. "On one hand, I was sorry this happened. Monsieur Brach showed so much promise. Bringing the goods in by air was *excellante*. So much faster than by land. I regret the failure, which brings me to this meeting today. We must be assured the security for the *next* operation will be as 'bulletproof' as your Mercedes."

———

The clock on the wall read 11:21 as Lauren Stahling stepped into the lobby of the Hart Senate Office Building on Capitol Hill on Tuesday morning. She was nine minutes early, but Chad Marltyn was already waiting.

"Lauren," Marltyn shouted the moment she walked in the door. "Over here"

"Hi Chad, great to see you. I'd like to put this big bag of conference paperwork junk in a coin locker."

"You don't have to do that," he said. "Here, I'll carry your heavy bag and we'll go right up."

As Agnes Wickfield had done for Maxime Evrémonde that same morning at Hambledon, Marltyn escorted Lauren around the security checkpoints and directly to an elevator reserved for congressional staff. It was discreetly *not* covered by CCTV cameras.

"You look nice," he said as he pushed the button for private staff entrance on the sixth floor.

"Thank you, she said, returning his smile. Under her fall coat, she wore a businesslike burgundy dress with a mid-length skirt and a conservative neckline, the sort of attire someone might wear to an assessors' conference.

"How was the conference this morning?" Marltyn asked.

"It was, um, interesting," she said. "But I'm sure not nearly as interesting as what the senator has to say."

"I told him about you," Marltyn said eagerly. "He's anxious to meet you."

They passed through the outer office and went directly into Olconian's private office with its outward-facing windows.

"Senator, this is Lauren Ransdell," Marltyn said as Olconian stood and came around his desk.

"How do you do, sir," she said.

"Miss Ransdell," he said, shaking her gloved hand. "I'm always happy to meet a member of the public who's well-informed about the environmental issues with which we grapple."

He was a big man of ample girth and sallow complexion who apparently spent little time actually experiencing the great outdoors.

"It's exciting to see what you are doing so much with the nonprofits and NGOs," she said, steering him toward the basket of beneficiaries of his legislation which included Hambledon Global—without actually mentioning Hambledon.

"There's been a public-private partnership in public land stewardship for years," he said, obviously used to pontificating on the topic.

Like most people in Olconian's line of work, he liked to talk, and with his schedule open for the early afternoon, he happily persisted, liberally encouraged by Lauren's feigned, but friendly, interest. Knowing what she did of his backstory in human trafficking, she found this more than a little bit strange. Finally the jovial orator handed her the perfect opportunity.

"The nonprofits can raise money from private donors, and they've taken over dozens of infrastructure and visitor experience projects in national parks, and on public and private land," he said. "With donor funding, the nonprofits are taking over responsibility and authority for public and private spaces, especially in areas where less public oversight exists."

"In Montana," she interrupted, "we recently had an unseemly incident with a nonprofit called Sunrise Land Holdings, who were a part of one of your partners called Hambledon Global."

"Oh, that was terrible, wasn't it?" Olconian said with dismay. "But let me quickly add that Sunrise was not a *part* of Hambledon, they were merely associated, *briefly* associated, with Hambledon."

That's not what it said in the Hambledon brochure Tom R. Brach handed me in Billings, Lauren thought, though she continued to smile.

"You can be assured Hambledon has moved quickly to distance themselves from Sunrise, which I understand has been shut down," Olconian said in a reassuring tone.

When he saw her expression was one of skepticism, he moved quickly to reclaim her affability.

"Let me show you how conscientious and committed our nonprofit partners are," he said, putting his hand on her knee—at which she winced. "The philanthropist behind Hambledon Global is coming to Washington. I'm meeting him informally for a private meeting at an undisclosed location *tonight.*"

"That sounds very mysterious," Lauren said with a smile.

"It is, but I'll be able to tell you all about it tomorrow," Olconian said with a wink as he stepped out of the office, promising to have coffee sent in.

———

Jim Hammer looked at his phone as it pinged with an incoming text message.

Sntr confirmed he'll be at house for meet,

Lauren wrote.

I'm almost done here.

Hammer returned a "thumbs up" emoticon and went back to scanning the rural landscape forty-some miles southwest of Capitol Hill.

He was back out on Route 28 surveying the ground approaches to the airport a dozen miles south of Marshalton. This being a small airport, there was no control tower, so things were generally quiet, with people who hangared their private planes here making touch-and-go practice landings. He saw the approach to the single runway was northwest to southeast. This meant that if you were about to take off in a business jet and needed a lot of runway, you'd begin your takeoff roll as far to the northwest as possible.

There was a paved road about a half mile to the north, and a gravel road through an open field connecting this thoroughfare to the tarmac. If someone was planning to board a bizjet just before takeoff, this was the place to be. If one was to be watching this transpire, a pile of discarded shipping pallets Hammer found lying in a field provided an ideal observation place—or sniper stand. Hammer spent about fifteen minutes rearranging the pallets—just in case it was he who needed to use this pile of pallets.

Nobody noticed or cared.

When he was finished, he climbed back into his pickup and headed north.

On Wednesday, when he had tailed Milino and Foullon northbound from here, they had taken Route 28, the "main road," following it up through Manassas to Braddock Road and east to the Ravensworth house. Why would they *not* go this way? It *was* the main highway. All the navigation apps on any phone took you this way. It was more than intuitive; it was the *only* way.

Or was it?

Hammer had long ago learned the intuitive way was never the *only* way, and very often it was not the *best* way. As he studied his paper highway map, tracing a straight line between the airport and the Ravensworth house, he could see the main highway did not follow a straight line. There was another minor road, actually a succession of minor roads, which was a straighter, shorter connection.

Should he check it out? Why not?

As he turned onto it and began driving it, he discovered a surprising lack of stop signs to slow his progress. As he cruised along, he recalled the "main highway" was complicated by a frustrating number of traffic lights and intersections, not to mention the road work between Gainesville and Manassas. The weatherman on the radio was talking about a big storm which would be moving in later tonight with a lot of rain, so this would complicate traffic through construction zones.

It was open country, so there were relatively few cars, and almost no small towns requiring him to slow down. What he did see were a sizable number of small trucks and delivery vans. This told him people who drove from place to place for a living favored this route for its efficiency, and for the time it saved driving point to point.

Time is money, and if Jim Hammer needed it, he could put his money on this as the ideal shortcut between Ravensworth and the airport.

CHAPTER
THIRTY

AS AUSTIN Olconian lumbered through the private reception room outside his private office to rejoin his guest, Chad Marltyn took him aside.

"Senator, a word?"

"Yes, Chad?"

"You weren't supposed to tell *anyone* about tonight," Marltyn whispered. "You and I are the only ones in this office who are supposed to know the sheikh is coming to town. Carker was very explicit that we can't let anybody in on this information until *after* he goes back to Doha. You just told her about him."

"What can it hurt?" the senator said. "Lauren…Miss Ransdell…she's a friend of yours, right? She's okay. I didn't name names…didn't not tell her *who* he was. I don't even know *where* this meeting is going to be. You can just tell her to keep those pretty lips of hers sealed. You don't think she's going to figure out from *this* that our friends are importing girls for naughty purposes, do you? Who in the world would even guess such a thing? Don't worry. She'll never know. It's a meeting. Everybody on the Hill has ten or twelve meetings every day."

"But..."

"Listen, I've got an idea," Olconian interrupted. "I'll handle it. I'll just invite her to join me when the Hambledon driver comes to take me to the meeting. That way, we've got an eye on her so we *know* she doesn't tell anybody."

"How are you going to get her to agree to this?"

"She likes me," Olconian said with a sly wink. "I can tell. I have a way with women. Send in some lunch."

"Miss Ransdell," the senator said, announcing his return. "Are you hungry? I'm starving. I just told Mr. Marltyn to have the girl send in some sandwiches. They usually send in a selection. Are there any you especially like or don't like?"

"I'm, um, easy," Lauren said with a smile. She decided not to tell him that being around him left her with not much of an appetite.

As the sandwiches arrived, Lauren picked a ham and cheddar and Olconian resumed his discussion of the wonderful things which flowed from Senate Bill this, or Senate Bill that.

As she nibbled a sea salt potato chip, she tried to square his flowery words with the darker portrait painted by Tim Tommis. As he occasionally touched her leg to emphasize this point or that, she recalled Tommis having said he imagined himself a ladies' man. When he stood up to grab some papers from his desk, she recrossed her legs and pulled the hem of her skirt over her knee.

It came as a surprise when he said it—but it almost made sense.

"Listen, Ms. Ransdell," he said with a sparkle in his eye. "I have an idea. As I told you, I'm meeting the generous contributor behind Hambledon Global tonight for a private meeting. The Hambledon car will be picking me up. Why don't *you* join me? We can continue our conversation on the way, and then you'll have a chance to meet this man. The driver will be coming straight back to the district. We can drop you at your hotel."

"Thank you," she said hesitantly. "This is very generous of you."

"Not at all."

She rapidly weighed all the pros and cons in her mind. Hammer's plan was to disrupt the party at the Ravensworth house, and Lauren was determined not to be left out. This way, she would not have to interrupt what he was doing with the necessity of a rendezvous because she would *already* be there.

Why not? It's a crazy idea, but then this whole adventure is a crazy idea. Again, as so often in the past week, she surprised herself with how she was feeling more excitement than apprehension.

"Sure, that would be great," she said, smiling. "I'd like it. Will Mr. Marltyn be joining us?"

"He'll be meeting us there about eight o'clock," the senator said. "He'll be going down separately to meet our philanthropist's private jet. They're getting in around sevenish at a small airport down there. We'll be leaving here in an hour or so. Your cup is empty. I'll have more coffee brought in."

———

Chad Marltyn met the Hambledon Global car and driver on Maryland Avenue a block east of his office at half past four. As he'd been told, it was a dark blue Acura TLX with Virginia plates, the type of anonymous sedan common on the Hill. He said hello to the driver, hoping for conversation, but the man said nothing.

Marltyn had no idea where they were going. It wasn't

a major airport, like Dulles, and there were numerous small general aviation fields all over that part of the state.

They turned south on Fourteenth Street and crawled onto the George Mason Bridge; their destination could have been anywhere in northern Virginia.

Within a half hour, they passed through Manassas and continued south on Route 28, deeper into the rural countryside. Finally, just over a rolling hill and around a corner, Marltyn saw the airport—a long straight strip of asphalt lined by lights.

There was a cluster of metal buildings near one end of the single runway, but the driver continued on the road parallel to the runway to a place where there was just a single building. Here, he turned into a large gravel parking lot. The few vehicles parked here and there around the buildings seemed unattended, but at the edge of the parking lot near the paved taxiway, a large black Mercedes S-Class luxury sedan was idling.

Marltyn's driver pulled in next to the S-Class, leaned over his shoulder and spoke for the first time.

"Mr. Evrémonde would like to see you," he said, nodding to the black car.

As soon as Marltyn had stepped out of the Acura, the driver pulled away and drove toward the nearby building.

The left rear door of the long black car opened and the man inside gestured to Marltyn to get in.

"My name is Maxime Evrémonde," he said in a noticeable, though not thick, French accent. "I understand Monsieur Carker briefed you on our meeting today with Hamad bin-Sharia?"

"He said Mr. bin-Sharia was flying in today, and I guess this is the airport where he's arriving. Mr. Carker told me he and I would be meeting him. He didn't mention you."

"*C'est bon. C'est très bien,*" Evrémonde replied with a guttural laugh. "This is just as well. Enough to say that I am a business colleague of the sheikh. I source merchandise on behalf of the sheikh which Monsieur Carker imports into America."

"Is Mr. Carker here yet?"

"He's late," Evrémonde said in a perturbed tone, as he glanced at his Emile Pequignet Royale Titane wristwatch. "That's not like him. Englishmen are usually punctual. Is your boss, the senator, meeting us at the house?"

"Yes, of course, he's looking forward to it."

"We, the sheikh and I greatly appreciate the work he does to shield us from your government agencies that do what you call 'oversight.' This has been helpful and will be much more appreciated and we expand our operations in America and begin importing our products and services on a much larger scale."

"The senator certainly appreciates the sheikh's generous donations to his electoral campaigns through Hambledon Global. Of course he can't say too much publicly about foreign donations, especially from that part of the world, but he really is thankful."

"I hope he appreciates the female companionship Monsieur bin-Sharia and Monsieur Carker have provided for him from time to time," Evrémonde said with an expression which came as close a smile as the wily Frenchman could bring to his impassive face.

"He has been personally quite lonely since the divorce, yes."

"And the ladies to whom Monsieur bin-Sharia introduced *you* at the conference in Geneva last year? Evrémonde said. "Did they meet with your approval?"

"Of course," Marltyn said nervously. He was still intimidated by the high society hookers to whom he had been introduced. *I'm no longer in Yakima,* he had thought to himself.

"*Très bien.*"

"The aircraft is on final approach," the driver said through the intercom from the front. Marltyn and Evrémonde looked up. The landing lights were just coming into view in the distance.

Evrémonde again looked at his Emile Pequignet Royale Titane.

"It is not yet 1800. The flight is more than one hour early," Evrémonde complained. "*Où est ce maudit homme?* Where is Carker? He asked to meet me here at 1700, and he cannot be troubled to be on time!"

The sleek white jet, 99.9 feet of polished luxury, with its gracefully upturned wingtips barely kissed the runway in a perfect landing. The G650ER, the extended range version of the basic Gulfstream G650, has a nonstop capability of 8,600 miles, 1,700 miles farther than the straight line distance from Doha. With its extra fuel, the ER needs 6,300 feet of runway to take off, but with most of the fuel expended, the sheikh's Gulfstream used much less distance for landing. The aircraft was on the taxiway within moments.

As soon as the pilot throttled back the engines, the door popped open and the airstair unfolded. Two bearded men emerged to cautiously survey the scene. Each carried a sidearm and was wearing a black windbreaker with a logo depicting swords crossed over a palm tree. By the way they shuddered slightly, Marltyn sensed they had not dressed for a climate entirely different from Qatar.

When the driver of the S-Class stepped out of the car and Evrémonde followed, Marltyn decided this was his cue to do the same.

The driver walked briskly toward the two armed

men, who recognized him. By the time they had shaken hands, Evrémonde had reached them, and he too was greeted cordially.

"This is Monsieur Marltyn, he is chief of staff to Senator Olconian, who we will be meeting shortly," Evrémonde said in introduction. "These gentlemen are Monsieur bin-Sharia's *gardes du corps*, his *défenseurs*."

Neither of the bodyguards smiled nor spoke.

Only when they signaled toward the Gulfstream door did Hamad Abdallah bin-Sharia appear on the airstair. He was a man of medium height and stout girth, with a clipped black mustache and cautious expression. Marltyn half expected him to be dressed in the flowing robes of the stereotypical sheikh, but he wore a business suit, expensive but not ostentatious, with a dark blue tie. Like many businessmen, he carried a large laptop case.

Marltyn saw in him a man in command of his business universe, yet who was apprehensive of his immediate surroundings. He was a larger-than-life character who sought secret meetings with people whom he theoretically trusted—because he was never really sure *anyone* could be trusted.

He descended the steps and walked directly toward Evrémonde. After a perfunctory handshake, Evrémonde introduced Marltyn, whose hand the sheikh shook while maintaining cold, riveting eye contact. Evrémonde ushered him into the S-Class, closed the door and ordered his driver to go to where the blue Acura was parked.

Marltyn and the two bodyguards were left to walk the short distance to the big building. As they arrived, the roll-up door was being raised and the two cars driven inside. Sharing the space was a vehicle which reminded Marltyn or a large Jeep or Land Rover. He heard Evrémonde describe it to the sheikh as an armored Mercedes G63 with three rows of seating.

"Bulletproof?" bin-Sharia asked.

"They tell me it is rated at armor level BR6."

"Which means?"

"Impervious to 7.62mm assault rifle bullets. The underside is protected from hand grenades. Carker promised he would put a bottle of Macallan forty-year inside."

"Where *is* Carker?" bin-Sharia asked, looking around.

"He's late."

"We won't wait," the sheikh said. "Call him. Tell him to meet us at the rendezvous site. Let us go *immediately*."

Marltyn was tucked into the third row between one of the sheikh's bodyguards and one of the Hambledon drivers, while the other driver took the wheel next to the second bodyguard. Evrémonde and the sheikh took the comfortable middle row, the one which had the bar. The Scotch had, it fact, been delivered, but bin-Sharia showed no interest.

As the roll-up door descended, the G63 left the airport area and headed north toward Route 28.

CHAPTER
THIRTY-ONE

WESTLEY CARKER RECEIVED the news of Hamad bin-Sharia's early arrival in a phone call from one of the Hambledon drivers at the airport. There had been no communication from the Gulfstream as the sheikh always insisted on radio silence while traveling.

Carker had been trying to get out of his office in McLean for the better part of an hour, but one thing after another kept popping up. It was a Thursday afternoon, and all of the people in the office who were planning to take Friday off were nagging him for attention.

Finally, it was just a matter of shuffling a few papers into piles. As he reached to pull his coat and hat from the rack, the intercom buzzed.

"*Yes*," he said impatiently as he picked up the phone.

"You have a visitor, sir," Agnes Wickfield said.

"I'm in a hurry, Miss Wickfield, and I am *not* expecting a visitor."

"She says it's urgent. Promises it won't take long."

"What's her name?"

"It's Mavis Carlsruud, sir."

"What? *Mavis* Carlsruud?" Carker said, taken aback.

"There was a *Davis* Carlsruud. He was one of the Minnesota gangsters who murdered our people in Montana, but he's *dead*. I do not know a *Mavis* Carlsruud."

"She says she is his *sister*," Agnes explained. "She does promise it won't take long."

"Okay, in that case, send her in," Carker said impatiently. "But I only have a moment. I'm overdue at the Marshalton Airport and I have to drive *myself*."

If it had been anyone else, he would have sent her away, but this was *Mavis* Carlsruud, and her presence piqued his interest. Curiosity has a strong pull.

Closing the door behind her, Mavis entered Carker's rosewood paneled office almost timidly. Whereas Davis Carlsruud was big and brash, his sister was what anyone might expect of a quiet, understated, middle-aged Midwesterner. She had rosy cheeks, blue Scandinavian eyes, and a reserved smile.

"Miss Carlsruud," Carker said, extending his hand cordially. "I'm pleased to make your acquaintance. I didn't know Davis had a sister, but I can see the resemblance. Let me convey my condolences to your family on his passing."

She came around Carker's desk, approaching him as though she wanted to give him a hug.

How sweet, how pitifully sweet, Carker thought as he stood to embrace her.

It was only after it was too late he saw her pulling a seven-inch knife made of bone or antler out of her coat.

Of course it was a *bone-bladed* weapon! There was a metal detector downstairs.

This was the last thing that ever crossed his mind—both literally and figuratively.

"You people murdered my brother," she whispered calmly as she plunged the sharp point into the base of his throat, through his jugular vein and through his wind-pipe. "I cannot let this go."

Easing the dying man gently back into his large, leather executive chair, she twisted the knife, pulled it out and wiped it thoroughly on his shoulder. As the knife came out, blood spurted and dribbled down his front and onto the carpeting.

When the spurting stopped, indicating his heart had also stopped, she calmly put the knife into her handbag and went back into the office where Agnes Wickfield was on the phone.

Mavis heard the sound of her own name being whispered but pretended she had not.

With a calm Midwestern smile, Mavis gently patted the receptionist's head.

Then, without warning, she took a fistful of Agnes's hair, jerked her head powerfully upward and slammed it back down on the edge of her desk with such force her skull was crushed like a hard-boiled egg falling onto a tile floor.

As Mavis exited the Hambledon Global suite, no one in the outer office paid more than passing notice to the quiet, understated, middle-aged Midwesterner.

———

Assistant Deputy Director Joe Foullon was at the wheel of his Lincoln Town Car when he took the call from Agnes Wickfield. In the midst of the Thursday afternoon rush, New York Avenue was a parking lot, but the on-ramp to Highway 395 looked even worse. Unlike Carker, who had to drive all the way to the Marshalton Airport, Foullon only had to go as far as the Ravensworth house, where Vince Milino was setting up a perimeter. Still, it was going to be a long commute.

"What is it, Agnes?" Foullon said impatiently. "I'm stuck in traffic."

"Mr. Carker just took a visitor who you should know about."

"Who could this be?"

"It's Mavis Carlsruud," Agnes said in a conspiratorial whisper.

"That's *Davis* Carlsruud," Foullon said, rolling his eyes for the benefit of no one. "And he's *dead*."

"No. It's *Mavis* Carlsruud. It's his sister."

"*What*? What *sister*?"

"She's in with Mr. Carker now. She's a very nice lady. Complimented me on the floral arrangement here on my desk."

All sorts of thoughts went through Foullon's mind, but nothing in his imagination could have pictured what was *really* happening at that moment inside the Hambledon Global inner sanctum in McLean.

"Have Carker call me the minute he is done with her."

"I certainly will…wait, I think Mavis is coming out now."

Foullon heard Agnes say something and then there was a loud, dull thump.

"Agnes…*Agnes*? Are you still there?"

After a short pause, the phone hung up.

Foullon dialed back immediately, but Agnes's ATF burner phone went straight to voicemail.

He had decided to take New York Avenue to Fourteenth Street instead of 395, and traffic was finally moving again. Foullon had lost so much time he decided to pay attention to his driving and to make all the traffic lights he could.

It was nearly fifteen minutes before he had a red light

and was able to dial back. He tried Agnes again, and then he tried Carker's cell phone. Voicemail.

What the hell was going on?

He was across the Fourteenth Street Bridge and out into Fairfax County when he decided to pull over and try to find the Hambledon office landline number. When he finally got through, the office had mostly emptied out. It was the end of the day, and everybody was dreading the same traffic mess that was inconveniencing Foullon.

"Hambledon Global," answered the small voice of the last young intern left in the office. "How may I direct your call?"

Foullon asked for Carker, and after a long pause, the intern came back on to say he was not picking up.

"Has he left for the day?"

"I did not see him leave. No, sir."

"Could you just pop into his office and tell him Joe Foullon wants to speak with him?"

"I'm afraid I do not have authorization to 'just pop into' his office. Only senior staff are permitted to do that."

"Ask a senior person to do it."

"They've all left for the day."

"Is Agnes Wickfield there?"

"I believe so."

"Then ask *her!*" Foullon said with growing frustration.

"I'm afraid that I do not have authorization."

"*Please* just ask her. This is *urgent.*"

"Okay," the small voice said after a long pause.

Foullon did not expect what came next.

"*Oh my god!*"

"What happened?"

"Miss Wickfield must have had a stroke. Her head is on her desk and she does not seem to be breathing."

"Call 9-1-1 and go look in on Carker," Foullon

demanded. "I'll take all responsibility for you breaking protocol. You will *not* get fired for doing this."

When the small voice came back, it was with graphic descriptions of "blood everywhere" punctuated by panic-stricken sobs.

———

Not yet alerted to the early arrival of Hamad bin-Sharia's Gulfstream,

Vince Milino and Cory Sykes had stopped at a coffee place at a quarter to six for some pastry and sixteen-ounce double cappuccinos. As they had been briefed, the sheikh's airplane was not expected until around seven o'clock, so they had time.

It was going to be a long night, but between the sheikh's bodyguards and Carker's men, security for the meeting was in good hands. Milino had thoroughly scrutinized the Ravensworth house and its approaches. If all went well, the long night would be a slow night for Milino and Sykes.

Milino had just bitten into his bear claw when his phone buzzed with a text message. Assuming it was a routine call from Foullon, he took a long sip of hot cappuccino before he looked to see who it was.

Aron Kruegher!

What?

He had not heard from Kruegher since he disappeared during the gravel pit shootout in Montana a week ago. The message read:

> I'm here in DC

> I know what's going down. We need to talk. Now.

Where have you been all this time?

Milino replied, typing feverishly.

Why did you not return my calls?

I barely escaped. Everybody else got shot by the Minnesota gang.

How did you get back here? What are you doing?

I'll tell you in person. We have to meet.

When?

One hour.

I'm in the middle of something.

I know. BUT we need to meet before Sheikh shows up. Urgent.

Ok Where?

You know Ensign Ernie's?

Yes.

Text me when you arrive. This is important!

Vince Milino stared at his screen trying to imagine what Kruegher was talking about and why he'd been silent for a week.

"Who's that?" Sykes asked.

"Somebody from Montana. Agent Aron Kruegher. He was in the shootout where all those Hambledon people died. He survived. He's been off the grid since. He's here. Wants to meet...now."

"Do we have time?"

"We better *make time*. If you knew Krueger, you'd understand. He can be a real intense demon, and not in a good way."

About forty miles south, at the side of a country road in rural Fairfax County, Jim Hammer lay Aron Kruegher's cell phone next to several others on the passenger seat of his blue Chevy pickup, covered them carefully with an old sweatshirt, and started the ignition.

The radio came on with a weather update. It would be clear for the next few hours, but the storm which was blowing in around midnight would be bringing enough rain for "localized small stream flooding." Hammer expected to be through with his work by then, but he knew weather reports, like life itself, were all too often subject to change.

CHAPTER
THIRTY-TWO

"THERE IT IS," Senator Austin Olconian said, pointing to a mailbox at the side of Braddock Road with a weathered wooden duck decoy mounted as a decoration on top. The Hambledon Global driver who had picked them up at the Hart Senate Office Building was already signaling.

"You've been here before, then?" Lauren asked.

"No, but Chad told me what they told him. They mentioned the duck."

"A lot of duck hunting around here?"

"Chesapeake Bay," he said, patting her on her knee again. He must have thought she was being friendly and conversational. "Tidewater country. I've been out a few times myself. Donors like to take you shooting."

After a five-minute drive on a winding gravel road through thick stands of red maple and ash, the nondescript silver Audi A6 came to a stop in front of a white, two-story, federal-style home adjacent to a smaller outbuilding.

Tired of the senator's playful pats, Lauren was happy to be out of the car.

"This is a fine old house, isn't it," he said. "This is part of William Fitzhugh's old Ravensworth plantation from the early 1700s. It was the biggest land grant ever in Fairfax County, but they broke it up after the Revolutionary War. They tell me this house was built by a prominent Virginia family in the 1850s. I don't remember the name."

"Slave holders?" Lauren asked.

"Probably," he replied, missing her intended irony.

"They tell me the CIA once used this place to interrogate Russian spies," he said in a theatrical tone.

"Oh, how fun," Lauren said sarcastically.

The driver, a man in his late twenties with a man-bun and close-cropped black beard that looked painted on, went up the steps ahead of them, unlocked the door and went in.

When Lauren started to follow, Olconian touched her on the arm and cautioned her to wait.

"It looks like we're the first to arrive," he said. "Our young man needs to check everything."

"I see what you were saying about this being a *secret* meeting," she said.

"He's very careful. Our philanthropist friend is… well…a bit paranoid."

"Better safe than sorry, I guess."

When man-bun returned and gave them the high sign, Lauren and the senator ascended the stairs. She let him go up first, while man-bun perched himself like buzzard of the porch, keeping a watch on the long driveway that disappeared into the trees.

The house had a two-story foyer, with exposed beams and colonial crown molding, and the two rooms of the double parlor were separated by an overstated archway. There were fireplaces in both rooms, but neither was lit. A furnace coughed from somewhere within the house, but it was only slightly warmer in here than outside. Lauren had a good excuse to leave her gloves on.

There were several pieces of upholstered furniture in one of the rooms, including a short couch, while the room at the front of the house contained a well-worn dining table with six chairs perched on a large, faded rug. The senator took a seat on the couch in the farther room and slyly gestured for Lauren to join him. She pretended she did not notice his subtle invitation and took a seat in one of the upholstered chairs across the room from his teasing fingers.

"While we're waiting, why don't you tell me about Hambledon's mysterious benefactor," she said. "I'm so very intrigued, and you haven't even told me his name."

"He's very careful about his identity and his dealings. Like I said, he's kind of obsessed. But since you're going to meet him anyway, I don't see any harm in your knowing about him."

"I'm all ears."

"His name is Hamad Abdallah bin-Sharia. He's from a family of wealthy Middle Eastern oil sheikhs from Qatar. He has generously endowed the charitable work of the Hambledon Global Advocacy Group, who in turn have also been very kind in their donations to my past and upcoming campaigns. Chad can give you all the details if you're interested."

"I can see why he's so secretive," Lauren said. "It might not look good to have an oil sheikh donating to a senatorial campaign."

"Everything is legal," Olconian assured her. "It goes through Hambledon's North American operations, and they're a registered Virginia company. All the paperwork is in order. We've had lawyers go through everything."

"You said his family is in oil," Lauren said. "Is he in the family business himself?"

"He's into philanthropy, mainly. He gives away a lot to NGOs, mainly through Hambledon. It's intricate. He also has an international personnel business. He arranges employment contracts. He does this through the Hambledon Global offices in London and Doha."

"What kind of employment? Like high tech?"

"It's complicated, but mainly on the lower end of the pay scale."

"How low on the pay scale?"

"They do things differently over there. Throughout the Gulf States, not just Qatar, but everywhere from Kuwait to Bahrain, they use an employment sponsorship system called '*kafala*.'"

"I've heard the term," Lauren said, curious to get him to elaborate on bin-Sharia's part in the scheme. "But maybe you could explain it to me."

"Basically, it's a simple sponsorship program, but that's not out of the ordinary. All over the world, even in this country, you have people paying fees to recruiters or employment agencies to get them jobs. *Kafala* is used particularly with seasonal or even full-time low-wage and low-skilled workers, especially domestic workers, from developing countries. These kinds of temporary labor programs are used all over the world, where employees are tied to their sponsoring employer, who pays their travel expense to get them to the places where the jobs are, and the workers pay them back."

"I've heard they have to work for the same people until they pay off what they owe their bosses?"

"Of course."

"Doesn't *that* smack of indentured servitude?"

"Some people might say so, but it's a different culture in other parts of the world. There are international human rights organizations who look into these things all the time. Even the UN agency regulating international labor standards says *kafala* should not be eliminated. Workers get hired, they do their jobs and they *do* get paid. Millions of them."

"You have to admit it's a system ripe for exploitation of people," Lauren asserted. "And here we are, in a house built two hundred years ago by slave traders. Ironic, isn't it."

"These people are not slaves, *per se*," Olconian replied defensively. "They signed up of their own accord because they were eager to send cash to sustain their families back home. There are domestic workers in *this* country who…"

"This country?" Lauren said pointedly. "This reminds me of what we were talking about in your office…the Hambledon subsidiary…Sunrise Holdings. I'm sure you heard the stories about sex trafficking being involved. Did the sheikh know about this?"

"Well…"

"Isn't human trafficking a sordid first cousin to temporary labor contracting?"

"I'm not prepared to say…listen, let's just call it food for thought and pick up the conversation later," he said smoothly. "If you'd excuse me, I have a few text messages to send before it gets too late."

––––––––

It was getting dark as Vince Milino wheeled the big black Escalade into the gravel lot outside Ensign Eddie's Crab Shack. He parked in a space in the lot about as far as possible from the low tumbledown building where they served blue crab by the bucket. He studied the parked cars, imagining which one Aron Kruegher might be driving. Most of the plates were local, Virginia and Maryland, and one from Pennsylvania. None from out west.

"Let's take a look," Milino told Agent Cory Sykes. "Cover me while I go peek into the windows."

Milino peered in but saw no familiar faces. He was about to step inside for a closer look when his phone buzzed.

> I saw you park way over there

read the message that popped up with Kruegher's name.

> Come around back. Picnic tables.

"He's on the other side of the building," Milino told Sykes. "Let's go see what he wants."

There was a group of tables out there which were probably filled to capacity during warm summer evenings, but which now lay unused with a scatter of fallen leaves on them. The scene was dark and forlorn. Strings of outdoor lights hung above the tables, but they were turned off. The only light came from the steamed-up kitchen windows of the restaurant. It was a world away.

"Okay, Kruegher," Milino announced. "We're here. Where are you and what's going on. We don't have a lot of time."

Suddenly, a tall man with a heavy gray coat and a gray ball cap stepped quietly out of the shadows. He was more unshaven than bearded, but his whiskers were too long and scruffy to be fashionable.

"I'm afraid Kruegher couldn't be here tonight," Jim Hammer said, holding up the cell phone he had picked out of Kruegher's overcoat pocket before he tossed it over the cliff in Montana.

"Where's Kruegher?" Milino said insistently. "He's been texting me all afternoon about a meeting."

"He couldn't make it, but his phone did," Hammer said, tossing the phone onto the table with a gloved hand.

"Where is he?"

"Under at least two feet of snow in a crevice at the bottom of a cliff in Montana. Feeding coyotes, I suppose."

"And if I understand it right, you're admitting to the killing of a federal agent?"

"Is that a rhetorical question?"

"One more question before you follow him into oblivion," Milino asked as he and Sykes reached for their guns. "Who are *you*?"

"I'm the last man…" Hammer started to say.

By the time that the two agents had their weapons out, they were staring into the silencer on the muzzle of an ATF-issued Glock 19M—Aron Kruegher's own sidearm.

Thwop! Thwop!

The two shots were delivered in such rapid succession that by the sound, they came as one.

"I'm the last man…" Hammer continued, completing his sentence for the benefit of no other living creature within earshot. "I'm the last man who Kruegher ever saw. I guess I am the same for you."

With this, he pulled Milino's cell phone out of his pocket, unlocked it with Tim Tommis's magic algorithm and retrieved the personal numbers for Deputy Director Darwin Farthers and Assistant Deputy Director Joe Foullon.

Picking up Kruegher's phone again, Hammer composed a group text to both Farthers and Foullon, timing it to be sent in one hour.

"I'm meeting Agent Milino in a few minutes," it read.

"I will be coming to find each of you soon. Yours, Kruegher."

He powered Kruegher's phone off and gently placed it back in his pocket. The ghost of Aaron Kruegher may or may not be finished with his mischievous messaging from the netherworld.

Next, Hammer heaved Kruegher's Glock into the woods—not so far it would never be found, but far enough that whoever found it would have a sense of accomplishment in having located it.

CHAPTER
THIRTY-THREE

"ANY IDEA when they might be coming?" Lauren Stahling asked.

After they had reached their impasse in the discussion of the world of "sponsored labor," Senator Austin Olconian had decided he'd said enough, and had started fiddling with his cell phone. Lauren decided to make herself scarce, so she left the parlor area to idly explore the foyer and other rooms on the first floor. When she finally circled back, he had looked up.

"Soon," the senator answered, glancing up. "I got a text from Chad. They made the pick up at the airport and they are on their way."

"Good," she said. "I can't wait to meet Mr. bin-Sharia. By the way, how does one address a sheikh? Do you say 'Your Majesty' or something?"

"It's just Sheikh."

"All right, then." She smiled. "Sheikh it is."

She strolled idly into the kitchen, which was musty and uninviting. It had the look of a major remodeling perhaps twenty years earlier, but it looked as though it had hardly been used since. Maybe the CIA, or whatever agency had been using the place, no longer served lunch to the spies they interrogated here.

Lauren felt good about making the senator uneasy, and now she was feeling more anticipation than foreboding about meeting the sheikh.

She took out her phone and sent a quick text message to Hammer.

> At house w str. Others coming fr airport now.

The reply popped up a moment later.

> Early!!!

> This is what I'm told. Will stall best I can.

She touched her "send" button, took a breath, and deleted the messages. Looking up and glancing out the kitchen window, Lauren could see a large, lumbering vehicle through the trees. It was moving up the long driveway.

"Looks like they're here," she said, calmly strolling toward the front of the house.

With its four-liter turbo V6, the Mercedes G63 moved easily on the highway, but on a damp, spongy, gravel road, it trudged like a tortoise under the weight of an extra ton of bulletproofing.

The driver made a wide loop and pointed the big vehicle back down the road before he stopped near the Hambledon sedan. Man-bun was already down the front stairs to greet them. First out of the vehicle was the driver, a bearded man in a windbreaker with a crossed swords logo Lauren assumed was the sheikh's trademark. Next, from the passenger's side was a man with a Hambledon jacket like the one which man-bun wore.

Lauren watched as they ceremoniously opened the doors on each side of the middle row of seats. From these emerged two men whom she immediately recognized from the headshots Tim Tommis had shown her—Hamad Abdallah bin-Sharia on the left, clutching his laptop bag as a mother might clutch a child, and Maxime Evrémonde on the right.

Here they are. The Sheikh and the Devil…walking side by side.

The sheikh was soft and rounded in his perfectly tailored suit and a blue necktie that was probably worth its weight in gold. The Devil was taller and harder, with a cold, rough expression on his scarred face.

Scrambling from the third row of seats came another round of men in logo wear, a Hambledon coat, and a crossed swords jacket. Last to emerge was Chad Marltyn in the suit he'd been wearing when Lauren last saw him on the Hill.

The senator was already at the front door as they ascended the front steps. Lauren took this as her cue to retire to the back of the room with the upholstered furniture—to be as far as possible from the meeting table to which she was not invited. A fly on the wall, as it were.

She also wanted to be out of the way when Hammer opened fire. She hoped this would be soon.

First into the house, the two bearded men with the crossed swords jackets did a thorough visual sweep of the rooms, as one would expect of bodyguards, and talked briefly with man-bun. It was apparently decided that, despite their lighter jackets, they would stand guard outside, while the three Hambledon men would position themselves inside.

Only when all of this was in place, did bin-Sharia,

Evrémonde and Marltyn come into the house. When Senator Olconian greeted the Sheikh and the Devil with businesslike handshakes, it was clear that they knew one another, but equally clear this was a serious meeting. There were neither smiles nor good-natured chatter.

The two main attractions remained standing, each scrutinizing the double parlor for himself. The sheikh spoke first.

"Who is this woman?" bin-Sharia asked, glancing at Olconian and nodding toward Lauren. "Is she yours, or is she for *me*?"

Lauren found his directness startling, but not surprising. She was not frightened, but she *did* wish Hammer would get here soon.

"Oh, this is Miss Ransdell," the senator said. "She's an old friend of Mr. Marltyn. She has an interest in the work Hambledon is doing with open space preservation. She was in my office today as we were getting ready to come out here. Since we wanted the fewest number of people to know about this meeting *ahead of time*, I decided to simply ask her to join us. I hope this is acceptable to you gentlemen."

They both nodded slightly, but their expressions conveyed the notion that her presence was not desirable —although they *would* tolerate the unexpected woman.

"Shall we?" Chad Marltyn said, gesturing to the table.

The sheikh naturally took the chair at the head of the table, and Evrémonde the one to his right. The senator sat on bin-Sharia's left, with Marltyn next to him.

Nodding to Olconian, bin-Sharia said. "I appreciate all the work you have done this year on behalf of Hambledon Global."

As with many sons of sheikhs, many years of British boarding school had given him a firm grasp of the language and even a touch of an upper-class accent.

"As I appreciate your own generous donations through Hambledon Global to my reelection last year," Olconian said with an obsequious smile. "And yes, my committee has made a great deal of progress in making public land available for projects such as yours, and to shield your use of the land from public scrutiny."

"Let us look at the status of these projects here in America," the sheikh said, looking at Evrémonde.

"It seems we have an empty chair at the table, *mes ami*," Evrémonde said, glancing at his watch and glowering at the Hambledon men standing in the room. "Where is your boss? Where is Monsieur Carker? We need his report, *non*? He was supposed to meet us at the airport, yet he was late. He was supposed to be *here*, but he is not. I tried to phone him. He does not answer. *Where is he*?"

"I'll try him myself," man-bun said, his usual sullenness overtaken by uneasiness.

Everyone listened as the phone call, amplified on speaker, rang, rang, and defaulted to voicemail.

"*D'accord*," Evrémonde said, rolling his eyes. "We arranged this meeting to hear from *him*, and all about his plans for Hambledon Global in America, but he is not here. Then it must fall to me to report second hand on my meeting with Monsieur Carker yesterday, when he talked of public land in New Mexico and the next phase of his plans for Hambledon Global in America."

"His plans for Hambledon Global in America," bin-Sharia mimicked. "A year ago we were lulled by the promise of his proposal to bring our goods into a desolate corner of America by air. This sounded too good to be true, and it failed in a most exaggerated way before it had barely begun. My accountants are still adding up *my* financial losses."

"As I understand it, this failure was on account of

buyers from Minnesota who got greedy," Olconian interjected.

"It was a failure of Monsieur Brach, the Hambledon man in Montana, to properly scrutinize the Minnesota people," Evrémonde interjected.

"Where is Brach now?" bin-Sharia asked.

"He was murdered by a mugger here in Washington," Evrémonde answered.

"You Americans, and your English cousins, have a saying about a 'final straw,'" bin-Sharia said. "For me, this tardiness by Mr. Carker is the last in a series of intolerable episodes, the final straw for Hambledon Global's American operations. As Mr. Evrémonde is aware, my intention at this meeting was to give Westley Carker *one last chance* to convince me *not* to close down everything in America once and for all. I have already set the wheels in motion with our bankers and our international partners. Only I can stop those wheels, and I see no reason to do so."

"Could we give Carker a deadline to meet with us?" Olconian asked, eager not to see a cash cow go away. "Twenty-four hours?"

"Twenty-four hours?" bin-Sharia repeated, glancing at Evrémonde, who shrugged as though to ask *why not?*

"Twenty-four hours," the sheikh said reluctantly. "No more. I had great hopes for this country as a market, but the less time I spend here the better. Twenty-four hours and it is over. If Carker cannot relieve my apprehensions, we will shut down this."

Just then there was a commotion on the porch, and one of the bodyguards opened the door.

Evrémonde stood from his chair as the guard escorted ATF Assistant Deputy Director Joseph Foullon into the room. One hand gripped the left sleeve of Foullon's overcoat, and the other held a drawn pistol. In his right hand, the federal agent held his badge and ID.

"Is this man okay?" the guard asked in a heavy Middle Eastern accent.

"*Oui,*" Evrémonde said succinctly, taking Foullon's left sleeve from the guard.

"Why are *you* here?" bin-Sharia asked.

"We agreed you and your people would stand off unless needed," Evrémonde said, slightly confused but mostly perturbed. "Do we need you?"

"We have a problem," Foullon said.

"Aside from a breach of procedure, what is the problem?" Evrémonde asked scornfully, underscoring his perception of himself as higher up the food chain than any mere assistant deputy director.

"To begin with, *your friend* Westley Carker has been murdered," Foullon said defiantly. "So that would make this more *your* problem than mine."

No wonder he couldn't make the meeting, Lauren thought to herself.

"*When? Where?*" Olconian asked as he rose to his feet.

"About an hour ago in his office," Foullon said.

"How can you be sure?" Chad Marltyn asked nervously as he too stood.

"Because I was on the phone with his secretary when she was attacked by the same assailant. She's dead too. I confirmed this with another call to the office. I was on the line with an intern when she found Carker's body!"

Silence descended on the room for a moment, until bin-Sharia asked the obvious next question.

"*Who did this?*"

"Before she died, the secretary identified the killer as Mavis Carlsruud."

"Wasn't the head of the Minnesota group who killed

those Hambledon people in Montana named Carlsruud?" Evrémonde asked.

"His name was *Davis* Carlsruud," Foullon said.

"*Davis*? *Mavis*?" Marltyn muttered.

"Hambledon killed her brother. I guess she was out for revenge," Foullon speculated.

"What happened to the Carlsruud woman? Where did she go?"

The conversation was now between Marltyn and Foullon.

"She disappeared. She used a knife to kill Carker and slammed Agnes's skull on a desk. No gunshots. Nobody in the outer office heard anything. They barely noticed a sweet little old lady with a Midwest accent coming and going. She walked away."

"You have to…"

"It's out of our hands. The police were called. They will be handling it. We can't get involved. Not this close to DC. Too suspicious. ATF meddling would kick up too many red flags."

"You said 'to begin with, Carker was murdered.' What other problems were you talking about?" Marltyn asked.

"Agent Vincent Milino, who is supposed to be part of the detail keeping an eye on this place, is missing. This is why I came here myself. I really should not be here."

"*Missing*?"

"He's supposed to be near here and reachable, but he's *not*."

"What happened?" Evrémonde said, inserting himself into the dialogue.

"He told me he was meeting with an agent named Aron Kruegher."

"Who's this?" Evrémonde demanded. "Why did he leave his post to meet this man?"

"Kruegher is one of ours, but he's been off the grid and unreachable since the shootout in Montana a week ago. He never checked in...until he showed up back here *today*. Now Milino's missing as well."

"*Incroyable!*" Evrémonde cursed furiously. "*Putain. Putain! Quel désastre. Quel désastre!*"

"We are finished here," bin-Sharia said angrily. He was the only one at the table who remained seated, and the only one to show no emotion throughout Foullon's narrative and Evrémonde's outburst. "We will leave for the airport *now*. Contact the aircraft. Tell them to prepare for departure *now*."

Slowly standing, he turned to the others and spoke.

"I have long wanted to be part of the American market, where I see a vast appetite for young female servants, for concubines. Why is it so hard to launch a distribution network in this country as I have done on a large scale in the Gulf States and in Europe?"

"Because it's illegal? Because it's *slavery*, and because we abolished slavery in this country a long time ago!"

Lauren Stahling had been biting her tongue all through the earlier conversation, but suddenly she decided she had to speak up. The final straw for her was watching how eagerly Senator Austin Olconian nodded when bin-Sharia mentioned launching "a distribution network."

"You paint yourselves as an international entrepreneur here, and a dignified legislator there, but you're all just a bunch of filthy slave-trading pimps, sitting here so smug in this house built by slave traders two hundred years ago!"

She glared at each of them. Chad Marltyn returned an expression of embarrassment, and Olconian one of defensive awkwardness as the wheels in his head spun for a duplicitous retort. Evrémonde displayed to reaction at all.

Hamad bin-Sharia stared at Lauren angrily.

"It is not permitted for a woman to speak to a man is such a callous manner," he said firmly. "This is the problem with American women. It is their undisciplined tongues. If my wives or my concubines used such ugly language."

"Such as calling a pimp a *pimp*?" Lauren asked rhetorically, matching his firmness.

"You suggest the women for whom I supply employment are somehow abused?"

"*Somehow abused*? I've seen the cages with my own eyes. I've seen Korean teenagers crammed into dog crates and shipped into this country by your Hambledon Global *pimps*. If this is not slavery..."

"All to enjoy a better life under the care of new masters," bin-Sharia said calmly.

"Are you hearing this?" Lauren asked, scowling at the senator and his chief of staff. "This is what you're facilitating. Do you really enjoy being part of this?"

Olconian turned away, while Chad Marltyn just stared into space with a look of chagrin, like a child who never expected to be caught being naughty.

"I've had enough," bin-Sharia said. "We're going to the airport *now*."

Turning to the three Hambledon men, he ordered them to eliminate the source of his displeasure.

"A woman never, ever speaks to *any man* this way," he said, his voice quavering slightly from rage. "Take her outside and *punish her severely*. You may dispose of the body as you see fit, but *leave no trace*."

Two of the three men hesitated slightly, but man-bun stepped forward eagerly, pushing past Olconian while reaching for his sidearm.

As he came toward her, Lauren slid her hand into her purse and took out her .44-caliber revolver.

Many hours earlier in the day, when she had gone into the Hart Senate Office Building, she had intended to stash the weapon in a coin locker before passing through the metal detector. However, Chad Marltyn had appeared and had generously escorted her *around* the metal detector and up the members-only private elevator with no CCTV coverage.

Startled by the sight of the pistol, man-bun raised his own 9mm automatic.

But it was too late.

She squeezed her trigger as his finger closed upon his.

B'Boom!

Two nearly simultaneous shots thundered in a room stilled by uneasiness.

One went wild. One impacted man-bun squarely in the forehead, ripping through a brain whose last thought was disbelief, and carrying away the bun as it exited.

The adrenaline surging through Lauren's arteries compromised neither her skill nor her determination.

Two further men with sidearms partially drawn succumbed to slugs of .44-caliber lead—one which ripped through a chin, and another which disappeared into a left eye socket.

Like most people in law enforcement, ATF Assistant Deputy Director Joseph Foullon had never fired his service weapon outside the range. Yet for decades, as he working his way up through the ranks, and as he allowed himself to be lured into his secret side job in the service of those whom this impetuous woman called "pimps," he had spent many long hours at the ATF gun range.

He was good, he knew what to do, and he did it.

But nobody had ever taught him any of the rules of a *real* gunfight.

For example, you don't draw your gun against someone whose weapon is already raised, and you *never* draw against a woman who was just told she needed to be *punished*.

Foullon was so good, and so fast he had already pulled his Glock 19M from his shoulder holster by the time Lauren's round struck his chin, twisting his head sideways and turning his face into a frothy smudge the color of nearly ripe watermelon pulp.

But alas, this was to be Lauren's last shot.

Two hands seized her wrist as though in a vise.

She felt the gun being twisted from her hand, and her body being hurled off balance and through the air.

As she crashed to the floor, a driving pain shot through her arm from the impact to her right elbow.

She opened her eyes and brushed away her hair in time to watch Maxime Evrémonde slam his boot into her solar plexus with full force.

The room was spinning, and she briefly yearned to just pass out and go numb, but this didn't happen.

As she lay there immobile, she heard the loud, sharp sounds of bin-Sharia's bodyguards bursting through the front door. She heard the echo of shuffling feet and the murmur of voices.

Amid the jumble of sounds in the blurry, whirling world around her, there was a mournful, almost inanimate, squeal. She finally pulled her head together, opened her eyes, and saw the source of the plaintive cry. As Lauren lay crumpled in one corner of the room, another figure lay in the opposite corner.

Several of the others were staring down at Senator Austin Olconian, who had been pulled into a sitting position. He was seated in a pool of his own blood, which slowly flowed from a wound in his inner thigh in regular bubbling spurts, pumped by his failing heart.

The stray 9mm shot which man-bun had fired before he died had struck Olconian in the crotch. Somebody had shoved a wad of cloth, ripped from furniture somewhere, into the wound and this slowed the bleeding.

"What can we do?" Marltyn said in desperation. *"We can't let him die!* We have to call 9-1-1."

"We obviously *cannot* call the ambulance," Evrémonde corrected him disapprovingly.

"He'll die," Marltyn insisted.

Lauren watched as Evrémonde pulled Marltyn aside and whispered in the frightened bureaucrat's ear.

"The bullet cut *l'artère fémorale,* the femoral artery. He cannot be saved. To call the ambulance is futile and endangers the rest of us."

Lauren rose on her good elbow and looked into Chad Marltyn's familiar face, half expecting him to extend his hand to help her up. Instead, he glared at her with an expression of both disbelief and contempt.

"Jesus, Lauren, I can't believe what just happened. You have just so totally...so *totally* fucked this up...you just fucked up *everything.* I can't believe..."

As she stared up at the man she once knew, a man she once knew intimately, Maxime Evrémonde stepped between them and stared down at Lauren with his expressionless face.

"You are a spirited harlot, *n'est ce pas*?" Evrémonde said resolutely as Lauren looked up into the Devil's ice-blue eyes. "You were told *no one* has ever spoken to Sheikh Hamad Abdallah bin-Sharia this way without punishment, but you spoke without fear. From petty servants to self-styled aristocrats, they all face punishment. Yet *you* have fought back as no woman has ever fought back. I can see in *you* something different, something requiring closer examination."

As she staggered to stand up, Lauren was trying to fathom what this meant.

"This woman is not an ordinary insulting whore, nor

a disobedient concubine who must be beaten to death as discipline," the Devil said, turning to the sheikh. "This one is a *jument sauvage*, a rare wild mare in need of careful taming, a *créature sauvage*, which must be *broken*. With your permission, of course, I wish to *keep* this one, to *possess* and break this one. If nothing else, she may be of use to us later as a hostage."

With a nod and a toss of his hand, bin-Sharia turned away and was hustled out the front door by his bodyguards. Evrémonde picked up the revolver, which had fallen in the middle of the room.

"Take this," he said, handing it to Marltyn. "If *mon petite fille* misbehaves at any time as we travel to the airport, press the muzzle into her gut and pull the trigger."

CHAPTER
THIRTY-FOUR

IN THE CENTURY BEFORE LAST, a Prussian field marshal named Helmuth von Moltke, famously coined the phrase "no plan of operations extends with certainty beyond the first encounter with the enemy." Like Murphy's Law, which has a similar idea, it's been paraphrased countless times ever since.

Jim Hammer had been through this before and now he was about to be living it again. He was on his way from Ensign Ernie's to the Ravensworth house when he received Lauren's text message about the *hour-early* arrival of bin-Sharia's Gulfstream. Now he was trying to make up the time and hoping to restore a measure of certainty to his plan of operations.

He drove west on Braddock Road and made a right turn onto the country road he had previously scouted. In daylight, he had also reconnoitered the dirt road off this country road which was like a back door into the Ravensworth house compound. At night, it was completely invisible—but Hammer knew where it was, and he had memorized it well enough to drive the last part of it without lights.

He stopped in a place about thirty yards from the house, pointed his pickup toward the main entrance driveway for a fast exit, killed the ignition and began looking things over with his Oberwerk HD II binoculars. In the light from the house, he could see two cars parked outside. There was a midsize Audi sedan and the Lincoln Town Car, which Foullon had been driving on Wednesday.

He opened Tommis's laptop and launched the real-time global satellite imagery from the GIS satellites. The screen immediately popped up his location with the Ravensworth house beside it. He turned on the infrared, scrolled up and zeroed in.

What he saw startled him.

He had expected to see a house blazing with the heat signatures of multiple people. Instead, he saw only the pinpricks of table lamps and the signatures of just one person whose body temperature was near normal. Four others were much cooler. Hammer had seen enough of these images to understand the situation—four bodies, recently dead, and one person left alive.

Lauren's in there! Hammer thought, momentarily allowing himself to feel an emotion. He caught himself from tipping into panic. He could *not* think this way.

Think analytically. Think and act carefully, tactically.

I'm no good to anyone if I fall into this trap.

As he made his way toward the house, he thought about von Moltke's axiom, and he thought about his own plan for the Ravensworth house. His plan A had gone south at the first encounter with his enemy. Of course, Hammer still held one advantage: His enemies did not even know they were being stalked by a deadly and determined foe.

The situation Hammer now faced wasn't ideal, but he could cope. He had long ago learned that those who are most likely to be blindsided by the laws of Murphy or von Moltke are those without a well-considered plan B.

His plan A had been to end it all at the Ravensworth house, of course, but he had built a sniper's stand at the airport, and he had timed a shortcut to get there if he needed to finish the mission down there.

Hammer checked his Colt M1911 and pocketed two M114 thermite incendiary hand grenades. The last element of his original plan A had been to burn the place down when all had been said and done. This would now be part of plan B.

He carefully approached the Ravensworth house, pausing before ascending the broad stairway. The front door, flanked by cheerily illuminated windows, was inviting, but was it *too* inviting?

Hammer stopped to inspect the whole area for booby traps. After cautiously making his way to the top, he peeked into the interior to look it over visually through the window. What he saw confirmed what he had already seen on infrared. There were bodies scattered on the floor. The person who was alive was in the corner of the second room of a double parlor.

He scrutinized the door for any kind of possible IED, then gently turned the knob. It was unlocked and swung open. He held his breath. Nothing happened. Sometimes, things which seem too good to be true actually *are* that good. In this case, his enemy was operating in ignorance of his presence on the field of operations.

Hammer stepped inside, glanced at the bodies and breathed a sigh of relief when he saw all were male.

"You can lower your weapon, sir," came a feeble voice from the corner as he moved into the double parlor. "I'm the only one left, and I'm in no position to threaten you."

It took Hammer a moment to recognize Senator Austin Olconian. He looked pale and pitiful. His trousers and the lower part of his once-crisp white shirt were soaked in blood.

"What happened here?" Hammer asked.

"That *woman* shot all these people...hidden gun...are they all dead?"

"It looks that way...everyone except you."

"It won't take long," the senator said, speaking from within the cobwebs of an endorphin-fueled haze. "I've lost a lot of blood, haven't I?"

"What *woman*?" Hammer asked, going back to the earlier topic.

"She came to my office this morning...friend of my chief of staff...very attractive...very articulate. We had to invite her to this meeting. Couldn't have her tell anybody about it while the sheikh was in town. Very secret."

"Where is she now? Where is the sheikh? Is he one of these bodies?"

"Evrémonde got the gun away from her before she could shoot the sheikh. She did shoot Foullon. He's the deputy something director of the ATF."

"Did she shoot *you*?"

"No. It was one of the Hambledon people. That one there. His gun went off when she shot *him*. It was a damned accident!"

Olconian chortled a scratchy, rasping laugh at his own comment. He did not have long to live.

"Is that her phone on the table?" Hammer asked, recognizing Lauren's phone.

"Evrémonde took that from her. Left it behind. Says that when the cops come, it will implicate her in her own killing spree."

"Where did they take her?" Hammer asked. "Where did they go?"

"Airport...not Dulles. Some small airport down in

Virginia. Flying back to Doha tonight…taking the woman."

"How many in the car?"

"Sheikh…Evrémonde…a couple bodyguards…in a big, huge Jeep…and the woman, and my chief of staff… my chief of staff *abandoned* me. He took the gun she used."

"How long ago?"

"I don't know. Maybe only five minutes? I thought you were them coming back for me. How long do I have?"

"Unless somebody called 9-1-1 for you an hour ago…"

"Do me a favor?"

"What's that?"

"Put me out of my misery."

"Did you ever think about the misery of those girls who you helped traffic?"

"I'm not *directly* involved."

"Oh sure."

"Fuck you."

"Famous last words," Hammer mused.

And so they were. By the time Hammer walked back from examining the sprawled remains of the dead, the senator had joined them in the past tense.

As he had done at the scenes of the shootouts in Montana, he used the guns of the deceased to put 9mm rounds into the other deceased—just to misdirect any future forensic examination of this massacre. The last bullet was one from Foullon's distinctive ATF-issue Glock 19M. It was fired into the remains of the senator himself.

Hammer took one last look around and retrieved both Lauren's phone and the one that had belonged to Foullon. He opened Foullon's and saw that the delayed group text from the phone of Aron Kruegher to Foullon and

Deputy Director Darwin Farthers had just arrived. Hammer had intended this as a cynical measure to enhance the illusion that Kruegher was still at large, and to put the two men on edge. Having Foullon turn up deceased would double this effect on Farthers.

Hammer walked back through the front door and threw one of the M114 incendiaries into the Ravensworth house. Burning at 4,000 degrees Fahrenheit, it would be well on the way to taking the whole place down before the rainstorm arrived. The forensic team would inherit a nearly impossible mess, but shreds of DNA would probably be found. So too would the jacketed 9mm rounds. The fifty-year-old soft lead .44 rounds from Lauren's pistol would deform into forensically useless globs.

He tossed Foullon's phone into the crevice next to the driver's seat of his Town Car—where it would eventually be discovered "where Foullon had dropped it"—and walked back to his pickup to get his plan B on the road.

———

As he rolled down the long driveway, Jim Hammer turned on his GPS cell phone locator app and keyed in the number for the burner phone Lauren had zipped into the back of one of her tall black boots this morning. To his relief, the blinking light popped up on his phone immediately. The vehicle in which she was riding was only about a dozen miles away and traveling westward on Braddock Road at a cautiously modest speed. Olconian had called it a "big, huge Jeep," so Hammer pictured a large SUV of some kind.

Hammer put his phone into its dashboard holder so he could watch the progress of the other vehicle, and made the left turn *off* Braddock onto his shortcut road. The race was on.

As he drove through the hills and vales of Prince William County, cautiously minding the speed limit signs, Hammer focused his mind on his plan B.

"*No plan extends with certainty beyond the first encounter.*"

That's why they invented plans B.

It is also axiomatic that when a door closes, a window opens. Hammer hoped so. He had his windows picked out, and he hoped for the best.

He focused his mind on the mission, as had always been his practice when running an operation in wartime. *This is wartime*, he said to himself, while knowing it was a war declared by two people obsessed with righting a *very* egregious wrong.

He thought about Lauren Stahling, with whom he had declared this war. *Of course he did*. How could he not? He was both pleased and awed by her coolness, the way she had made this war her own. He tried *not* to think about how he *felt* about her. *Of course he thought this*. How could he not?

Mostly, he thought about the precarious predicament in which Lauren was at *this moment*—and he tried very hard to think about this *without* feelings. He was no good to anyone if he fell into that trap.

Think analytically. Think and act carefully, tactically.

He switched his mind to thoughts about mileage and about relative speed He noticed the white Ford SUV with Fauquier County Sherriff markings was parked near a diner, and *this* made him think about the arsenal of guns and grenades he carried beneath his camper shell.

Two miles under the speed limit, more or less.

———

Throughout their entire drive, Lauren Stahling stared out the window and considered her situation. Naturally, when one ponders a predicament, the phrase "what if" enters into the contemplation. For Lauren, it was "what if I hadn't shot off my mouth" at the men in the room back there? When she had done it, it was to give them something to think about. She did know that for five of them, it was one of the last things they *ever* thought about.

Where would she be now if she had not.?

Either way, they would never have let her walk away, so she supposed whatever she had said or done, she would probably still be in the back seat of a big Jeep—or dead. The irony was she may well be alive *because* of her tirade, an outburst in which Evrémonde had been perversely impressed with her impudence.

As she gently massaged her injured wrist, she thought about Hammer. Was she was in this madness because of him? *No*, she had run headlong into it. But she *had* run headlong into it because of her craving for the kind of adventure which *he* represented, and which was not part of her life before he walked back into it.

She tried not to think about how she felt when he had casually showed up at her office two weeks ago—and back into her life. She tried not to think how he still, after twenty years, had the power to turn her life upside down. On that day, she had tried so hard not to succumb to her feelings, and she continued to try in the days which followed—until their amazing night in Sioux City.

With each milepost flicking by the window, she hoped and prayed that Hammer would appear, but she realized this was the ridiculous craving of a little girl waiting for a prince to come. She knew in the real world, a damsel in distress had to create her own solutions.

Solutions. She had quickly ruled out one option. There was no way in hell she would be getting on the sheikh's airplane. There was no way in hell she would become the Devil's plaything. She would *die* first. She would force them to shoot her or, failing that, she would attack the Devil one-on-one with her fingers in his eyes and let him have to kill her with his own bare hands.

The most obvious escape was to jump out of the car, but she and Marltyn were in the third-row seats, which did not have doors. The only way out was through the second row where bin-Sharia and Evrémonde were seated.

With none of the other choices being possible or desirable, she began to formulate a plan to manipulate Marltyn. If somehow she could get the two of them separated from the Sheikh and the Devil, maybe she could convince him *not* to kill her. Or maybe it would come down to daring him to kill her and hoping he would chicken out and let her get away.

––––––––

For nearly an hour, the two-lane blacktop raced beneath the pickup as the pulsing light being broadcast from Lauren's boot edged its way through the traffic snarl around Manassas and pressed south toward Fauquier County.

Hammer resisted the temptation to put the pedal to the metal and get it over with. Like that night in Helmand Province, when it was below zero and he waited all night for a flock of drug-running mullahs to spill out of a house across the valley. That night had ended well, and he convinced himself that tonight would end well too. At least it was not nearly so cold.

He reached the airport turnoff just as the other vehicle cleared the town of Catlett, eight miles up the road, and headed south on Route 28. He followed the paved road to a point about a half mile from the north end of the lone runway of the Marshalton Airport. From here, he turned onto the gravel road through the open field which led the tarmac.

He could see it now. As he had predicted, the Gulfstream G650ER was parked at the extreme north end of the runway, less than half a mile away. Planning ahead, the aircraft would have been fueled the moment it landed and would have been ready to go whenever the sheikh or Evrémonde, or one of their minions, had called ahead to request a departure. It was in position to use maximum runway for a heavily fueled takeoff.

The most direct way to reach the G650ER from the north was on this gravel road, so Hammer saw he had positioned his sniper stand in an ideal place.

Did he dare allow himself to think his plan B might be coming together as hoped? Fingers crossed.

He parked his pickup in a copse of trees h had scouted earlier and pointed it north for a fast getaway should it be necessary. He carefully took out a backpack full of rifle magazines and other gear, as well as the case containing his Barrett Mk22 sniper rifle, with its ATN Ultra HD day and night vision scope.

Hammer attached his bipod, lay down at his stand, sighted his rifle and took a deep breath. He slotted in a ten-round magazine. He imagined he would probably need fewer rounds, but when you're down to plan B, you don't take chances.

It did not take long for headlights to appear on the paved road. As the vehicle approached, he saw it was more than just any SUV. Sizing up his next steps, he identified it as a bulletproofed Mercedes G63, which has an armored gas tank enclosure. He might be able to puncture this, but he wasn't about to blow up the car Lauren was riding in. He needed to stop it, not destroy it.

Shoot the tires? The G63 has a military-grade "run-flat" system with solid polycarbonate inserts reinforcing the rims so it can continue running unhindered even if the tires are penetrated.

No, he had to kill the driver, but the military-grade ballistic glass was a challenge. It was designed to shrug off 9mm pistol rounds, 7.62mm assault rifle rounds, or numerous other calibers that might be thrown at it. However, Hammer had anticipated such a contingency and had a magazine loaded with ten high-velocity .338-caliber jacketed AP529 armor-piercing rounds. Fingers crossed.

As the driver turned off the paved road, he doused his headlights and ran dark. This actually made Hammer's job easier because the glare did not interfere with his night scope view of the cab.

He knew windshields typically have thicker ballistic glass than side windows, so he decided on the latter option. Through the windshield, he could see two bearded men with their eyes glued to the Gulfstream. As they came closer, the windshield filled his view through the scope, and as they began to move past his point of view, the square of the driver's side window moved forward. For a split second, it was in perfect perpendicular alignment to his crosshairs.

CHAPTER
THIRTY-FIVE

INSIDE THE MERCEDES, Lauren Stahling had finally glimpsed the sinister white Gulfstream sitting on the runway in the distance. Soon, if she was lucky, fate would offer her an opportunity to seize her "now or never" moment.

She hoped for a miracle.

She felt the bumps and the lurching of the heavy vehicle as it left the paved road. She heard the sound of gravel spattering against the underside and sensed when the driver began to slow to a crawl.

For some reason, she held her breath.

None of the six people in the G63 were prepared for the sound which came next, nor for the jolt that rocked the vehicle suddenly and violently.

It was an indescribable combination of hissing, buzzing and tearing that came and went in an ear-splitting split second. It was immediately overlapped by a sound like a bowl of chili being hurled violently at a wall.

The initial sound heard through the back two rows was that of an AP529 armor-piercing round with its extra-hard tungsten carbide-based penetrator hitting the driver's side window square-on at a velocity of better than 2,700 feet per second, then exiting the opposite window before hurtling into the oblivion of distant darkness.

As it tore directly through the heads of the two bearded men in the front seat, the second sound was that of all the matter comprising those heads being splattered uniformly in every direction—especially on the inside of the windshield and the panel of bulletproof glass separating them from bin-Sharia and Evrémonde in the second row.

Lauren winced and ducked impulsively. Marltyn gasped in terror and gripped the pistol ever more firmly. She couldn't see the initial reaction of bin-Sharia or Evrémonde.

They all felt the G63 stumble, jerk and come to an abrupt stop. It had been running in third gear, but the driver's foot was suddenly no longer on the accelerator or the clutch.

For a moment after this, no one in the last two rows moved or spoke. Then, abruptly, Evrémonde opened his door and scrambled out. His intention was to jerk open the driver's side door, pull out the driver, climb in and get the G63 moving again. They were still at least a quarter mile from the Gulfstream.

The door was locked and would not open. Lauren could see his frustration as he pounded on the window to no avail. Despite the small hole punched by the armor-piercing round, the damaged ballistic glass was designed to resist, and not to shatter.

The sheikh climbed out and tried the opposite door. It too was also locked, of course.

"We must run," Evrémonde shouted. "We can make it. *Dépêchez-vous, courez vite, Hurry!*"

Clutching his all-important laptop case, bin-Sharia

followed Evrémonde as he made his way hurriedly toward the waiting plane.

"Keep your head down, there's a shooter out there," Evrémonde cautioned, though bin-Sharia obviously did not have to be told his life was in danger.

Both men had forgotten about their "hostage" and the senator's chief of staff.

Out of the corner of her eye, Lauren could see Marltyn was still stunned. She knew this would not last. She had to make her move *now*.

She scrambled clumsily through the space between the second row seats, nearly catching the strap of her purse, which was still over her shoulder beneath her coat, on an armrest. She finally made it and dove out the open door.

Now that she was outside, she could hear the idling aircraft engines and knew this foreshadowed a takeoff. She wanted no part of this. The only thing on her mind at this moment was to *not* be on that airplane.

She smoothed her skirt and began running back up the gravel road in the direction from which the G63 had come, and away from the runway. She made reasonably good progress with the two-inch heels of boots better suited to a senate office building than a muddy road, but soon she heard faster-running feet behind her. Finally, she just stopped and turned to face Marltyn.

He ran a few more steps and stopped about twenty feet away from her. His expression was one of insecurity, of someone acting in response to a situation not fully within his grasp. Though his head was backlit by the lights of the Gulfstream, she could see his face reasonably well.

She glowered angrily, knowing her expression, illuminated by those same lights, was clearly visible—and *unambiguous*.

"What are you chasing after me for," she said irritably. "Your friends are running for their airplane. They're all headed back to their magic kingdoms of luxury lives and captive women to service their manly needs. You need to hurry if you're going to catch your flight."

"I won't let you get away," he said with a mixture of anger and desperation. She was surprised by how out of breath he seemed.

"I'm not going on that airplane, and I am *certainly* not going with you!" Lauren shouted emphatically.

"I won't let you get away," he repeated. She could see he was still holding her revolver.

"Oh...and this from the man who did not even notice when I walked out on you fifteen years ago."

"I was at an important moment in my career..."

"What *career*? It was *college* politics, and you were not even the candidate. You were *oh so impressed* with your own importance in a campaign where you *weren't* important."

"This is not about that, and it's not about *you*," he replied, catching his breath and stepping closer. "This is much bigger. You are just too small-minded and provincial to understand. This is global and you so totally fucked things up tonight, you stupid *bitch*. Now, come with me!"

"*No.*"

"I don't have time to argue. I *will not* let you go. I *will not* let you tell *anyone* about what you've seen and heard tonight. You better come with me *now* if you know what's good for you!"

"I'm not going with you," she repeated furiously, standing her ground. "You'll have to shoot me."

Ouch. She wished she hadn't said this. She was only emphasizing the point that she would not go with him.

"I wish I didn't have to do this, but if this is the only

way to stop you," Marltyn said, raising the pistol. *"Jesus, Lauren*...I can't believe it came to this."

He was only about twelve feet away now, and they both knew he would not miss at this distance. He carefully aimed and closed one eye, taking his time.

The *cra-a-ack* of a pistol shot thundered into the night.

A pink froth of blood erupted into the air.

The sharp, throbbing wedge of pain had not yet reached his brain as Marltyn stared with uncomprehending bewilderment at his wrist—a wrist without a hand.

Lauren Stahling stared in disbelief at this man without a hand, this man without a gun.

From the shadows, there emerged another man, a man *with* a gun—a menacing-looking retro M1911 Colt .45.

"Damn it, Hammer," she said angrily as tears of emotion flowed down her cheeks. "Could you have *not* waited until the *last minute*?"

As he approached, she grabbed him, held him tight, and felt his arms envelop her.

"I was at the Ravensworth house..." she started to say after what only *seemed* to be a very long time. "I got myself kidnapped."

"I know," he interrupted. "I missed you by about five minutes. Sorry."

"It worked out," she said, squeezing him and feeling secure at last.

"You left quite a bloodbath there," he said after about a minute.

"They were trying to kill me," she said, letting go of Hammer and picking up the pistol from where it had fallen from the grasp of the severed extremity. "I shot a bunch of them."

"So I heard," He said. "The senator told me."

" He was in a bad way when we left," Lauren said."

"He won't be telling anyone anything…anymore."

"They took my phone," she said with sudden urgency. "It's still there. It could be a problem if it's found."

"This one?" Hammer said with a smile, handing her the phone from his pocket.

She was in the midst of kissing him when she suddenly remembered where they were, and *why*.

"The Sheikh and the Devil," she said urgently. "*They're getting away!*"

"Oh…not just yet," he replied.

As they started to walk away, she paused for a last look at Chad Marltyn.

His radial artery, the one immediately beneath the skin on the inner side of his wrist, was spewing blood in regular bursts.

He was on the ground, squirming in a sizable pool of blood, his squeals of pain sounding more animal than human. They reminded her of a coyote caught in a trap as it tries to chew off its own leg to escape.

Then she remembered her father using this same gun to put a trapped coyote out of its misery.

As she raised the muzzle, she remembered Marltyn's words.

"*Too small-minded and provincial to understand…you totally fucked things up tonight, you stupid bitch…you better come with me now if you know what's good for you!*"

"No, Chad," she whispered as she looked down at a man close to death. "This woman *does* know what's good for her, without anyone whatsoever telling her."

With that, she released the cocked hammer on her father's pistol, returned it to her purse, and followed Hammer across the field.

———

As this Thursday edged toward its close, Lauren Stahling had a lot in common with Mavis Carlsruud.

For those with whom the two women had interacted today—those who were still alive, of course—these women were like ghosts, like two wisps of smoke. Both Lauren and Mavis had passed through a suite of offices, seen but unnoticed by busy staffers and interns who forgot them in the way you forget a passerby on the street, or someone with whom you share a supermarket checkout line.

Each woman, each ghost, had interacted with just two people in those respective offices who had heard their voices and heard their names—and none of those people would ever speak of it again.

Those who had seen but not noticed Mavis were already racking their memories for the details which were confused and fuzzy at best.

For Lauren, she would not even be a fading twinkle of memory tomorrow morning when the disappearances of a senator and a chief of staff would be discovered.

CHAPTER
THIRTY-SIX

WITH EACH STEP they took as they dashed toward the waiting Gulfstream G650ER, Hamad Abdallah bin-Sharia and Maxime Evrémonde wondered why the sniper who had shot into the front seat of the Mercedes had not fired at them again. They cautiously took this as a good sign. They'd worry about wondering *why* later.

As the distant sound of a pistol shot reverberated through the dark, they paused and looked back.

"He shot her," bin-Sharia said as though surprised that the bureaucrat would actually kill the harlot. "The aide of the senator shot the woman, just as you ordered him to do."

"Or our *créature sauvage* killed *him*," Evrémonde said. "Either way, it's not our problem. *Au revoir l'Amérique.*"

As bin-Sharia and Evrémonde reached the tarmac, one of the members of the three-man flight crew was on the Gulfstream's airstair waiting for them, and the other two were in the cockpit going through their preflight ritual. All three pilots were veterans of countless flights in the service of the sheikh and his nefarious enterprise. They had started out flying 737 or A320 freighters filled with cages of captive organ donors or hapless comfort women into and out of East Africa and the Middle East and had worked their way up to become the sheikh's own personal aerial chauffeurs. They were anxious to be on their way. They had been shot at before, but it had been a long time, and they were hoping to dodge trouble tonight.

The man on the stairs stepped back as bin-Sharia and Evrémonde settled into the plush heart of the luxurious executive aircraft. They each took a seat and strapped in, anxious to put distance between themselves and what had happened at the Mercedes. While both men were exhausted by their dash, Evrémonde was reasonably fit and caught his breath quickly, while bin-Sharia, who never exercised, gasped for several moments. Evrémonde relaxed when he heard his companion announce in English that he needed a drink.

While this was ongoing, neither of them noticed the pilot at the door was having trouble stowing the airstair so the door could be secured. This was normally the duty of the cabin crew, but the cabin crewmen had been doubling as drivers tonight, and they had died in the front seat of the G63. This pilot was grappling with an unfamiliar task.

There was a crackle on the intercom as one of the pilots on the flight deck asked what was wrong with the door. Hissing angrily, Evrémonde unstrapped his seat belt and went to help. Finally, after considerable pushing and pulling, the stairway was folded away, and the door was closed and secured.

The third pilot went forward to the flight deck jump seat, while the French slave trader returned to his seat. Hamad bin-Sharia, who had paid little attention to the fiasco with the door, had poured a glass of brandy. The moment he handed this generous pour to his companion, the aircraft shook as the left-seat pilot throttled up the two Rolls-Royce Pearl 700 turbofan engines to begin the takeoff roll.

Suddenly, the glass fell into Evrémonde's lap, spilling the brandy all over the front of his trousers.

"*Bordel de merde!*" Evrémonde exclaimed as the Gulfstream slowly rolled forward. "*Putain de merde!*"

————

Lauren's eyes were riveted to the Gulfstream as it idled at the end of the runway with its door open. She was in the midst of wondering why when it finally slammed shut.

Hammer was lying prone at his shooting stand, about fifty yards from the aircraft, inserting a fresh magazine into his MRAD. She noticed he had marked it with the letters "INCEN" written on a piece of blue painter's tape.

Suddenly, the engines accelerated with a horrible shriek.

She jammed her fingers into her ears and gritted her teeth as the sleek white aircraft started to roll. She could see the orange glow in the two tail-mounted engines as the jet gained speed.

Over the sound of the engines, Lauren did not hear the sound of Hammer taking his first shot, but she saw the slight jerk of the recoil against his shoulder and a hint of muzzle flash.

The "INCEN" label on Hammer's magazine stood for ten API571 armor-piercing incendiary rounds. Hammer did not need the armor-piercing characteristics to penetrate a thin-skinned aluminum and carbon composite airplane. He really *needed* only that they were incendiary rounds, but when you are down to plan B, you don't take chances.

Emitting an observable burst as it hit, the first API571

struck the Gulfstream with a velocity of around 2,700 feet per second.

Lauren watched as Hammer squinted through his ATN 4K scope and fired again. When she looked up, she saw tongues of flame licking from the left wing. She knew enough about airplanes to know he was shooting into the fuel tanks, and they are extremely vulnerable to people on the ground shooting at them.

To give the G650ER its extended range, an additional 4,000 pounds of fuel capacity augmented the twenty-two tons of the basic G650, turning the sheikh's jet into a rolling gas can. As Hammer knew, the detonation of fuel-air vapors above the fuel in the main tank would burst it and flood the interior of the aircraft, immersing bin-Sharia and Evrémonde, along with the sheikh's all-important laptop, in liquid fire.

As the two Montanans watched, the Gulfstream raced down the runway with flames beginning to engulf the wing and fuselage. They could feel the heat even though the fireball was moving away rapidly.

A split second later, the left wing fell away from the rest of the aircraft. With this, the aircraft rolled over and corkscrewed down the runway, looking like a bug dwarfed by an enveloping cocoon of fire. The massive and catastrophic explosion about halfway down the runway was almost anticlimactic.

The flames showed no sign of slackening. The airport was unattended at night, so it would take a long time for the fire department to get all the way out here.

Lauren felt an exhilarating sense of relief and triumph, as every tense nerve in her body unspooled.

———

Hammer felt himself relax as he extracted his finger from the trigger guard.

His mind raced ahead to the last loose end which would wrap up his plan B. Chad Marltyn and his disconnected hand would be tossed into the Mercedes G63 minus his wallet and cell phone, but together with an M114 incendiary grenade. The rigidity of the blast-resistant armored body would contain both the explosion and the ensuing fire, turning the vehicle into the oven of its own demise.

The impending heavy rainstorm would come after the fires at both ends of the runway had consumed most of the human remains, and they would wash away the extraneous blood from around the Mercedes and tidy up the scene.

Just as Hammer was starting to unwind, he felt his body being aggressively dragged away from his sniper stand.

Before he was able to respond, he was manhandled onto his back, where he found himself staring up into the smiling face of his companion, illuminated by the firelight from down the runway. Lauren was now sitting on his body, clamping it between her knees and looking at him as she unfastened the buttons of his shirt.

A man knows never to tell a woman she looks good when her hair is hopelessly mussed, but this did not stop him from thinking it.

"*You're crazy,*" he told her while trying to suppress a grin

"Watch who you're calling 'crazy,' mister," Lauren replied, breathing heavily as she slid her hands inside his shirt and leaned her face close to his. "I'm not the one who just turned a fifty-million-dollar airplane into a Duraflame log."

EPILOGUE

LINDA STAHLING STEPPED into the Black Rock Café and brushed the dry flakes of snow from her coat. Across the room, she spotted her friend, Charlotte Hendricksen, at the booth where they met for coffee a couple of times a week.

"I see you're reading the paper," Linda said. "I thought you'd be working on your Wordle."

"I got it on the second try this morning," Charlotte said with a sense of triumph.

"What was the word?"

"It was 'flame.' For some reason, I started with 'floss' instead of 'audio.' Maybe it was because I have to go to the dentist next week."

"Congratulations," Linda said.

"Thanks," Charlotte said, nodding first to Linda, then to Kristin as she dropped a couple of cups of coffee to the table.

"Did you hear about Jenna Tolliver?" Linda asked.

"Oh that poor girl," Charlotte replied. "Kidnapped by those terrible people, and then she *escaped*! Last I heard was she was moved up here to the Logan County Hospital. What have you heard?"

"I saw her mom at the supermarket yesterday," Linda said with a sense of triumph. "She's out of the hospital and doing great. Anxious to get back to work."

"I'm sure Mike is over the moon."

"The good news is there's no lasting damage physically from the hypothermia or frostbite," Linda said apprehensively. "The bad news, or maybe not so bad, is she doesn't *remember* anything about what happened. The doctors say this can happen...trauma-induced amnesia or something."

"Is she okay otherwise?"

"It seems so. Maybe she doesn't really *need* to remember all that."

"And the poor girl drove herself to the hospital. It's like a miracle," Charlotte declared.

"What's in the paper today?" Linda asked after they had each ordered a cinnamon roll.

"Well, it's the *Gazette*, so it's mostly Billings news."

"What's going on down there?"

"Nothing much. The usual. But there's an interesting story on the national page."

"Hmmm."

"Remember that senator who went missing back in Washington last week?"

"Oh, yeah."

"Well they found him."

"*Where?*"

"He died in a house fire somewhere out in the countryside down in Virginia."

"Oh, that's awful," Linda said sadly. "Wait a minute, how did they not know that he was at this house? I'll bet there was a woman involved."

"Apparently several people were killed, and it turns

out nobody knew it was the senator until they started trying to identify bodies. The fire was really bad. Burned them almost beyond recognition. If there hadn't been a big storm back there, everything would have burned up."

"That's terrible."

"Here's the weird thing," Charlotte continued. "One of the other bodies they identified was the director or something of the ATF."

"How was it that they misplaced both him and a senator for over a week?" Linda said, shaking her head. "Doesn't give you much confidence in whoever's running the government, does it?"

"The thing that's got the conspiracy hounds chirping is that here they've got a senator from *one party*, and a high-muck-de-muck from the Justice Department of the *other party*, and nobody knew anything about them being there."

"That's interesting."

"Both sides are really embarrassed," Charlotte said with a laugh.

Kristin came by to top off their coffee, and the conversation continued.

"Speaking of fires back east," Linda asked. "Is there anything more about that plane crash last week?"

"Everything was burned up," Charlotte said. "They're still piecing together the five bodies. It was a private jet that's owned by a Middle Eastern oilman, a Sheikh Somebody-or-Other. And get this, he was somehow mixed up in the parent company of that same outfit who bought the old Tredquist place."

"Small world," Linda said. "I heard yesterday at the hardware store that Logan County is going to use eminent domain to take over the property."

"About time," Charlotte said emphatically. "I suppose this will take up a lot of Lauren's time down at the assessor's office when she gets back from her hunting trip with James."

"Speaking of which," Linda said with a sly smile. "Well, I drove by her place this morning. I've been watering her plants every few days while she was gone… and you know what?"

"What?"

"*His* truck was parked in *her* driveway," Linda said, winking. "I decided not to stop today."

"Well I certainly hope they had a nice, relaxing time up there in the mountains," Charlotte said with a smile. "It must be a huge relief to get away from it all for a change."

A LOOK AT BOOK TWO:

THE NEXT TO LAST MOONRAKER INTO BROUILLECOURT PARISH

They thought the war was over, but Jim Hammer never left the battlefield.

A decade ago, Captain Jim Hammer hunted Afghan warlords with a sniper's focus and a soldier's resolve. He and his team brought justice to the mountains of Kandahar— almost. One corrupt U.S. bureaucrat escaped the crosshairs, and now, halfway across the world, the war is back on.

In the shadowed bayous of Brouillecourt Parish, Louisiana, there are whispers of a large-scale smuggling operation protected by federal agents. Former members of Hammer's old Special Ops team and Nicole Kirbye, a young accountant, are unwittingly dragged into the mysterious intrigue. When a murdered whistleblower's warning is whispered to the anxious Nicole and killers close in, who can they call?

Jim Hammer is plunged into a deadly, high-stakes chase across Mississippi, Arkansas, and Louisiana—where the moonrakers aren't smuggling rum or even drugs, but weapons of war. U.S. military hardware—once abandoned in Afghanistan—will soon find new life on American soil, smuggled by a network of rogue defense officials, shadowy enforcers, and a Taliban-connected conman playing both sides.

At the center: Wallace "Wally" Gusche, a crooked DOD logistics boss; Abed Qalandar, a slippery war profiteer with Taliban ties; and Alexis Mondtrom, a government insider selling death to cartels. Backed by a loyal circle of his old war buddies and ordinary citizens turned patriots, Hammer launches a ruthless campaign to dismantle a conspiracy embedded deep within the U.S. government.

When the operation spirals into chaos—ambushes, double-crosses, cartel uprisings, and fiery shootouts— Hammer learns that justice doesn't come with rules. It comes at a cost.

AVAILABLE DECEMBER 2025

ABOUT THE AUTHOR

 Bill Yenne is the award-winning author of three dozen books on historical topics especially non-fiction books on military history and hardware. His various works have been translated into six languages.
He has contributed to encyclopedias of both world wars, and his work has been selected for the official Chief of Staff of the Air Force Reading List. Yenne has appeared in documentaries airing on the History Channel, the National Geographic Channel, the Smithsonian Channel, ARD German Television, and NHK Japanese Television. His book signings have been covered by C-SPAN.

Among his fiction works are the Raptor Force action-adventure series and the Bladen Cole Western series, both published by Berkley (PenguinRandomHouse).

He is the recipient of the Air Force Association's Gill Robb Wilson Award for the "most outstanding contribution in the field of arts and letters [as an] author whose [many] works have shaped how thousands of Americans understand and appreciate airpower." (Previous Gill Robb Wilson Awardees include Edward R. Murrow, Ted Koppel, Tom Brokaw and Tom Clancy.)

Bill Yenne grew up inside Montana's remote and rugged Glacier National Park, where his father was the supervisor of backcountry trails. He spent his summers on foot or on horseback in the remote mountains, and his winters becoming a voracious reader and history buff.

In the course of gathering material for his books, Yenne has traveled far and wide. He followed the entire 3,000 miles of the Lewis and Clark Trail; he flew in the jump seat of a B-52 bomber on a training flight for a classified Cold War mission; he fired a Thompson submachine gun in an organized shooting competition (and did pretty well); and he has climbed to the top of two dozen Gothic cathedrals across Europe. He is also an amateur silver medalist in the annual Kauai Canoe Club outrigger races.